FLORA THOMPSON

Lark Rise

PENGUIN BOOKS

PENGUIN CLASSICS

Published by the Penguin Group
Penguin Books Ltd, 80 Strand, London WC2R ORL, England
Penguin Group (USA) Inc., 375 Hudson Street, New York, New York 10014, USA
Penguin Group (Canada), 90 Eglinton Avenue East, Suite 700, Toronto, Ontario, Canada M4P 2Y3
(a division of Pearson Penguin Canada Inc.)
Penguin Ireland, 25 St Stephen's Green, Dublin 2, Ireland
(a division of Penguin Books Ltd)
Penguin Group (Australia), 250 Camberwell Road, Camberwell, Victoria 3124, Australia
(a division of Pearson Australia Group Pty Ltd)
Penguin Books India Pvt Ltd, 11 Community Centre, Panchsheel Park, New Delhi – 110 017, India
Penguin Group (NZ), 67 Apollo Drive, Rosedale, North Shore 0632, New Zealand
(a division of Pearson New Zealand Ltd)
Penguin Books (South Africa) (Pty) Ltd, 24 Sturdee Avenue, Rosebank, Johannesburg 2196, South Africa

Penguin Books Ltd, Registered Offices: 80 Strand, London WC2R ORL, England

www.penguin.com

First published by Oxford University Press 1939
Published in Penguin Classics 2009
This film and TV tie-in edition published 2009
By arrangement with the BBC
BBC © BBC 1996
The BBC logo is a registered trademark of the
British Broadcasting Corporation and is used under license.
1

Set in 10.5/13 pt PostScript Monotype Dante
Typeset by Rowland Phototypesetting Ltd, Bury St Edmunds, Suffolk
Printed in England by Clays Ltd, St Ives plc

978-0-141-19014-3

www.greenpenguin.co.uk

Lark Rise

Flora Jane Thompson was born in 1876 at Juniper Hill, a hamlet on the borders of Oxfordshire and Northamptonshire. After leaving school she was sent as assistant to the postmistress (who also kept the forge) to a town eight miles away, and was for some time employed to carry the letters in a locked leather bag to the big house nearby. So began her long connection with the Post Office. She married young and her husband later became a postmaster. His work took them to Bournemouth, where she obtained from the public library the Greek and Roman classics in translation, as well as Ibsen and the English poets, novelists and critics – especially Shaw and Yeats. Her first book was a collection of poems, *Bog Myrtle and Peat*. However, she is best remembered for three auto-biographical volumes: *Lark Rise* (1939), *Over to Candleford* (1941) and *Candleford Green* (1943), reissued in one volume as *Lark Rise to Candleford* (1945). A fourth volume, *Still Glides the Stream*, was published posthumously in 1948. Flora Thompson died at Brixham, Devon, on 21 May 1947.

Contents

I

Poor People's Houses

The hamlet stood on a gentle rise in the flat, wheat-growing north-east corner of Oxfordshire. We will call it Lark Rise because of the great number of skylarks which made the surrounding fields their springboard and nested on the bare earth between the rows of green corn.

All around, from every quarter, the stiff, clayey soil of the arable fields crept up; bare, brown and windswept for eight months out of the twelve. Spring brought a flush of green wheat and there were violets under the hedges and pussy-willows out beside the brook at the bottom of the 'Hundred Acres'; but only for a few weeks in later summer had the landscape real beauty. Then the ripened cornfields rippled up to the doorsteps of the cottages and the hamlet became an island in a sea of dark gold.

To a child it seemed that it must always have been so; but the ploughing and sowing and reaping were recent innovations. Old men could remember when the Rise, covered with juniper bushes, stood in the midst of a furzy heath – common land, which had come under the plough after the passing of the Enclosure Acts. Some of the ancients still occupied cottages on land which had been ceded to their fathers as 'squatters' rights', and probably all the small plots upon which the houses stood had originally been so ceded. In the eighteen-eighties the hamlet consisted of about thirty cottages and an inn, not built in rows, but dotted down anywhere within a more or less circular group. A deeply rutted cart track surrounded the whole, and separate houses or groups of houses were connected by a network of pathways. Going from one part of the hamlet to another was called 'going round the Rise', and the plural of 'house' was not 'houses', but 'housen'. The only shop was a small general one kept in the back kitchen of the inn. The church and school were in the mother village, a mile and a half away.

A road flattened the circle at one point. It had been cut when the heath was enclosed, for convenience in fieldwork and to connect the main Oxford road with the mother village and a series of other villages beyond. From the hamlet it led on the one hand to church and school, and on the other to the main road, or the turnpike, as it was still called, and so to the market town where the Saturday shopping was done. It brought little traffic past the hamlet. An occasional farm wagon, piled with sacks or square-cut bundles of hay; a farmer on horseback or in his gig; the baker's little old white-tilted van; a string of blanketed hunters with grooms, exercising in the early morning; and a carriage with gentry out paying calls in the afternoon were about the sum of it. No motors, no buses, and only one of the old penny-farthing high bicycles at rare intervals. People still rushed to their cottage doors to see one of the latter come past.

A few of the houses had thatched roofs, whitewashed outer walls and diamond-paned windows, but the majority were just stone or brick boxes with blue-slated roofs. The older houses were relics of pre-enclosure days and were still occupied by descendants of the original squatters, themselves at that time elderly people. One old couple owned a donkey and cart, which they used to carry their vegetables, eggs, and honey to the market town and sometimes hired out at sixpence a day to their neighbours. One house was occupied by a retired farm bailiff, who was reported to have 'well feathered his own nest' during his years of stewardship. Another aged man owned and worked upon about an acre of land. These, the innkeeper, and one other man, a stonemason who walked the three miles to and from his work in the town every day, were the only ones not employed as agricultural labourers.

Some of the cottages had two bedrooms, others only one, in which case it had to be divided by a screen or curtain to accommodate parents and children. Often the big boys of a family slept downstairs, or were put out to sleep in the second bedroom of an elderly couple whose own children were out in the world. Except at holiday times, there were no big girls to provide for, as they were all out in service. Still, it was often a tight fit, for children swarmed, eight, ten, or even more in some families, and although they were seldom all at home together, the eldest often being married before the youngest was born, beds and shakedowns were often so closely packed that the inmates had to climb over one bed to get into another.

But Lark Rise must not be thought of as a slum set down in the country. The inhabitants lived an open-air life; the cottages were kept clean by much scrubbing with soap and water, and doors and windows stood wide open when the weather permitted. When the wind cut across the flat land to the east, or came roaring down from the north, doors and windows had to be closed; but then, as the hamlet people said, they got more than enough fresh air through the keyhole.

There were two epidemics of measles during the decade, and two men had accidents in the harvest field and were taken to hospital; but, for years together, the doctor was only seen there when one of the ancients was dying of old age, or some difficult first confinement baffled the skill of the old woman who, as she said, saw the beginning and end of everybody. There was no cripple or mental defective in the hamlet, and, except for a few months when a poor woman was dying of cancer, no invalid. Though food was rough and teeth were neglected, indigestion was unknown, while nervous troubles, there as elsewhere, had yet to be invented. The very word 'nerve' was used in a different sense to the modern one. 'My word! An' 'aven't she got a nerve!' they would say of any one who expected more than was reasonable.

In nearly all the cottages there was but one room downstairs, and many of these were poor and bare, with only a table and a few chairs and stools for furniture and a superannuated potato-sack thrown down by way of hearthrug. Other rooms were bright and cosy, with dressers of crockery, cushioned chairs, pictures on the walls and brightly coloured hand-made rag rugs on the floor. In these there would be pots of geraniums, fuchsias, and old-fashioned sweet-smelling musk on the window-sills. In the older cottages there were grandfathers' clocks, gate-legged tables, and rows of pewter, relics of a time when life was easier for country folk.

The interiors varied, according to the number of mouths to be fed and the thrift and skill of the housewife, or the lack of those qualities; but the income in all was precisely the same, for ten shillings a week was the standard wage of the farm labourer at that time in that district.

Looking at the hamlet from a distance, one house would have been seen, a little apart, and turning its back on its neighbours, as though about to run away into the fields. It was a small grey stone cottage with a thatched roof, a green-painted door and a plum tree trained up the wall to the eaves. This was called the 'end house' and was the home of the stonemason and his family. At the beginning of the decade there were two children: Laura, aged three, and Edmund, a year and a half younger. In some respects these children, while small, were more fortunate than their neighbours. Their father earned a little more money than the labourers. Their mother had been a children's nurse and they were well looked after. They were taught good manners and taken for walks, milk was bought for them, and they were bathed regularly on Saturday nights and, after 'Gentle Jesus' was said, were tucked up in bed with a peppermint or clove ball to suck. They had tidier clothes, too, for their mother had taste and skill with her needle and better-off relations sent them parcels of outgrown clothes. The other children used to tease the little girl about the lace on her drawers and led her such a life that she once took them off and hid them in a haystack.

Their mother at that time used to say that she dreaded the day when they would have to go to school; children got so wild and rude and tore their clothes to shreds going the mile and a half backwards and forwards. But when the time came for them to go she was glad, for, after a break of five years, more babies had begun to arrive, and, by the end of the 'eighties, there were six children at the end house.

As they grew, the two elder children would ask questions of anybody and everybody willing or unwilling to answer them. Who planted the buttercups? Why did God let the wheat get blighted?

Who lived in this house before we did, and what were their children's names? What's the sea like? Is it bigger than Cottisloe Pond? *Why* can't we go to Heaven in the donkey-cart? Is it farther than Banbury? And so on, taking their bearings in that small corner of the world they had somehow got into.

This asking of questions teased their mother and made them unpopular with the neighbours. 'Little children should be seen and not heard', they were told at home. Out of doors it would more often be 'Ask no questions and you'll be told no lies.' One old woman once handed the little girl a leaf from a pot plant on her window-sill. 'What's it called?' was the inevitable question. ''Tis called mind your own business,' was the reply; 'an' I think I'd better give a slip of it to your mother to plant in a pot for you.' But no such reproofs could cure them of the habit, although they soon learned who and who not to question.

In this way they learned the little that was known of the past of the hamlet and of places beyond. They had no need to ask the names of the birds, flowers, and trees they saw every day, for they had already learned these unconsciously, and neither could remember a time when they did not know an oak from an ash, wheat from barley, or a Jenny wren from a blue-tit. Of what was going on around them, not much was hidden, for the gossips talked freely before children, evidently considering them not meant to hear as well as not to be heard, and, as every house was open to them and their own home was open to most people, there was not much that escaped their sharp ears.

The first charge on the labourers' ten shillings was house rent. Most of the cottages belonged to small tradesmen in the market town and the weekly rents ranged from one shilling to half a crown. Some labourers in other villages worked on farms or estates where they had their cottages rent free; but the hamlet people did not envy them, for 'Stands to reason,' they said, 'they've allus got to do just what they be told, or out they goes, neck and crop, bag and baggage.' A shilling, or even two shillings a week, they felt, was not too much to pay for the freedom to live and vote as they liked and to go to church or chapel or neither as they preferred.

Every house had a good vegetable garden and there were allotments for all; but only three of the thirty cottages had their own water supply. The less fortunate tenants obtained their water from a well on a vacant plot on the outskirts of the hamlet, from which the cottage had disappeared. There was no public well or pump. They just had to get their water where and how they could; the landlords did not undertake to supply water.

Against the wall of every well-kept cottage stood a tarred or green-painted water butt to catch and store the rain-water from the roof. This saved many journeys to the well with buckets, as it could be used for cleaning and washing clothes and for watering small, precious things in the garden. It was also valued for toilet purposes and women would hoard the last drops for themselves and their children to wash in. Rain-water was supposed to be good for the complexion, and, though they had no money to spend upon beautifying themselves, they were not too far gone in poverty to neglect such means as they had to that end.

For drinking water, and for cleaning water, too, when the water butts failed, the women went to the well in all weathers, drawing up the buckets with a windlass and carting them home suspended from their shoulders by a yoke. Those were weary journeys 'round the Rise' for water, and many were the rests and endless was the gossip, as they stood at corners in their big white aprons and crossover shawls.

A few of the younger, more recently married women who had been in good service and had not yet given up the attempt to hold themselves a little aloof would get their husbands to fill the big red store crock with water at night. But this was said by others to be 'a sin and a shame', for, after his hard day's work, a man wanted his rest, not to do ''ooman's work'. Later on in the decade it became the fashion for the men to fetch water at night, and then, of course, it was quite right that they should do so and a woman who 'dragged her guts out' fetching more than an occasional load from the well was looked upon as a traitor to her sex.

In dry summers, when the hamlet wells failed, water had to be fetched from a pump at some farm buildings half a mile distant.

Those who had wells in their gardens would not give away a spot, as they feared if they did theirs, too, would run dry, so they fastened down the lids with padlocks and disregarded all hints.

The only sanitary arrangement known in the hamlet was housed either in a little beehive-shaped building at the bottom of the garden or in a corner of the wood and toolshed known as 'the hovel'. It was not even an earth closet; but merely a deep pit with a seat set over it, the half-yearly emptying of which caused every door and window in the vicinity to be sealed. Unfortunately, there was no means of sealing the chimneys!

The 'privies' were as good an index as any to the characters of their owners. Some were horrible holes; others were fairly decent, while some, and these not a few, were kept well cleared, with the seat scrubbed to snow-whiteness and the brick floor raddled. One old woman even went so far as to nail up a text as a finishing touch, 'Thou God seest me' – most embarrassing to a Victorian child who had been taught that no one must even see her approach the door.

In other such places health and sanitary maxims were scrawled with lead pencil or yellow chalk on the whitewashed walls. Most of them embodied sound sense and some were expressed in sound verse, but few were so worded as to be printable. One short and pithy maxim may pass: 'Eat well, work well, sleep well, and — well once a day.'

On the wall of the 'little house' at Laura's home pictures cut from the newspapers were pasted. These were changed when the walls were whitewashed and in succession they were 'The Bombardment of Alexandria', all clouds of smoke, flying fragments, and flashes of explosives; 'Glasgow's Mournful Disaster: Plunges from Life from the *Daphne*', and 'The Tay Bridge Disaster', with the end of the train dangling from the broken bridge over a boiling sea. It was before the day of Press photography and the artists were able to give their imagination full play. Later, the place of honour in the 'little house' was occupied by 'Our Political Leaders', two rows of portraits on one print; Mr Gladstone, with hawk-like countenance and flashing eyes, in the middle of the top row, and kind, sleepy-looking Lord Salisbury in the other. Laura loved that picture because Lord

Randolph Churchill was there. She thought he must be the most handsome man in the world.

At the back or side of each cottage was a lean-to pigsty and the house refuse was thrown on a nearby pile called 'the muck'll'. This was so situated that the oozings from the sty could drain into it; the manure was also thrown there when the sty was cleared, and the whole formed a nasty, smelly eyesore to have within a few feet of the windows. 'The wind's in the so-and-so,' some woman indoors would say, 'I can smell th' muck'll,' and she would often be reminded of the saying, 'Pigs for health', or told that the smell was a healthy one.

It was in a sense a healthy smell for them; for a good pig fattening in the sty promised a good winter. During its lifetime the pig was an important member of the family, and its health and condition were regularly reported in letters to children away from home, together with news of their brothers and sisters. Men callers on Sunday afternoons came, not to see the family, but the pig, and would lounge with its owner against the pigsty door for an hour, scratching piggy's back and praising his points or turning up their own noses in criticism. Ten to fifteen shillings was the price paid for a pigling when weaned, and they all delighted in getting a bargain. Some men swore by the 'dilling', as the smallest of a litter was called, saying it was little and good, and would soon catch up; others preferred to give a few shillings more for a larger young pig.

The family pig was everybody's pride and everybody's business. Mother spent hours boiling up the 'little taturs' to mash and mix with the pot-liquor, in which food had been cooked, to feed to the pig for its evening meal and help out the expensive barley-meal. The children, on their way home from school, would fill their arms with sow thistle, dandelion, and choice long grass, or roam along the hedgerows on wet evenings collecting snails in a pail for the pig's supper. These piggy crunched up with great relish. 'Feyther', over and above farming out the sty, bedding down, doctoring, and so on, would even go without his nightly half-pint when, towards the end, the barley-meal mounted until 'it fair frightened anybody'.

Sometimes, when the weekly income would not run to a sufficient quantity of fattening food, an arrangement would be made with the baker or miller that he should give credit now, and when the pig was killed receive a portion of the meat in payment. More often than not one-half the pig-meat would be mortgaged in this way, and it was no uncommon thing to hear a woman say, 'Us be going to kill half a pig, please God, come Friday,' leaving the uninitiated to conclude that the other half would still run about in the sty.

Some of the families killed two separate half pigs a year; others one, or even two, whole ones, and the meat provided them with bacon for the winter or longer. Fresh meat was a luxury only seen in a few of the cottages on Sunday, when six-pennyworth of pieces would be bought to make a meat pudding. If a small joint came their way as a Saturday night bargain, those without oven grates would roast it by suspending it on a string before the fire, with one of the children in attendance as turnspit. Or a 'pot-roast' would be made by placing the meat with a little lard or other fat in an iron saucepan and keeping it well shaken over the fire. But, after all, as they said, there was nothing to beat a 'toad'. For this the meat was enclosed whole in a suet crust and well boiled, a method which preserved all the delicious juices of the meat and provided a good pudding into the bargain. When some superior person tried to give them a hint, the women used to say, 'You tell us how to get the victuals; we can cook it all right when we've got it': and they could.

When the pig was fattened – and the fatter the better – the date of execution had to be decided upon. It had to take place some time during the first two quarters of the moon; for, if the pig was killed when the moon was waning the bacon would shrink in cooking, and they wanted it to 'plimp up'. The next thing was to engage the travelling pork butcher, or pig-sticker, and, as he was a thatcher by day, he always had to kill after dark, the scene being lighted with lanterns and the fire of burning straw which at a later stage of the proceedings was to singe the bristles off the victim.

The killing was a noisy, bloody business, in the course of which the animal was hoisted to a rough bench that it might bleed thoroughly and so preserve the quality of the meat. The job was often bungled, the pig sometimes getting away and having to be chased; but country people of that day had little sympathy for the sufferings of animals, and men, women, and children would gather round to see the sight.

After the carcass had been singed, the pig-sticker would pull off the detachable, gristly, outer coverings of the toes, known locally as 'the shoes', and fling them among the children, who scrambled for, then sucked and gnawed them, straight from the filth of the sty and blackened by fire as they were.

The whole scene, with its mud and blood, flaring lights and dark shadows, was as savage as anything to be seen in an African jungle. The children at the end house would steal out of bed to the window. 'Look! Look! It's hell, and those are the devils,' Edmund would whisper, pointing to the men tossing the burning straw with their pitchforks; but Laura felt sick and would creep back into bed and cry: she was sorry for the pig.

But, hidden from the children, there was another aspect of the pig-killing. Months of hard work and self-denial were brought on that night to a successful conclusion. It was a time to rejoice, and rejoice they did, with beer flowing freely and the first delicious dish of pig's fry sizzling in the frying-pan.

The next day, when the carcass had been cut up, joints of pork were distributed to those neighbours who had sent similar ones at their own pig-killing. Small plates of fry and other oddments were sent to others as a pure compliment, and no one who happened to be ill or down on his luck at these occasions was ever forgotten.

Then the housewife 'got down to it', as she said. Hams and sides of bacon were salted, to be taken out of the brine later and hung on the wall near the fireplace to dry. Lard was dried out, hog's puddings were made, and the chitterlings were cleaned and turned three days in succession under running water, according to ancient ritual. It was a busy time, but a happy one, with the larder full and something over to give away, and all the pride and importance of owning such riches.

On the following Sunday came the official 'pig feast', when fathers and mothers, sisters and brothers, married children and grandchildren who lived within walking distance arrived to dinner.

If the house had no oven, permission was obtained from an old couple in one of the thatched cottages to heat up the big bread-baking oven in their wash-house. This was like a large cupboard with an iron door, lined with brick and going far back into the wall. Faggots of wood were lighted inside and the door was closed upon them until the oven was well heated. Then the ashes were swept out and baking tins with joints of pork, potatoes, batter puddings, pork pies, and sometimes a cake or two, were popped inside and left to bake without further attention.

Meanwhile, at home, three or four different kinds of vegetables would be cooked, and always a meat pudding, made in a basin. No feast and few Sunday dinners were considered complete without that item, which was eaten alone, without vegetables, when a joint was to follow. On ordinary days the pudding would be a roly-poly containing fruit, currants, or jam; but it still appeared as a first course, the idea being that it took the edge off the appetite. At the pig feast there would be no sweet pudding, for that could be had any day, and who wanted sweet things when there was plenty of meat to be had!

But this glorious plenty only came once or at most twice a year, and there were all the other days to provide for. How was it done on ten shillings a week? Well, for one thing, food was much cheaper than it is today. Then, in addition to the bacon, all vegetables, including potatoes, were home-grown and grown in abundance. The men took great pride in their gardens and allotments and there was always competition amongst them as to who should have the earliest and choicest of each kind. Fat green peas, broad beans as big as a halfpenny, cauliflowers a child could make an armchair of, runner beans and cabbage and kale, all in their seasons went into the pot with the roly-poly and slip of bacon.

Then they ate plenty of green food, all home-grown and freshly pulled; lettuce and radishes and young onions with pearly heads and leaves like fine grass. A few slices of bread and home-made lard, flavoured with rosemary, and plenty of green food 'went down good' as they used to say.

Bread had to be bought, and that was a heavy item, with so many growing children to be fed; but flour for the daily pudding and an occasional plain cake could be laid in for the winter without any cash outlay. After the harvest had been carried from the fields, the women and children swarmed over the stubble picking up the ears of wheat the horse-rake had missed. Gleaning, or 'leazing', as it was called locally.

Up and down and over and over the stubble they hurried, backs bent, eyes on the ground, one hand outstretched to pick up the ears, the other resting on the small of the back with the 'handful'. When this had been completed, it was bound round with a wisp of straw and erected with others in a double rank, like the harvesters erected their sheaves in shocks, beside the leazer's water-can and dinner-basket. It was hard work, from as soon as possible after daybreak until nightfall, with only two short breaks for refreshment; but the single ears mounted, and a woman with four or five strong, well-disciplined children would carry a good load home on the head every night. And they enjoyed doing it, for it was pleasant in the fields under the pale blue August sky, with the clover springing green in the stubble and the hedges bright with hips and haws and feathery with traveller's joy. When the rest-hour came, the children would wander off down the hedgerows gathering crab-apples or sloes, or searching for mushrooms, while the mothers reclined and suckled their babes and drank their cold tea and gossiped or dozed until it was time to be at it again.

At the end of the fortnight or three weeks that the leazing lasted, the corn would be thrashed out at home and sent to the miller, who paid himself for grinding by taking toll of the flour. Great was the excitement in a good year when the flour came home – one bushel, two bushels, or even more in large, industrious families. The mealy-white sack with its contents was often kept for a time on show on a chair in the living-room and it was a common thing for a passer-by to be invited to 'step inside an' see our little bit o' leazings'. They liked to have the product of their labour before their own eyes and to let others admire it, just as the artist likes to show his picture and the composer to hear his opus played. 'Them's better'n any o' yer oil-paintin's,' a man would say, pointing to the flitches on his wall, and the women felt the same about the leazings.

Here, then, were the three chief ingredients of the one hot meal a day, bacon from the flitch, vegetables from the garden, and flour for the roly-poly. This meal, called 'tea', was taken in the evening, when the men were home from the fields and the children from school, for neither could get home at midday.

About four o'clock, smoke would go up from the chimneys, as the fire was made up and the big iron boiler, or the three-legged pot, was slung on the hook of the chimney-chain. Everything was cooked in the one utensil; the square of bacon, amounting to little more than a taste each; cabbage, or other green vegetables in one net, potatoes in another, and the roly-poly swathed in a cloth. It sounds a haphazard method in these days of gas and electric cookers; but it answered its purpose, for, by carefully timing the putting in of each item and keeping the simmering of the pot well regulated, each item was kept intact and an appetising meal was produced. The water in which the food had been cooked, the potato parings, and other vegetable trimmings were the pig's share.

When the men came home from work they would find the table spread with a clean whitey-brown cloth, upon which would be knives and two-pronged steel forks with buckhorn handles. The vegetables would then be turned out into big round yellow crockery dishes and the bacon cut into dice, with much the largest cube upon Feyther's plate, and the whole family would sit down to the chief meal of the day. True, it was seldom that all could find places at the central table; but some of the smaller children could sit upon stools with the seat of a chair for a table, or on the doorstep with their plates on their laps.

Good manners prevailed. The children were given their share of the food, there was no picking and choosing, and they were expected to eat it in silence. 'Please' and 'Thank you' were permitted, but nothing more. Father and Mother might talk if they wanted to; but usually they were content to concentrate upon their enjoyment of the meal. Father might shovel green peas into his mouth with his knife, Mother might drink her tea from her saucer, and some of the children might lick their plates when the food was devoured; but who could eat peas with a two-pronged fork, or wait for tea to cool after the heat and flurry of cooking, and licking the plates passed as a graceful compliment to Mother's good dinner. 'Thank God for my good dinner. Thank Father and Mother. Amen' was the grace used in one family, and it certainly had the merit of giving credit where credit was due.

For other meals they depended largely on bread and butter, or, more often, bread and lard, eaten with any relish that happened to be at hand. Fresh butter was too costly for general use, but a pound was sometimes purchased in the summer, when it cost tenpence. Margarine, then called 'butterine', was already on the market, but was little used there, as most people preferred lard, especially when it was their own home-made lard flavoured with rosemary leaves. In summer there was always plenty of green food from the garden and home-made jam as long as it lasted, and sometimes an egg or two, where fowls were kept, or when eggs were plentiful and sold at twenty a shilling.

When bread and lard appeared alone, the men would spread mustard on their slices and the children would be given a scraping of black treacle or a sprinkling of brown sugar. Some children, who preferred it, would have 'sop' – bread steeped in boiling water, then strained and sugar added.

Milk was a rare luxury, as it had to be fetched a mile and a half from the farmhouse. The cost was not great: a penny a jug or can, irrespective of size. It was, of course, skimmed milk, but hand-skimmed, not separated, and so still had some small proportion of cream left. A few families fetched it daily; but many did not bother about it. The women said they preferred their tea neat, and it did not seem to occur to them that the children needed milk. Many of them never tasted it from the time they were weaned until they went out in the world. Yet they were stout-limbed and rosy-cheeked and full of life and mischief.

The skimmed milk was supposed by the farmer to be sold at a penny a pint, that remaining unsold going to feed his own calves and pigs. But the dairymaid did not trouble to measure it; she just filled the proffered vessel and let it go as 'a pen'orth'. Of course, the jugs and cans got larger and larger. One old woman increased the size of her vessels by degrees until she had the impudence to take a small, new, tin cooking boiler which was filled without question. The children at the end house wondered what she could do with so much milk, as she had only her husband and herself at home. 'That'll make you a nice big rice pudding, Queenie,' one of them said tentatively.

'Pudden! Lor' bless 'ee!' was Queenie's reply. 'I don't ever make no rice puddens. That milk's for my pig's supper, an', my! ain't 'ee just about thrivin' on it. Can't hardly see out of his eyes, bless him!'

'Poverty's no disgrace, but 'tis a great inconvenience' was a common saying among the Lark Rise people; but that put the case too mildly, for their poverty was no less than a hampering drag upon them. Everybody had enough to eat and a shelter which, though it fell far short of modern requirements, satisfied them. Coal at a shilling a hundredweight and a pint of paraffin for lighting *had* to be squeezed out of the weekly wage; but for boots, clothes, illness, holidays, amusements, and household renewals there was no provision whatever. How did they manage?

Boots were often bought with the extra money the men earned in the harvest field. When that was paid, those lucky families which were not in arrears with their rent would have a new pair all round, from the father's hobnailed dreadnoughts to little pink kid slippers for the baby. Then some careful housewives paid a few pence every week into the boot club run by a shopkeeper in the market town. This helped; but it was not sufficient, and how to get a pair of new boots for 'our young Ern or Alf' was a problem which kept many a mother awake at night.

Girls needed boots, too, and good, stout, nailed ones for those rough and muddy roads; but they were not particular, any boots would do. At a confirmation class which Laura attended, the clergyman's daughter, after weeks of careful preparation, asked her catechumens: 'Now, are you sure you are all of you thoroughly prepared for tomorrow. Is there anything you would like to ask me?'

'Yes, miss,' piped up a voice in a corner, 'me mother says have you got a pair of your old boots you could give me, for I haven't got any fit to go in.'

Alice got her boots on that occasion; but there was not a confirmation every day. Still, boots were obtained somehow; nobody went barefoot, even though some of the toes might sometimes stick out beyond the toe of the boot.

To obtain clothes was an even more difficult matter. Mothers of families sometimes said in despair that they supposed they would have to black their own backsides and go naked. They never quite came to that; but it was difficult to keep decently covered, and that was a pity because they did dearly love what they called 'anything a bit dressy'. This taste was not encouraged by the garments made by the girls in school from material given by the Rectory people – roomy chemises and wide-legged drawers made of unbleached calico, beautifully sewn, but without an inch of trimming; harsh, but strong flannel petticoats and worsted stockings that would almost stand up with no legs in them – although these were gratefully received and had their merits, for they wore for years and the calico improved with washing.

For outer garments they had to depend upon daughters, sisters, and aunts away in service, who all sent parcels, not only of their own clothes, but also of those they could beg from their mistresses. These were worn and altered and dyed and turned and ultimately patched and darned as long as the threads hung together.

But, in spite of their poverty and the worry and anxiety attending it, they were not unhappy, and, though poor, there was nothing sordid about their lives. 'The nearer the bone the sweeter the meat', they used to say, and they were getting very near the bone from which their country ancestors had fed. Their children and children's children would have to depend wholly upon whatever was carved for them from the communal joint, and for their pleasure upon the mass enjoyments of a new era. But for that generation there was still a small picking left to supplement the weekly wage. They had their home-cured bacon, their 'bit o' leazings', their small wheat or barley patch on the allotment; their knowledge of herbs for their homely simples, and the wild fruits and berries of the countryside for jam, jellies, and wine, and round about them as part of their lives were the last relics of country customs and the last echoes of country songs, ballads, and game rhymes. This last picking, though meagre, was sweet.

II

A Hamlet Childhood

Oxford was only nineteen miles distant. The children at the end house knew that, for, while they were small, they were often taken by their mother for a walk along the turnpike and would never pass the milestone until the inscription had been read to them: OXFORD XIX MILES.

They often wondered what Oxford was like and asked questions about it. One answer was that it was 'a gert big town' where a man might earn as much as five and twenty shillings a week; but as he would have to pay 'pretty near' half of it in house rent and have nowhere to keep a pig or to grow many vegetables, he'd be a fool to go there.

One girl who had actually been there on a visit said you could buy a long stick of pink-and-white rock for a penny and that one of her aunt's young gentlemen lodgers had given her a whole shilling for cleaning his shoes. Their mother said it was called a city because a bishop lived there, and that a big fair was held there once a year, and that was all she seemed to know about it. They did not ask their father, although he had lived there as a child, when his parents had kept an hotel in the city (his relations spoke of it as an hotel, but his wife once called it a pot-house, so probably it was an ordinary public-house). They already had to be careful not to ask their father too many questions, and when their mother said, 'Your father's cross again', they found it was better not to talk at all.

So, for some time, Oxford remained to them a dim blur of bishops (they had seen a picture of one with big white sleeves, sitting in a high-backed chair) and swings and shows and coconut shies (for they knew what a fair was like) and little girls sucking pink-and-white rock and polishing shoes. To imagine a place without pigsties and vegetable gardens was more difficult. With no bacon or cabbage, what could people have to eat?

But the Oxford road with the milestone they had known as long as they could remember. Round the Rise and up the narrow hamlet road they would go until they came to the turning, their mother pushing the baby carriage ('pram' was a word of the future) with Edmund strapped in the high, slippery seat, or, later, little May, who was born when Edmund was five, and Laura holding on at the side or darting hither and thither to pick flowers.

The baby carriage was made of black wickerwork, something like an old-fashioned bath-chair in shape, running on three wheels and pushed from behind. It wobbled and creaked and rattled over the stones, for rubber tyres were not yet invented and its springs, if springs it had, were of the most primitive kind. Yet it was one of the most cherished of the family possessions, for there was only one other baby carriage in the hamlet, the up-to-date new bassinet which the young wife at the inn had recently purchased. The other mothers carried their babies on one arm, tightly rolled in shawls, with only the face showing.

As soon as the turning was passed, the flat, brown fields were left behind and they were in a different world with a different atmosphere and even different flowers. Up and down went the white main road between wide grass margins, thick, berried hedgerows and overhanging trees. After the dark mire of the hamlet ways, even the milky-white road surface pleased them, and they would splash up the thin, pale mud, like uncooked batter, or drag their feet through the smooth white dust until their mother got cross and slapped them.

Although it was a main road, there was scarcely any traffic, for the market town lay in the opposite direction along it, the next village was five miles on, and with Oxford there was no road communication from that distant point in those days of horse-drawn vehicles. Today, past that same spot, a first-class, tar-sprayed road, thronged with motor traffic, runs between low, closely trimmed hedges. Last year a girl of eighteen was knocked down and killed by a passing car at that very turning. At that time it was deserted for hours together. Three miles away trains roared over a viaduct, carrying those who would, had they lived a few years before or later, have used the turnpike. People were saying that far too much money was being spent on keeping such roads in repair, for their day was over; they were only needed now for people going from village to village. Sometimes the children and their mother would meet a tradesman's van, delivering goods from the market town at some country mansion, or the doctor's tall gig, or the smart turn-out of a brewer's traveller; but often they walked their mile along the turnpike and back without seeing anything on wheels.

The white tails of rabbits bobbed in and out of the hedgerows; stoats crossed the road in front of the children's feet – swift, silent, stealthy creatures which made them shudder; there were squirrels in the oak-trees, and once they even saw a fox curled up asleep in the ditch beneath thick overhanging ivy. Bands of little blue butterflies flitted here and there or poised themselves with quivering wings on the long grass bents; bees hummed in the white clover blooms, and over all a deep silence brooded. It seemed as though the road had been made ages before, then forgotten.

The children were allowed to run freely on the grass verges, as wide as a small meadow in places. 'Keep to the grinsard,' their mother would call. 'Don't go on the road. Keep to the grinsard!' and it was many years before Laura realized that that name for the grass verges, in general use there, was a worn survival of the old English 'greensward'.

It was no hardship to her to be obliged to keep to the greensward, for flowers strange to the hamlet soil flourished there, eyebright and harebell, sunset-coloured patches of lady's-glove, and succory with vivid blue flowers and stems like black wire.

In one little roadside dell mushrooms might sometimes be found, small button mushrooms with beaded moisture on their cold milk-white skins. The dell was the farthest point of their walk; after searching the long grass for mushrooms, in season and out of season – for they would not give up hope – they turned back and never reached the second milestone.

Once or twice when they reached the dell they got a greater thrill than even the discovery of a mushroom could give; for the gipsies were there, their painted caravan drawn up, their poor old skeleton horse turned loose to graze, and their fire with a cooking pot over it, as though the whole road belonged to them. With men making pegs, women combing their hair or making cabbage nets, and boys and girls and dogs sprawling around, the dell was full of dark, wild life, foreign to the hamlet children and fascinating, yet terrifying.

When they saw the gipsies they drew back behind their mother and the baby carriage, for there was a tradition that once, years before, a child from a neighbouring village had been stolen by them. Even the cold ashes where a gipsy's fire had been sent little squiggles of fear down Laura's spine, for how could she know that they were not still lurking near with designs upon her own person? Her mother laughed at her fears and said, 'Surely to goodness they've got children enough of their own,' but Laura would not be reassured. She never really enjoyed the game the hamlet children played going home from school, when one of them went on before to hide and the others followed slowly, hand in hand, singing:

'I hope we shan't meet any gipsies tonight!
I hope we shan't meet any gipsies tonight!'

And when the hiding-place was reached and the supposed gipsy sprung out and grabbed the nearest, she always shrieked, although she knew it was only a game.

But in those early days of the walks fear only gave spice to excitement, for Mother was there, Mother in her pretty maize-coloured gown with the rows and rows of narrow brown velvet sewn round the long skirt, which stuck out like a bell, and her second-best hat with the honeysuckle. She was still in her twenties and still very pretty, with her neat little figure, rose-leaf complexion and hair which was brown in some lights and golden in others. When her family grew larger and troubles crowded upon her and the rose-leaf complexion had faded and the last of the pre-marriage wardrobe had worn out, the walks were given up; but by that time

Edmund and Laura were old enough to go where they liked, and, though they usually preferred to go farther afield on Saturdays and other school holidays, they would sometimes go to the turnpike to jump over and over the milestone and scramble about in the hedges for blackberries and crab-apples.

It was while they were still small they were walking there one day with a visiting aunt; Edmund and Laura, both in clean, white, starched clothes, holding on to a hand on either side. The children were a little shy, for they did not remember seeing this aunt before. She was married to a master builder in Yorkshire and only visited her brother and his family at long intervals. But they liked her, although Laura had already sensed that their mother did not. Jane was too dressy and 'set up' for her taste, she said. That morning, her luggage being still at the railway station, she was wearing the clothes she had travelled in, a long, pleated dove-coloured gown with an apron arrangement drawn round and up and puffed over a bustle at the back, and, on her head, a tiny toque made entirely of purple velvet pansies.

Swish, swish, swish, went her long skirt over the grass verges; but every time they crossed the road she would relinquish Laura's hand to gather it up from the dust, thus revealing to the child's delighted gaze a frilly purple petticoat. When she was grown up she would have a frock and petticoat just like those, she decided.

But Edmund was not interested in clothes. Being a polite little boy, he was trying to make conversation. He had already shown his aunt the spot where they had found the dead hedgehog and the bush where the thrush had built last spring and told her the distant rumble they heard was a train going over the viaduct, when they came to the milestone.

'Aunt Jenny,' he said, 'what's Oxford like?'

'Well, it's all old buildings, churches and colleges where rich people's sons go to school when they're grown up.'

'What do they learn there?' demanded Laura.

'Oh, Latin and Greek and suchlike, I suppose.'

'Do they all go there?' asked Edmund seriously.

'Well, no. Some go to Cambridge; there are colleges there as well. Some go to one and some to the other,' said the aunt with a smile that meant 'Whatever will these children want to know next?'

Four-year-old Edmund pondered a few moments, then said, 'Which college shall I go to when I am grown up, Oxford or Cambridge?' and his expression of innocent good faith checked his aunt's inclination to laugh.

'There won't be any college for you, my poor little man,' she explained. 'You'll have to go to work as soon as you leave school; but if I could have *my* way, you should go to the very best college in Oxford,' and, for the rest of the walk she entertained them with stories of her mother's family, the Wallingtons.

She said one of her uncles had written a book and she thought Edmund might turn out to be clever, like him. But when they told their mother what she had said she tossed her head and said she had never heard about any book, and what if he had, wasting his time. It was not as if he was like Shakespeare or Miss Braddon or anybody like that. And she hoped Edmund would not turn out to be clever. Brains were no good to a working man; they only made him discontented and saucy and lose his jobs. She'd seen it happen again and again.

Yet she had brains of her own and her education had been above the average in her station in life. She had been born and brought up in a cottage standing in the churchyard of a neighbouring village, 'just like the little girl in *We are Seven*', she used to tell her own children. At the time when she was a small girl in the churchyard cottage the incumbent of the parish had been an old man and with him had lived his still more aged sister. This lady, whose name was Miss Lowe, had become very fond of the pretty, fair-haired little girl at the churchyard cottage and had had her at the Rectory every day out of school hours. Little Emma had a sweet voice and she was supposed to go there for singing lessons; but she had learned other things, too, including old-world manners and to write a beautiful antique hand with delicate, open-looped pointed letters and long 's's', such as her instructress and other young ladies had been taught in the last quarter of the eighteenth century.

Miss Lowe was then nearly eighty, and had long been dead when

Laura, at two and a half years old, had been taken by her mother to see the by then very aged Rector. The visit was one of her earliest memories, which survived as an indistinct impression of twilight in a room with dark green walls and the branch of a tree against the outside of the window; and, more distinctly, a pair of trembling, veiny hands putting something smooth and cold and round into her own. The smooth cold roundness was accounted for afterwards. The old gentleman, it appeared, had given her a china mug which had been his sister's in her nursery days. It had stood on the mantelpiece at the end house for years, a beautiful old piece with a design of heavy green foliage on a ground of translucent whiteness. Afterwards it got broken, which was strange in that careful home; but Laura carried the design in her mind's eye for the rest of her life and would sometimes wonder if it accounted for her lifelong love of green and white in conjunction.

Their mother would often tell the children about the Rectory and her own home in the churchyard, and how the choir, in which her father played the violin, would bring their instruments and practise there in the evening. But she liked better to tell of that other rectory where she had been nurse to the children. The living was small and the Rector was poor, but three maids had been possible in those days, a cook-general, a young housemaid, and Nurse Emma. They must have been needed in that large, rambling old house, in which lived the Rector and his wife, their nine children, three maids, and often three or four young men pupils. They had all had such jolly, happy times she said; all of them, family and maids and pupils, singing glees and part songs in the drawing-room in the evening. But what thrilled Laura most was that she herself had had a narrow escape from ever having been born at all. Some relatives of the family who had settled in New South Wales had come to England on a visit and nearly persuaded Nurse Emma to go back with them. Indeed, it was all settled when, one night, they began talking about snakes, which, according to their account, infested their Australian bungalow and garden. 'Then,' said Emma, 'I shan't go, for I can't abear the horrid creatures,' and she did not go, but got married instead and became the mother of Edmund and Laura. But it seems that the call was genuine, that Australia had something for, or required something of, her descendants; for of the next generation her own second son became a fruit-farmer in Queensland, and of the next a son of Laura's is now an engineer in Brisbane.

The little Johnstones were always held up as an example to the end-house children. They were always kind to each other and obedient to their elders, never grubby or rowdy or inconsiderate. Perhaps they deteriorated after Nurse Emma left, for Laura remembered being taken to see them before they left the neighbourhood for good, when one of the big boys pulled her hair and made faces at her and buried her doll beneath a tree in the orchard, with one of the cook's aprons tied round his neck by way of a surplice.

The eldest girl, Miss Lily, then about nineteen, walked miles of the way back home with them and returned alone in the twilight (so Victorian young ladies were not always as carefully guarded as they are now supposed to have been!). Laura remembered the low murmur of conversation behind her as she rode for a lift on the front of the baby carriage with her heels dangling over the front wheel. Both a Sir George and a Mr Looker, it appeared, were paying Miss Lily 'particular attention' at the time, and their rival advantages were under discussion. Every now and then Miss Lily would protest, 'But, Emma, Sir George paid me *particular attention*. Many remarked upon it to Mamma,' and Emma would say, 'But, Miss Lily, my dear, do you think he is serious?' Perhaps he was, for Miss Lily was a lovely girl; but it was as Mrs Looker she became a kind of fairy godmother to the end-house family. A Christmas parcel of books and toys came from her regularly, and although she never saw her old nurse again, they were still writing to each other in the nineteen-twenties.

Around the hamlet cottages played many little children, too young to go to school. Every morning they were bundled into a piece of old shawl crossed on the chest and tied in a hard knot at the back, a slice of food was thrust into their hands and they were told to 'go play' while their mothers got on with the house-work. In winter, their little limbs purple-mottled with cold, they would stamp around playing horses or engines. In summer they would make mud pies in the dust, moistening them from their own most intimate water supply. If they fell down or hurt themselves in any other way, they did not run indoors for comfort, for they knew that all they would get would be 'Sarves ye right. You should've looked where you wer' a-goin'!'

They were like little foals turned out to grass, and received about as much attention. They might, and often did, have running noses and chilblains on hands, feet and ear-tips; but they hardly ever were ill enough to have to stay indoors, and grew sturdy and strong, so the system must have suited them. 'Makes 'em hardy,' their mothers said, and hardy, indeed, they became, just as the men and women and older boys and girls of the hamlet were hardy, in body and spirit.

Sometimes Laura and Edmund would go out to play with the other children. Their father did not like this; he said they were little savages already. But their mother maintained that, as they would have to go to school soon, it was better for them to fall in at once with the hamlet ways. 'Besides,' she would say, 'why shouldn't they? There's nothing the matter with Lark Rise folks but poverty, and that's no crime. If it was, we should likely be hung ourselves.'

So the children went out to play and often had happy times, outlining houses with scraps of broken crockery and furnishing them with moss and stones; or lying on their stomachs in the dust to peer down into the deep cracks dry weather always produced in that stiff, clayey soil; or making snow men or sliding on puddles in winter.

Other times were not so pleasant, for a quarrel would arise and kicks and blows would fly freely, and how hard those little two-year-old fists could hit out! To say that a child was as broad as it was long was considered a compliment by the hamlet mothers, and some of those toddlers in their knotted woollen wrappings were as near square as anything human can be. One little girl named Rosie Phillips fascinated Laura. She was plump and hard and as rosy-cheeked as an apple, with the deepest of dimples and hair like bronze wire. No matter how hard the other children bumped into her in the games, she stood foursquare, as firm as a little rock. She was a very hard hitter and had little, pointed, white teeth that bit. The two tamer children always came out worst in these conflicts. Then they would make a dash on their long stalky legs for their own garden gate, followed by stones and cries of 'Long-shanks! Cowardy, cowardy custards!'

During those early years at the end house plans were always being made and discussed. Edmund must be apprenticed to a good trade – a carpenter's, perhaps – for if a man had a good trade in his hands he was always sure of a living. Laura might become a school-teacher, or, if that proved impossible, a children's nurse in a good family. But, first and foremost, the family must move from Lark Rise to a house in the market town. It had always been the parents' intention to leave. When he met and married his wife the father was a stranger in the neighbourhood, working for a few months on the restoration of the church in a neighbouring parish and the end house had been taken as a temporary home. Then the children had come and other things had happened to delay the removal. They could not give notice until Michaelmas Day, or another baby was coming, or they must wait until the pig was killed or the allotment crops were brought in; there was always some obstacle, and at the end of seven years they were still at the end house and still talking almost daily about leaving it. Fifty years later the father had died there and the mother was living there alone.

When Laura approached school-going age the discussions became more urgent. Her father did not want the children to go to school with the hamlet children and for once her mother agreed with him. Not because, as he said, they ought to have a better education than they could get at Lark Rise; but because she feared they would tear their clothes and catch cold and get dirty heads going the mile and a half to and from the school in the mother village. So vacant cottages in the market town were inspected and often it seemed that the next week or the next month they would be leaving Lark Rise for ever; but, again, each time something would happen to prevent the removal, and, gradually, a new idea arose. To gain time, their father would teach the two eldest children to read and write, so that, if approached by the School Attendance Office, their mother could say they were leaving the hamlet shortly and, in the meantime, were being taught at home.

So their father brought home two copies of Mavor's First Reader and taught them the alphabet; but just as Laura was beginning on words of one syllable, he was sent away to work on a distant job, only coming home at week-ends. Laura, left at the 'C-a-t s-i-t-s on the m-a-t' stage, had then to carry her book round after her mother as she went about her housework, asking: 'Please, Mother, what does h-o-u-s-e spell?' or 'W-a-l-k, Mother, what is that?' Often when her mother was too busy or too irritated to attend to her, she would sit and gaze on a page that might as well have been printed in Hebrew for all she could make of it, frowning and poring over the print as though she would wring out the meaning by force of concentration.

After weeks of this, there came a day when, quite suddenly, as it seemed to her, the printed characters took on a meaning. There were still many words, even in the first pages of that simple primer, she could not decipher; but she could skip those and yet make sense of the whole. 'I'm reading! I'm reading!' she cried aloud. 'Oh, Mother! Oh, Edmund! I'm reading!'

There were not many books in the house, although in this respect the family was better off than its neighbours; for, in addition to 'Father's books', mostly unreadable as yet, and Mother's Bible and *Pilgrim's Progress*, there were a few children's books which the Johnstones had turned out from their nursery when they left the neighbourhood. So, in time, she was able to read Grimms' *Fairy Tales*, *Gulliver's Travels*, *The Daisy Chain*, and Mrs Molesworth's *Cuckoo Clock* and *Carrots*.

As she was seldom seen without an open book in her hand, it was not long before the neighbours knew she could read. They did not approve of this at all. None of their children had learned to read before they went to school, and then only under compulsion, and they thought that Laura, by doing so, had stolen a march on them. So they attacked her mother about it, her father conveniently being away. 'He'd no business to teach the child himself,' they said.

'Schools be the places for teaching, and you'll likely get wrong for him doing it when governess finds out.' Others, more kindly disposed, said Laura was trying her eyes and begged her mother to put an end to her studies; but, as fast as one book was hidden away from her, she found another, for anything in print drew her eyes as a magnet drew steel.

Edmund did not learn to read quite so early; but when he did, he learned more thoroughly. No skipping unknown words for him and guessing what they meant by the context; he mastered every page before he turned over, and his mother was more patient with his inquiries, for Edmund was her darling.

If the two children could have gone on as they were doing, and have had access to suitable books as they advanced, they would probably have learnt more than they did during their brief school-days. But that happy time of discovery did not last. A woman, the frequent absences from school of whose child had brought the dreaded Attendance Officer to her door, informed him of the end-house scandal, and he went there and threatened Laura's mother with all manner of penalties if Laura was not in school at nine o'clock the next Monday morning.

So there was to be no Oxford or Cambridge for Edmund. No school other than the National School for either. They would have to pick up what learning they could like chickens pecking for grain – a little at school, more from books, and some by dipping into the store of others.

Sometimes, later, when they read about children whose lives were very different from their own, children who had nurseries with rocking-horses and went to parties and for sea-side holidays and were encouraged to do and praised for doing just those things they themselves were thought odd for, they wondered why they had alighted at birth upon such an unpromising spot as Lark Rise.

That was indoors. Outside there was plenty to see and hear and learn, for the hamlet people were interesting, and almost every one of them interesting in some different way to the others, and to Laura the old people were the most interesting of all, for they told her about the old times and could sing old songs and remember old customs, although they could never remember enough to satisfy her. She sometimes wished she could make the earth and stones speak and tell her about all the dead people who had trodden upon them. She was fond of collecting stones of all shapes and colours, and for years played with the idea that, one day, she would touch a secret spring and a stone would fly open and reveal a parchment which would tell her exactly what the world was like when it was written and placed there.

There were no bought pleasures, and, if there had been, there was no money to pay for them; but there were the sights, sounds and scents of the different seasons: spring with its fields of young wheat-blades bending in the wind as the cloud-shadows swept over them; summer with its ripening grain and its flowers and fruit and its thunder-storms, and how the thunder growled and rattled over that flat land and what boiling, sizzling downpours it brought! With August came the harvest and the fields settled down to the long winter rest, when the snow was often piled high and frozen, so that the buried hedges could be walked over, and strange birds came for crumbs to the cottage doors and hares in search of food left their spoor round the pigsties.

The children at the end house had their own private amusements, such as guarding the clump of white violets they found blooming in a cleft of the brook bank and called their 'holy secret', or pretending the scabious, which bloomed in abundance there, had fallen in a shower from the mid-summer sky, which was exactly the same dim, dreamy blue. Another favourite game was to creep silently up behind birds which had perched on a rail or twig and try to touch their tails. Laura once succeeded in this, but she was alone at the time and nobody believed she had done it.

A little later, remembering man's earthy origin, 'dust thou art and to dust thou shalt return', they liked to fancy themselves bubbles of earth. When alone in the fields, with no one to see them, they would hop, skip and jump, touching the ground as lightly as possible and crying 'We are bubbles of earth! Bubbles of earth! Bubbles of earth!'

But although they had these private fancies, unknown to their elders, they did not grow into the ultra-sensitive, misunderstood, and thwarted adolescents who, according to present-day writers, were a feature of that era. Perhaps, being of mixed birth with a large proportion of peasant blood in them, they were tougher in fibre than some. When their bottoms were soundly smacked, as they often were, their reaction was to make a mental note not to repeat the offence which had caused the smacking, rather than to lay up for themselves complexes to spoil their later lives; and when Laura, at about twelve years old, stumbled into a rickyard where a bull was in the act of justifying its existence, the sight did not warp her nature. She neither peeped from behind a rick, nor fled, horrified, across country; but merely thought in her old-fashioned way, 'Dear me! I had better slip quietly away before the men see me.' The bull to her was but a bull performing a necessary function if there was to be butter on the bread and bread and milk for breakfast, and she thought it quite natural that the men in attendance at such functions should prefer not to have women or little girls as spectators. They would have felt, as they would have said, 'a bit okkard'. She just withdrew and went another way round without so much as a kink in her subconscious.

From the time the two children began school they were merged in the hamlet life, sharing the work and play and mischief of their younger companions and taking harsh or kind words from their elders according to circumstances. Yet, although they shared in the pleasures, limitations, and hardships of the hamlet, some peculiarity of mental outlook prevented them from accepting everything that existed or happened there as a matter of course, as the other children did. Small things which passed unnoticed by others interested, delighted, or saddened them. Nothing that took place around them went unnoted; words spoken and forgotten the next moment by the speaker were recorded in their memories, and the actions and reactions of others were impressed on their minds, until a clear, indelible impression of their little world remained with them for life.

Their own lives were to carry them far from the hamlet. Edmund's to South Africa, India, Canada, and, lastly, to his soldier's grave in

Belgium. Their credentials presented, they will only appear in this book as observers of and commentators upon the country scene of their birth and early years.

III

Men Afield

A mile and a half up the straight, narrow road in the opposite direction to that of the turnpike, round a corner, just out of sight of the hamlet, lay the mother village of Fordlow. Here, again, as soon as the turning of the road was passed, the scene changed, and the large open fields gave place to meadows and elm trees and tiny trickling streams.

The village was a little, lost, lonely place, much smaller than the hamlet, without a shop, an inn, or a post office, and six miles from a railway station. The little squat church, without spire or tower, crouched back in a tiny churchyard that centuries of use had raised many feet above the road, and the whole was surrounded by tall, windy elms in which a colony of rooks kept up a perpetual cawing. Next came the Rectory, so buried in orchards and shrubberies that only the chimney stacks were visible from the road; then the old Tudor farmhouse with its stone, mullioned windows and reputed dungeon. These, with the school and about a dozen cottages occupied by the shepherd, carter, blacksmith, and a few other superior farm-workers, made up the village. Even these few buildings were strung out along the roadside, so far between and so sunken in greenery that there seemed no village at all. It was a standing joke in the hamlet that a stranger had once asked the way to Fordlow after he had walked right through it. The hamlet laughed at the village as 'stuck up'; while the village looked down on 'that gipsy lot' at the hamlet.

Excepting the two or three men who frequented the inn in the evening, the villagers seldom visited the hamlet, which to them represented the outer wilds, beyond the bounds of civilization. The hamlet people, on the other hand, knew the road between the two places by heart, for the church and the school and the farmhouse which was the men's working headquarters were all in the village. The hamlet had only the inn.

Very early in the morning, before daybreak for the greater part of the year, the hamlet men would throw on their clothes, breakfast on bread and lard, snatch the dinner-baskets which had been packed for them overnight, and hurry off across fields and over stiles to the farm. Getting the boys off was a more difficult matter. Mothers would have to call and shake and sometimes pull boys of eleven or twelve out of their warm beds on a winter morning. Then boots which had been drying inside the fender all night and had become shrunk and hard as boards in the process would have to be coaxed on over chilblains. Sometimes a very small boy would cry over this and his mother to cheer him would remind him that they were only boots, not breeches. 'Good thing you didn't live when breeches wer' made o' leather,' she would say, and tell him about the boy of a previous generation whose leather breeches were so baked up in drying that it took him an hour to get into them. 'Patience! Have patience, my son', his mother had exhorted. 'Remember Job.' 'Job!' scoffed the boy. 'What did he know about patience? He didn't have to wear no leather breeches.'

Leather breeches had disappeared in the 'eighties and were only remembered in telling that story. The carter, shepherd, and a few of the older labourers still wore the traditional smock-frock topped by a round black felt hat, like those formerly worn by clergymen. But this old country style of dress was already out of date; most of the men wore suits of stiff, dark brown corduroy, or, in summer, corduroy trousers and an unbleached drill jacket known as a 'sloppy'.

Most of the young and those in the prime of life were thickset, red-faced men of good medium height and enormous strength who prided themselves on the weights they could carry and boasted of never having had 'an e-ache nor a pa-in' in their lives. The elders stooped, had gnarled and swollen hands and walked badly, for they felt the effects of a life spent out of doors in all weathers and of the rheumatism which tried most of them. These elders wore a fringe of grey whisker beneath the jaw, extending from ear to ear. The younger men sported drooping walrus moustaches. One or two, in advance of the fashion of their day, were clean-shaven; but as Sunday was the only shaving day, the effect of either style became blurred by the end of the week.

They still spoke the dialect, in which the vowels were not only broadened, but in many words doubled. 'Boy' was 'boo-oy', 'coal', 'coo-al', 'pail', 'pay-ull', and so on. In other words, syllables were slurred, and words were run together, as 'brenbu'er' for bread and butter. They had hundreds of proverbs and sayings and their talk was stiff with simile. Nothing was simply hot, cold, or coloured; it was 'as hot as hell', 'as cold as ice', 'as green as grass', or 'as yellow as a guinea'. A botched-up job done with insufficient materials was 'like Dick's hat-band that went half-way round and tucked'; to try to persuade or encourage one who did not respond was 'putting a poultice on wooden leg'. To be nervy was to be 'like a cat on hot bricks'; to be angry, 'mad as a bull'; or any one might be 'poor as a rat', 'sick as a dog', 'hoarse as a crow', 'as ugly as sin', 'full of the milk of human kindness', or 'stinking with pride'. A temperamental person was said to be 'one o' them as is either up on the roof or down the well'. The dialect was heard at its best on the lips of the few middle-aged men, who had good natural voices, plenty of sense, and a grave, dignified delivery. Mr Frederick Grisewood of the BBC gave a perfect rendering of the old Oxfordshire dialect in some broadcast sketches a few years ago. Usually, such imitations are maddening to the native born; but he made the past live again for one listener.

The men's incomes were the same to a penny; their circumstances, pleasures, and their daily field work were shared in common; but in themselves they differed, as other men of their day differed, in country and town. Some were intelligent, others slow at the uptake; some were kind and helpful, others selfish, some vivacious, others taciturn. If a stranger had gone there looking for the conventional Hodge, he would not have found him.

Nor would he have found the dry humour of the Scottish peasant, or the racy wit and wisdom of Thomas Hardy's Wessex. These men's minds were cast in a heavier mould and moved more slowly. Yet there were occasional gleams of quiet fun. One man who had found Edmund crying because his magpie, let out for her daily exercise, had not returned to her wicker cage, said: 'Doo'nt 'ee take on like that, my man. You goo an' tell Mrs Andrews about it [naming the village gossip] an' you'll hear where your Maggie's been seen, if 'tis as far away as Stratton.'

Their favourite virtue was endurance. Not to flinch from pain or hardship was their ideal. A man would say, 'He says, says he, that field o' oo-ats's got to come in afore night, for there's a rain a-comin'. But we didn't flinch, not we! Got the last loo-ad under cover by midnight. A'moost too fagged-out to walk home; but we didn't flinch. We done it!' Or, 'Ole bull he comes for me, wi's head down. But I didn't flinch. I ripped off a bit o' loose rail an' went for he. 'Twas him as did th' flinchin'. He! he!' Or a woman would say, 'I set up wi' my poor old mother six nights runnin'; never had me clothes off. But I didn't flinch, an' I pulled her through, for she didn't flinch neither.' Or a young wife would say to the midwife after her first confinement, 'I didn't flinch, did I? Oh, I do hope I didn't flinch.'

The farm was large, extending far beyond the parish boundaries; being, in fact, several farms, formerly in separate occupancy, but now thrown into one and ruled over by the rich old man at the Tudor farmhouse. The meadows around the farmstead sufficed for the carthorses' grazing and to support the store cattle and a couple of milking cows which supplied the farmer's family and those of a few of his immediate neighbours with butter and milk. A few fields were sown with grass seed for hay, and sainfoin and rye were grown and cut green for cattle food. The rest was arable land producing corn and root crops, chiefly wheat.

Around the farmhouse were grouped the farm buildings; stables for the great stamping shaggy-fetlocked carthorses; barns with doors so wide and high that a load of hay could be driven through; sheds for the yellow-and-blue painted farm wagons, granaries with outdoor staircases; and sheds for storing oilcake, artificial manures, and agricultural implements. In the rickyard, tall, pointed, elaborately thatched ricks stood on stone straddles; the dairy indoors, though small, was a model one; there was a profusion of all that was necessary or desirable for good farming.

Labour, too, was lavishly used. Boys leaving school were taken on at the farm as a matter of course, and no time-expired soldier or settler on marriage was ever refused a job. As the farmer said, he could always do with an extra hand, for labour was cheap and the land was well tilled up to the last inch.

When the men and boys from the hamlet reached the farmyard in the morning, the carter and his assistant had been at work for an hour, feeding and getting ready the horses. After giving any help required, the men and boys would harness and lead out their teams and file off to the field where their day's work was to be done.

If it rained, they donned sacks, split up one side to form a hood and cloak combined. If it was frosty, they blew upon their nails and thumped their arms across their chest to warm them. If they felt hungry after their bread-and-lard breakfast, they would pare a turnip and munch it, or try a bite or two of the rich, dark brown oilcake provided for the cattle. Some of the boys would sample the tallow candles belonging to the stable lanterns; but that was done more out of devilry than from hunger, for, whoever went short, the mothers took care that their Tom or Dicky should have 'a bit o' summat to peck at between meals' – half a cold pancake or the end of yesterday's roly-poly.

With 'Gee!' and 'Wert up!' and 'Who-a-a, now!' the teams would draw out. The boys were hoisted to the backs of the tall carthorses, and the men, walking alongside, filled their clay pipes with shag and drew the first precious puffs of the day, as with cracking of whips, clopping of hooves and jingling of harness, the teams went tramping along the muddy byways.

The field names gave the clue to the fields' history. Near the farmhouse, 'Moat Piece', 'Fishponds', 'Duffus [i.e. dovehouse] Piece', 'Kennels', and 'Warren Piece' spoke of a time before the Tudor house took the place of another and older establishment. Farther on, 'Lark Hill', 'Cuckoos' Clump', 'The Osiers', and 'Pond Piece' were named after natural features, while 'Gibbard's Piece' and 'Blackwell's' probably commemorated otherwise long-forgotten former occupants. The large new fields round the hamlet had been cut too late to be named and were known as 'The Hundred Acres', 'The Sixty Acres', and so on according to their acreage. One or two of the ancients persisted in calling one of these 'The Heath' and another 'The Racecourse'.

One name was as good as another to most of the men; to them it was just a name and meant nothing. What mattered to them about the fields in which they happened to be working was whether the road was good or bad which led from the farm to it; or if it was comparatively sheltered or one of those bleak open places which the wind hurtled through, driving the rain through the clothes to the very pores; and was the soil easily workable or of back-breaking heaviness or so bound together with that 'hemmed' twitch that a ploughshare could scarcely get through it.

There were usually three or four ploughs to a field, each of them drawn by a team of three horses, with a boy at the head of the leader and the ploughman behind at the shafts. All day, up and down they would go, ribbing the pale stubble with stripes of dark furrows, which, as the day advanced, would get wider and nearer together, until, at length, the whole field lay a rich velvety plum-colour.

Each plough had its following of rooks, searching the clods with sidelong glances for worms and grubs. Little hedgerow birds flitted hither and thither, intent upon getting their tiny share of whatever was going. Sheep, penned in a neighbouring field, bleated complainingly; and above the ma-a-ing and cawing and twittering rose the immemorial cries of the land-worker: 'Wert up!' 'Who-o-o-a!' 'Go it, Poppet!' 'Go it, Lightfoot!' 'Boo-oy, be you deaf, or be you hard of hearin', dang ye!'

After the plough had done its part, the horse-drawn roller was used to break down the clods; then the harrow to comb out and leave in neat piles the weeds and the twitch grass which infested those fields, to be fired later and fill the air with the light blue haze and the scent that can haunt for a lifetime. Then seed was sown, crops were thinned out and hoed and, in time, mown, and the whole process began again.

Machinery was just coming into use on the land. Every autumn appeared a pair of large traction engines, which, posted one on each side of a field, drew a plough across and across by means of a cable. These toured the district under their own steam for hire on the different farms, and the outfit included a small caravan, known as 'the box', for the two drivers to live and sleep in. In the 'nineties, when they had decided to emigrate and wanted to learn all that was possible about farming, both Laura's brothers, in turn, did a spell with the steam plough, horrifying the other hamlet people, who looked upon such nomads as social outcasts. Their ideas had not then been extended to include mechanics as a class apart and they were lumped as inferiors with sweeps and tinkers and others whose work made their faces and clothes black. On the other hand, clerks and salesmen of every grade, whose clean smartness might have been expected to ensure respect, were looked down upon as 'counter-jumpers'. Their recognized world was made up of landowners, farmers, publicans, and farm labourers, with the butcher, the baker, the miller, and the grocer as subsidiaries.

Such machinery as the farmer owned was horse-drawn and was only in partial use. In some fields a horse-drawn drill would sow the seed in rows, in others a human sower would walk up and down with a basket suspended from his neck and fling the seed with both hands broadcast. In harvest time the mechanical reaper was already a familiar sight, but it only did a small part of the work; men were still mowing with scythes and a few women were still reaping with sickles. A thrashing machine on hire went from farm to farm and its use was more general; but men at home still thrashed out their allotment crops and their wives' leazings with a flail and winnowed the corn by pouring from sieve to sieve in the wind.

The labourers worked hard and well when they considered the occasion demanded it and kept up a good steady pace at all times. Some were better workmen than others, of course; but the majority took a pride in their craft and were fond of explaining to an outsider that field work was not the fool's job that some townsmen considered it. Things must be done just so and at the exact moment, they said; there were ins and outs in good land work which took a man's lifetime to learn. A few of less admirable build would boast: 'We gets ten bob a week, a' we yarns every penny of it; but we doesn't yarn no more; we takes hemmed good care o' that!' But at team work, at least, such 'slack-twisted 'uns' had to keep in step, and the pace, if slow, was steady.

While the ploughmen were in charge of the teams, other men went singly, or in twos or threes, to hoe, harrow, or spread manure in other fields; others cleared ditches and saw to drains, or sawed wood or cut chaff or did other odd jobs about the farmstead. Two or three highly skilled middle-aged men were sometimes put upon piecework, hedging and ditching, sheep-shearing, thatching, or mowing, according to the season. The carter, shepherd, stockman, and blacksmith had each his own specialized job. Important men, these, with two shillings a week extra on their wages and a cottage rent free near the farmstead.

When the ploughmen shouted to each other across the furrows, they did not call 'Miller' or 'Gaskins' or 'Tuffrey' or even 'Bill', 'Tom' or 'Dick', for they all had nicknames and answered more readily to 'Bishie' or 'Pumpkin' or 'Boamer'. The origin of many of these names was forgotten, even by the bearers; but a few were traceable to personal peculiarities. 'Cockie' or 'Cock-eye' had a slight cast; 'Old Stut' stuttered, while 'Bavour' was so called because when he fancied a snack between meals he would say 'I must just have my mouthful of bavour', using the old name for a snack, which was rapidly becoming modernized into 'lunch' or 'luncheon'.

When, a few years later, Edmund worked in the fields for a time, the carter, having asked him some question and being struck with the aptness of his reply, exclaimed: 'Why, boo-oy, you be as wise as Solomon, an' Solomon I shall call 'ee!' and Solomon he was until he left the hamlet. A younger brother was called 'Fisher'; but the origin of this name was a mystery. His mother, who was fonder of boys than girls, used to call him her 'kingfisher'.

Sometimes afield, instead of the friendly shout, a low hissing whistle would pass between the ploughs. It was a warning note that meant that 'Old Monday', the farm bailiff, had been sighted. He would come riding across the furrows on his little long-tailed grey pony, himself so tall and his steed so dumpy that his feet almost touched the ground, a rosy, shrivelled, nut-cracker-faced old fellow, swishing his ash stick and shouting, 'Hi, men! Ho, men! What do you reckon you're doing!'

He questioned them sharply and found fault here and there, but was in the main fairly just in his dealings with them. He had one great fault in their eyes, however; he was always in a hurry himself and he tried to hurry them, and that was a thing they detested.

The nickname of 'Old Monday', or 'Old Monday Morning', had been bestowed upon him years before when some hitch had occurred and he was said to have cried: 'Ten o'clock Monday morning! Today's Monday, tomorrow's Tuesday, next day's Wednesday – half the week gone and nothing done!' This name, of course, was reserved for his absence; while he was with them it was 'Yes, Muster Morris' and 'No, Muster Morris', and 'I'll see what I can do, Muster Morris'. A few of the tamer-spirited even called him 'sir'. Then, as soon as his back was turned, some wag would point to it with one hand and slap his own buttocks with the other, saying, but not too loudly, 'My elbow to you, you ole devil!'

At twelve by the sun, or by signal from the possessor of one of the old turnip-faced watches which descended from father to son, the teams would knock off for the dinner-hour. Horses were unyoked, led to the shelter of a hedge or a rick and given their nosebags, and men and boys threw themselves down on sacks spread out beside them and tin bottles of cold tea were uncorked and red handkerchiefs of food unwrapped. The lucky ones had bread and cold bacon, perhaps the top or the bottom of a cottage loaf, on which the small cube of bacon was placed, with a finger of bread on top, called the thumbpiece, to keep the meat untouched by hand and in position for manipulation with a clasp-knife. The consumption of this food was managed neatly and decently, a small sliver of bacon and chunk of bread being cut and conveyed to the mouth in one movement. The less fortunate ones munched their bread and lard or morsel of cheese; and the boys with their ends of cold pudding were jokingly bidden not to get 'that 'ere treacle' in their ears.

The food soon vanished, the crumbs from the red handkerchiefs were shaken out for the birds, the men lighted their pipes and the boys wandered off with their catapults down the hedgerows. Often the elders would sit out their hour of leisure discussing politics, the latest murder story, or local affairs; but at other times, especially when one man noted for that kind of thing was present, they would while away the time in repeating what the women spoke of with shamed voices as 'men's tales'.

These stories, which were kept strictly to the fields and never repeated elsewhere, formed a kind of rustic *Decameron*, which seemed to have been in existence for centuries and increased like a snowball as it rolled down the generations. The tales were supposed to be extremely indecent, and elderly men would say after such a sitting, 'I got up an' went over to th' 'osses, for I couldn't stand no more on't. The brimstone fair come out o' their mouths as they put their rascally heads together.' What they were really like only the men knew; but probably they were coarse rather than filthy. Judging by a few stray specimens which leaked through the channel of eavesdropping juniors, they consisted chiefly of 'he said' and 'she said', together with a lavish enumeration of those parts of the human body then known as 'the unmentionables'.

Songs and snatches on the same lines were bawled at the plough-tail and under hedges and never heard elsewhere. Some of these ribald rhymes were so neatly turned that those who have studied the subject have attributed their authorship to some graceless son of the Rectory or Hall. It may be that some of these young scamps had a hand in them, but it is just as likely that they sprung direct from the soil, for, in those days of general churchgoing, the men's minds were well stored with hymns and psalms and some of them were very good at parodying them.

There was 'The Parish Clerk's Daughter', for instance. This damsel was sent one Christmas morning to the church to inform her father that the Christmas present of beef had arrived after he left home. When she reached the church the service had begun and the congregation, led by her father, was half-way through the psalms. Nothing daunted, she sidled up to her father and intoned:

'Feyther, the me-a-at's come, an' what's me mother to d-o-o-o w'it?'

And the answer came pat: 'Tell her to roast the thick an' boil th' thin, an' me-ak a pudden o' th' su-u-u-u-et.'

But such simple entertainment did not suit the man already mentioned. He would drag out the filthiest of the stock rhymes, then go on to improvise, dragging in the names of honest lovers and making a mock of fathers of first children. Though nine out of ten of his listeners disapproved and felt thoroughly uncomfortable, they did nothing to check him beyond a mild 'Look out, or them boo-oys'll hear 'ee!' or 'Careful! some 'ooman may be comin' along th' roo-ad.'

But the lewd scandalizer did not always have everything his own way. There came a day when a young ex-soldier, home from his five years' service in India, sat next to him. He sat through one or two such extemporized songs, then, eyeing the singer, said shortly, 'You'd better go and wash out your dirty mouth.'

The answer was a bawled stanza in which the objector's name figured. At that the ex-soldier sprung to his feet, seized the singer by the scruff of his neck, dragged him to the ground and, after a scuffle, forced earth and small stones between his teeth. 'There, that's a lot cleaner!' he said, administering a final kick on the buttocks as the fellow slunk, coughing and spitting, behind the hedge.

A few women still did field work, not with the men, or even in the same field as a rule, but at their own special tasks, weeding and hoeing, picking up stones, and topping and tailing turnips and mangel; or, in wet weather, mending sacks in a barn. Formerly, it was said, there had been a large gang of field women, lawless, slatternly creatures, some of whom had thought nothing of having four or five children out of wedlock. Their day was over; but the reputation they had left behind them had given most country-women a distaste for 'goin' afield'. In the 'eighties about half a dozen of the hamlet women did field work, most of them being respectable middle-aged women who, having got their families off hand, had spare time, a liking for an open-air life, and a longing for a few shillings a week they could call their own.

Their hours, arranged that they might do their housework before they left home in the morning and cook their husband's meal after they returned, were from ten to four, with an hour off for dinner. Their wage was four shillings a week. They worked in sunbonnets, hobnailed boots and men's coats, with coarse aprons of sacking enveloping the lower part of their bodies. One, a Mrs Spicer, was a pioneer in the wearing of trousers; she sported a pair of her husband's corduroys. The others compromised with ends of old trouser legs worn as gaiters. Strong, healthy, weather-beaten, hard as nails, they worked through all but the very worst weathers and declared they would go 'stark, staring mad' if they had to be shut up in a house all day.

To a passer-by, seeing them bent over their work in a row, they might have appeared as alike as peas in a pod. They were not. There was Lily, the only unmarried one, big and strong and clumsy as a carthorse and dark as a gipsy, her skin ingrained with field mould and the smell of the earth about her, even indoors. Years before she had been betrayed by a man and had sworn she would never marry until she had brought up the boy she had had by him – a quite superfluous oath, her neighbours thought, for she was one of the very few really ugly people in the world.

The 'eighties found her a woman of fifty, a creature of earth, earthy, whose life was a round of working, eating, and sleeping. She lived alone in a tiny cottage, in which, as she boasted, she could get her meals, eat them, and put the things away without leaving her seat by the hearth. She could read a little, but had forgotten how to write, and Laura's mother wrote her letters to her soldier son in India.

Then there was Mrs Spicer, the wearer of the trousers, a rough-tongued old body, but independent and upright, who kept her home spotless and boasted that she owed no man a penny and wanted nothing from anybody. Her gentle, henpecked, little husband adored her.

Very different from either was the comfortable, pink-cheeked Mrs Braby, who always carried an apple or a paper of peppermints in her pocket, in case she should meet a child she favoured. In her spare time she was a great reader of novelettes and out of her four shillings subscribed to *Bow Bells* and the *Family Herald*. Once when Laura, coming home from school, happened to overtake her, she enlivened the rest of the journey with the synopsis of a serial she was reading, called *His Ice Queen*, telling her how the heroine, rich, lovely, and icily virtuous in her white velvet and swansdown, almost broke the heart of the hero by her cool aloofness; then, suddenly melting, threw herself into his arms. But, after all, the plot could not have been quite as simple as that, for there was a villainous colonel in it. 'Oh! I do just about hate that colonel!' Mrs Braby ejaculated at intervals. She pronounced it 'col-on-el', as spelt, which so worked upon Laura that at last she ventured, 'But don't they call that word "colonel", Mrs Braby?' Which led to a spelling lesson: 'Col-on-el; that's as plain as the nose on your face. Whatever be you a-thinkin' of, child? They don't seem to teach you much at school these days!' She was distinctly offended and did not offer Laura a peppermint for weeks, which served her right, for she should not have tried to correct her elders.

One man worked with the field women or in the same field. He was a poor, weedy creature, getting old and not very strong and they had put him upon half-pay. He was known as 'Algy' and was not a native, but had appeared there suddenly, years before, out of a past he never mentioned. He was tall and thin and stooping, with watery blue eyes and long ginger side-whiskers of the kind then known as 'weepers'. Sometimes, when he straightened his back, the last vestiges of a military bearing might be detected, and there were other grounds for supposing he had at some time been in the Army. When tipsy, or nearly so, he would begin, 'When I was in the Grenadier Guards . . .' a sentence that always tailed off into silence. Although his voice broke on the high notes and often deteriorated into a squeak, it still bore the same vague resemblance to that of a man of culture as his bearing did to that of a soldier. Then, instead of swearing with 'd—s' and 'b—s' as the other men did, he would, when surprised, burst into a 'Bai Jove!' which amused everybody, but threw little light on his mystery.

Twenty years before, when his present wife had been a widow

of a few weeks' standing, he had knocked at her door during a thunderstorm and asked for a night's lodging, and had been there ever since, never receiving a letter or speaking of his past, even to his wife. It was said that during his first days at field work his hands had blistered and bled from softness. There must have been great curiosity in the hamlet about him at first; but it had long died down and by the 'eighties he was accepted as 'a poor, slack-twisted crittur', useful for cracking jokes on. He kept his own counsel and worked contentedly to the best of his power. The only thing that disturbed him was the rare visit of the German band. As soon as he heard the brass instruments strike up and the 'pom, pom' of the drum, he would stick his fingers in his ears and run, across fields, anywhere, and not be seen again that day.

On Friday evening, when work was done, the men trooped up to the farmhouse for their wages. These were handed out of a window to them by the farmer himself and acknowledged by a rustic scraping of feet and pulling of forelocks. The farmer had grown too old and too stout to ride horseback, and, although he still made the circuit of his land in his high dogcart every day, he had to keep to the roads, and pay-day was the only time he saw many of his men. Then, if there was cause for complaint, was the time they heard of it. 'You, there! What were you up to in Causey Spinney last Monday, when you were supposed to be clearing the runnels?' was a type of complaint that could always be countered by pleading, 'Call o' Nature, please, sir.' Less frequent and harder to answer was: 'I hear you've not been too smart about your work lately, Stimson. 'Twon't do, you know, 'twon't do! You've got to earn your money if you're going to stay here.' But, just as often, it would be: 'There, Boamer, there you are, my lad, a bright and shining golden half-sovereign for you. Take care you don't go spending it all at once!' or an inquiry about some wife in childbed or one of the ancients' rheumatism. He could afford to be jolly and affable: he paid poor old Monday Morning to do his dirty work for him.

Apart from that, he was not a bad-hearted man and had no idea he was sweating his labourers. Did they not get the full standard wage, with no deduction for standing by in bad weather? How they managed to live and keep their families on such a sum was their own affair. After all, they did not need much, they were not used to luxuries. He liked a cut off a juicy sirloin and a glass of good port himself; but bacon and beans were better to work on. 'Hard liver, hard worker' was a sound old country maxim, and the labouring men did well to follow it. Besides, was there not at least one good blow-out for everybody once a year at his harvest-home dinner, and the joint of beef at Christmas, when he killed a beast and distributed the meat, and soup and milk-puddings for anybody who was ill; they had only to ask for and fetch them.

He never interfered with his men as long as they did their work well. Not he! He was a staunch Conservative himself, a true blue, and they knew his colour when they went to vote; but he never tried to influence them at election times and never inquired afterwards which way they had voted. Some masters did it, he knew, but it was a dirty, low-down trick, in his opinion. As to getting them to go to church – that was the parson's job.

Although they hoodwinked him whenever possible and referred to him behind his back as 'God a'mighty', the farmer was liked by his men. 'Not a bad ole sort,' they said; 'an' does his bit by the land.' All their rancour was reserved for the bailiff.

There is something exhilarating about pay-day, even when the pay is poor and already mortgaged for necessities. With that morsel of gold in their pockets, the men stepped out more briskly and their voices were cheerier than ordinary. When they reached home they handed the half-sovereign straight over to their wives, who gave them back a shilling for the next week's pocket-money. That was the custom of the countryside. The men worked for the money and the women had the spending of it. The men had the best of the bargain. They earned their half-sovereign by hard toil, it is true, but in the open air, at work they liked and took an interest in, and in congenial company. The women, kept close at home, with cooking, cleaning, washing, and mending to do, plus their constant pregnancies and a tribe of children to look after, had also the worry of ways and means on an insufficient income.

Many husbands boasted that they never asked their wives what they did with the money. As long as there was food enough, clothes to cover everybody, and a roof over their heads, they were satisfied, they said, and they seemed to make a virtue of this and think what generous, trusting, fine-hearted fellows they were. If a wife got in debt or complained, she was told: 'You must larn to cut your coat accordin' to your cloth, my gal.' The coats not only needed expert cutting, but should have been made of elastic.

On light evenings, after their tea-supper, the men worked for an hour or two in their gardens or on the allotments. They were first-class gardeners and it was their pride to have the earliest and best of the different kinds of vegetables. They were helped in this by good soil and plenty of manure from their pigsties; but good tilling also played its part. They considered keeping the soil constantly stirred about the roots of growing things the secret of success and used the Dutch hoe a good deal for this purpose. The process was called 'tickling'. 'Tickle up old Mother Earth and make her bear!' they would shout to each other across the plots, or salute a busy neighbour in passing with: 'Just tickling her up a bit, Jack?'

The energy they brought to their gardening after a hard day's work in the fields was marvellous. They grudged no effort and seemed never to tire. Often, on moonlight nights in spring, the solitary fork of some one who had not been able to tear himself away would be heard and the scent of his twitch fire smoke would float in at the windows. It was pleasant, too, in summer twilight, perhaps in hot weather when water was scarce, to hear the *swish* of water on parched earth in a garden – water which had been fetched from the brook a quarter of a mile distant. 'It's no good stintin' th' land,' they would say. 'If you wants anything out you've got to put summat in, if 'tis only elbow-grease.'

The allotment plots were divided into two, and one half planted with potatoes and the other half with wheat or barley. The garden was reserved for green vegetables, currant and gooseberry bushes, and a few old-fashioned flowers. Proud as they were of their celery, peas and beans, cauliflowers and marrows, and fine as were the specimens they could show of these, their potatoes were their special care, for they had to grow enough to last the year round. They grew all the old-fashioned varieties – ashleaf kidney, early rose, American rose, magnum bonum, and the huge misshaped white elephant. Everybody knew the elephant was an unsatisfactory potato, that it was awkward to handle when paring, and that it boiled down to a white pulp in cooking; but it produced tubers of such astonishing size that none of the men could resist the temptation to plant it. Every year specimens were taken to the inn to be weighed on the only pair of scales in the hamlet, then handed round for guesses to be made of the weight. As the men said, when a patch of elephants was dug up and spread out, 'You'd got summat to put in your eye and look at.'

Very little money was spent on seed; there was little to spend, and they depended mainly upon the seed saved from the previous year. Sometimes, to secure the advantage of fresh soil, they would exchange a bag of seed potatoes with friends living at a distance, and sometimes a gardener at one of the big houses around would give one of them a few tubers of a new variety. These would be carefully planted and tended, and, when the crop was dug up, specimens would be presented to neighbours.

Most of the men sang or whistled as they dug or hoed. There was a good deal of outdoor singing in those days. Workmen sang at their jobs; men with horses and carts sang on the road; the baker, the miller's man, and the fish-hawker sang as they went from door to door; even the doctor and parson on their rounds hummed a tune between their teeth. People were poorer and had not the comforts, amusements, or knowledge we have today; but they were happier. Which seems to suggest that happiness depends more upon the state of mind – and body, perhaps – than upon circumstances and events.

IV

At the 'Wagon and Horses'

Fordlow might boast of its church, its school, its annual concert, and its quarterly penny reading, but the hamlet did not envy it these amenities, for it had its own social centre, warmer, more human, and altogether preferable, in the taproom of the 'Wagon and Horses'.

There the adult male population gathered every evening, to sip its half-pints, drop by drop, to make them last, and to discuss local events, wrangle over politics or farming methods, or to sing a few songs 'to oblige'.

It was an innocent gathering. None of them got drunk; they had not money enough, even with beer, and good beer, at twopence a pint. Yet the parson preached from the pulpit against it, going so far on one occasion as to call it a den of iniquity. ' 'Tis a great pity he can't come an' see what it's like for his own self,' said one of the older men on the way home from church. 'Pity he can't mind his own business,' retorted a younger one. While one of the ancients put in pacifically, 'Well, 'tis his business, come to think on't. The man's paid to preach, an' he's got to find summat to preach against, stands to reason.'

Only about half a dozen men held aloof from the circle and those were either known to 'have religion', or suspected of being 'close wi' their ha'pence'.

The others went as a matter of course, appropriating their own special seats on settle or bench. It was as much their home as their own cottages, and far more homelike than many of them, with its roaring fire, red window curtains, and well-scoured pewter.

To spend their evenings there was, indeed, as the men argued, a saving, for, with no man in the house, the fire at home could be let die down and the rest of the family could go to bed when the room got cold. So the men's spending money was fixed at a shilling a week, sevenpence for the nightly half-pint and the balance for other expenses. An ounce of tobacco, Nigger Head brand, was bought for them by their wives with the groceries.

It was exclusively a men's gathering. Their wives never accompanied them; though sometimes a woman who had got her family off hand, and so had a few halfpence to spend on herself, would knock at the back door with a bottle or jug and perhaps linger a little, herself, unseen, to listen to what was going on within. Children also knocked at the back door to buy candles or treacle or cheese, for the innkeeper ran a small shop at the back of his premises, and the children, too, liked to hear what was going on. Indoors, the innkeeper's children would steal out of bed and sit on the stairs in their nightgowns. The stairs went up from the taproom, with only the back of the settle between, and it gave the men a bit of a shock one night when what looked at first sight like a big white bird came flopping down among them. It was little Florrie, who had gone to sleep on the stairs and fallen. They nursed her on their knees, held her feet to the fire, and soon dried her tears, for she was not hurt, only frightened.

The children heard no bad language beyond an occasional 'B —' or 'd —', for their mother was greatly respected and the merest hint of anything stronger was hushed by nudges and whispers of 'Don't forget Landlady', or 'Mind! 'Ooman present'. Nor were the smutty songs and stories of the fields ever repeated there; they were kept for their own time and place.

Politics was a favourite topic, for, under the recently extended franchise, every householder was a voter, and they took their new responsibility seriously. A mild Liberalism prevailed, a Liberalism that would be regarded as hide-bound Toryism now, but was daring enough in those days. One man who had been to work in Northampton proclaimed himself a Radical; but he was cancelled out by the landlord, who called himself a 'true blue'. With the collaboration of this Left and Right, questions of the moment were thrashed out and settled to the satisfaction of the majority.

'Three Acres and a Cow', 'The Secret Ballot', 'The Parnell Commission and Crime', 'Disestablishment of the Church', were catchwords that flew about freely. Sometimes a speech by Gladstone or some other leader would be read aloud from a newspaper and punctuated by the fervent 'Hear! Hear!' of the company. Or Sam, the man with advanced opinions, would relate with reverent pride the story of his meeting and shaking hands with Joseph Arch, the farm-worker's champion. 'Joseph Arch!' he would cry. 'Joseph Arch is the man for the farm labourer!' and knock on the table and wave aloft his pewter mug, very carefully, for every drop was precious.

Then the landlord, standing back to the fireplace with legs astride, would say with the authority of one in his own house, 'It's no good you chaps think'n you're goin' against the gentry. They've got the land and they've got the money, *an'* they'll keep it. Where'd *you* be without them to give you work an' pay your wages, I'd like to know?' and this, as yet, unanswerable question would cast a chill over the company until some one conjured it away with the name of Gladstone. Gladstone! The Grand Old Man! The People's William! Their faith in his power was touching, and all voices would join in singing:

> God bless the people's William,
>   Long may he lead the van
> Of Liberty and Freedom,
>   God bless the Grand Old Man.

But the children, listening, without and within, liked better the evenings of tale-telling; when, with curdling blood and creeping spine, they would hear about the turnpike ghost, which, only a mile away from the spot where they stood, had been seen in the form of a lighted lantern, bobbing up and down in the path of a solitary wayfarer, the bearer, if any, invisible. And the man in a neighbouring village who, on his six-mile walk in the dark to fetch medicine for his sick wife, met a huge black dog with eyes of fire – the devil, evidently. Or perhaps the talk would turn to the old sheep-stealing days and the ghost which was said still to haunt the spot where the gibbet had stood; or the lady dressed in white and riding a white horse, but minus her head, who, every night as the clock struck twelve, rode over a bridge on the way to the market town.

One cold winter night, as this tale was being told, the doctor, an old man of eighty, who still attended the sick in the villages for miles around, stopped his dogcart at the inn gate and came in for hot brandy and water.

'You, sir, now,' said one of the men. 'You've been over Lady Bridge at midnight many's the time, I'll warrant. Can you say as you've ever seen anything?'

The doctor shook his head. 'No,' he replied, 'I can't say that I have. But,' and he paused to weigh his words, 'well, it's rather a curious thing. During the fifty years I've been amongst you I've had many horses, as you know, and not one of them have I got over that bridge at night without urging. Whether they can see more than we can see, of course, I don't know; but there it is for what it is worth. Good night, men.'

In addition to these public and well-known ghost stories, there were family tales of death warnings, or of a father, mother, or wife who had appeared after death to warn, counsel, or accuse. But it was all entertainment; nobody really believed in ghosts, though few would have chosen to go at night to haunted spots, and it all ended in: 'Well, well, if the livin' don't hurt us, the dead can't. The good wouldn't want to come back, an' the bad wouldn't be let to.'

The newspapers furnished other tales of dread. Jack the Ripper was stalking the streets of East London by night, and one poor wretched woman after another was found murdered and butchered. These crimes were discussed for hours together in the hamlet and everybody had some theory as to the identity and motive of the elusive murderer. To the children the name was indeed one of dread and the cause of much anguished sleeplessness. Father might be hammering away in the shed and Mother quietly busy with her sewing downstairs; but the Ripper! the Ripper! he might be nearer still, for he might have crept in during the day and be hiding in the cupboard on the landing!

One curious tale had to do with natural phenomena. Some years before, the people in the hamlet had seen a regiment of soldiers marching in the sky, all complete with drum and fife band. Upon inquiry it had been found that such a regiment had been passing at the time along a road near Bicester, six miles away, and it was concluded that the apparition in the sky must have been a freak reflection.

Some of the tales related practical jokes, often cruel ones, for even in the 'eighties the sense of humour there was not over-refined, and it had, in past times, been cruder still. It was still the practice there to annoy certain people by shouting after them a nickname or a catchword, and one old and very harmless woman was known as 'Thick and thin'. One winter night, years before, when the snowdrifts were knee-high and it was still snowing, a party of thoughtless youths had knocked at her cottage door and got her and her husband out of bed by telling them that their daughter, married and living three miles away, was brought to bed and had sent for her mother.

The old couple huddled on all the clothes they possessed, lighted their lantern, and set out, the practical jokers shadowing them. They struggled through the snowdrifts for some distance, but the road was all but impassable, and the old man was for turning back. Not so the mother. Determined to reach her child in her hour of need, she struggled onward, encouraging her husband the while by coaxing, 'Come on John. Through thick and thin!' and 'Thick and thin' she was ever after.

But tastes were changing, if slowly, by the 'eighties, and such a story, though it might be still current, no longer produced the loud guffaws it had formerly done. A few sniggers, perhaps, then silence; or 'I calls it a shame, sarvin' poor old people like that. Now let's have a song to te-ake the taste of it out of our mouths.'

All times are times of transition; but the eighteen-eighties were so in a special sense, for the world was at the beginning of a new era, the era of machinery and scientific discovery. Values and conditions of life were changing everywhere. Even to simple country people the change was apparent. The railways had brought distant parts of the country nearer; newspapers were coming into every home; machinery was superseding hand labour, even on the farms to some extent; food bought at shops, much of it from distant countries, was replacing the home-made and home-grown. Horizons were widening; a stranger from a village five miles away was no longer looked upon as 'a furriner'.

But, side by side with these changes, the old country civilization lingered. Traditions and customs which had lasted for centuries did not die out in a moment. State-educated children still played the old country rhyme games; women still went leazing, although the field had been cut by the mechanical reaper; and men and boys still sang the old country ballads and songs, as well as the latest music hall successes. So, when a few songs were called for at the 'Wagon and Horses', the programme was apt to be a curious mixture of old and new.

While the talking was going on, the few younger men, 'boychaps', as they were called until they were married, would not have taken a great part in it. Had they shown any inclination to do so, they would have been checked, for the age of youthful dominance was still to come; and, as the women used to say, 'The old cocks don't like it when the young cocks begin to crow.' But, when singing began they came into their own, for they represented the novel.

They usually had first innings with such songs of the day as had percolated so far. 'Over the Garden Wall', with its many parodies, 'Tommy, Make Room for Your Uncle', 'Two Lovely Black Eyes', and other 'comic' or 'sentimental' songs of the moment. The most popular of these would have arrived complete with tune from the outer world; others, culled from the penny song-book they most of them carried, would have to have a tune fitted to them by the singer. They had good lusty voices and bawled them out with spirit. There were no crooners in those days.

The men of middle age inclined more to long and usually mournful stories in verse, of thwarted lovers, children buried in snowdrifts, dead maidens, and motherless homes. Sometimes they would vary these with songs of a high moral tone, such as:

Waste not, want not,
  Some maxim I would teach;
Let your watchword be never despair
  And practise what you preach.
Do not let your chances like the sunbeams pass you by,
For you'll never miss the water till the well runs dry.

But this dolorous singing was not allowed to continue long. 'Now, then, all together, boys,' some one would shout, and the company would revert to old favourites. Of these, one was 'The Barleymow'. Trolled out in chorus, the first verse went:

Oh, when we drink out of our noggins, my boys,
  We'll drink to the barleymow.
We'll drink to the barleymow, my boys,
  We'll drink to the barleymow.
So knock your pint on the settle's back;
  Fill again, in again, Hannah Brown,
We'll drink to the barleymow, my boys,
  We'll drink now the barley's mown.

So they went on, increasing the measure in each stanza, from noggins to half-pints, pints, quarters, gallons, barrels, hogsheads, brooks, ponds, rivers, seas, and oceans. That song could be made to last a whole evening, or it could be dropped as soon as they got tired of it.

Another favourite for singing in chorus was 'King Arthur', which was also a favourite for outdoor singing and was often heard to the accompaniment of the jingling of harness and cracking of whips as the teams went afield. It was also sung by solitary wayfarers to keep up their spirits on dark nights. It ran:

When King Arthur first did reign
  He ru-led like a king;
He bought three sacks of barley meal
  To make a plum pud-ding.

The pudding it was made
   And duly stuffed with plums,
And lumps of suet put in it
   As big as my two thumbs.

The king and queen sat down to it
   And all the lords beside;
And what they couldn't eat that night
   The queen next morning fried.

Every time Laura heard this sung she saw the queen, a gold crown on her head, her train over her arm, and her sleeves rolled up, holding the frying-pan over the fire. Of course, a queen *would* have fried pudding for breakfast: ordinary common people seldom had any left over to fry.

Then Lukey, the only bachelor of mature age in the hamlet, would oblige with:

Me feyther's a hedger and ditcher,
   An' me mother does nothing but spin,
But I'm a pretty young girl and
   The money comes slowly in.
     Oh, dear! what can the matter be?
      Oh, dear! what shall I do?
    For there's nobody coming to marry,
     And there's nobody coming to woo.

They say I shall die an old maid,
   Oh, dear! how shocking the thought!
For then all my beauty will fade,
   And I'm sure it won't be my own fault.
     Oh, dear! what can the matter be?
      Oh, dear! what shall I do?
    There's nobody coming to marry,
     And there's nobody coming to woo!

This was given point by Luke's own unmarried state. He sang it as a comic song and his rendering certainly made it one. Perhaps, then, for a change, poor old Algy, the mystery man, would be asked for a song and he would sing in a cracked falsetto, which seemed to call for the tinkling notes of a piano as accompaniment:

> Have you ever been on the Penin-su-lah?
> If not, I advise you to stay where you haw,
>> For should you adore a
>> Sweet Spanish senor-ah,
> She may prove what some might call sin-gu-lah.

Then there were snatches that any one might break out with at any time when no one else happened to be singing:

> I wish, I wish, 'twer' all in vain,
> I wish I were a maid again!
> A maid again I ne'er shall be
> Till oranges grow on an apple tree

or:

> Now all you young chaps, take a warning by me,
> And do not build your nest at the top of any tree,
> For the green leaves they will wither and the flowers they will
>> decay,
> And the beauty of that fair maid will soon pass away.

One comparatively recent settler, who had only lived at the hamlet about a quarter of a century, had composed a snatch for himself, to sing when he felt homesick. It ran:

> Where be Dedington boo-oys, where be they now?
> They be at Dedington at the 'Plough';
> If they be-ent, they be at home,
> And this is the 'Wagon and Horses'.

But, always, sooner or later, came the cry, 'Let's give the old 'uns a turn. Here you, Master Price, what about "It was my father's custom and always shall be mine", or "Lord Lovell stood", or summat of that sort as has stood the testing o' time?' and Master Price would rise from his corner of the settle, using the stick he called his 'third leg' to support his bent figure as he sang:

Lord Lovell stood at his castle gate,
    Calming his milk-white steed,
When up came Lady Nancy Bell
    To wish her lover God-speed.

'And where are you going, Lord Lovell?' she said.
    'And where are you going?' said she.
'Oh, I'm going away from my Nancy Bell,
    Away to a far country-tre-tre;
    Away to a far coun-tre.'

'And when will you come back, Lord Lovell?' she said,
    'When will you come back?' said she.
'Oh, I will come back in a year and a day,
    Back to my Lady Nancy-ce-ce-ce.
    Back to my Lady Nan-cee.'

But Lord Lovell was gone more than his year and a day, much longer, and when he did at last return, the church bells were tolling:

'And who is it dead?' Lord Lovell, he said.
    'And who is it dead?' said he.
And some said, 'Lady Nancy Bell,'
    And some said, 'Lady Nancy-ce-ce-ce,'
    And some said, 'Lady Nan-cee.'

Lady Nancy died as it were to-day;
    And Lord Lovell, he died to-morrow,
And she, she died for pure, pure grief,
    And he, he died for sorrow.

And they buried her in the chancel high,
    And they buried him in the choir;
And out of her grave sprung a red, red rose,
    And out of his sprung a briar.

And they grew till they grew to the church roof,
    And then they couldn't grow any higher;
So they twined themselves in a true lovers' knot,
    For all lovers true to admire.

After that they would all look thoughtfully into their mugs. Partly because the old song had saddened them, and partly because by that time the beer was getting low and the one half-pint had to be made to last until closing time. Then some would say, 'What's old Master Tuffrey up to, over in his corner there? Ain't heard him strike up tonight', and there would be calls for old David's 'Outlandish Knight'; not because they wanted particularly to hear it – indeed, they had heard it so often they all knew it by heart – but because, as they said, 'Poor old feller be eighty-three. Let 'un sing while he can.'

So David would have his turn. He only knew the one ballad, and that, he said, his grandfather had sung, and had said that he had heard his own grandfather sing it. Probably a long chain of grandfathers had sung it; but David was fated to be the last of them. It was out of date, even then, and only tolerated on account of his age. It ran:

An outlandish knight, all from the north lands,
    A-wooing came to me,
He said he would take me to the north lands
    And there he would marry me.

'Go, fetch me some of your father's gold
    And some of your mother's fee,
And two of the best nags out of the stable
    Where there stand thirty and three.'

She fetched him some of her father's gold
    And some of her mother's fee,
And two of the best nags out of the stable
    Where there stood thirty and three.

And then she mounted her milk-white steed
    And he the dapple grey,
And they rode until they came to the sea-shore,
    Three hours before it was day.

'Get off, get off thy milk-white steed
    And deliver it unto me,
For six pretty maids I have drowned here
    And thou the seventh shall be.

'Take off, take off, thy silken gown,
    And deliver it unto me,
For I think it is too rich and too good
    To rot in the salt sea.'

'If I must take off my silken gown,
    Pray turn thy back to me,
For I think it's not fitting a ruffian like you
    A naked woman should see.'

He turned his back towards her
    To view the leaves so green,
And she took hold of his middle so small
    And tumbled him into the stream.

And he sank high and he sank low
    Until he came to the side.
'Take hold of my hand, my pretty ladye,
    And I will make you my bride.'

'Lie there, lie there, you false-hearted man,
  Lie there instead of me,
For six pretty maids hast thou drowned here
  And the seventh hath drowned thee.'

So then she mounted the milk-white steed
  And led the dapple grey,
And she rode till she came to her own father's door,
  An hour before it was day.

As this last song was piped out in the aged voice, women at their cottage doors on summer evenings would say: 'They'll soon be out now. Poor old Dave's just singing his "Outlandish Knight".'

Songs and singers all have gone, and in their places the wireless blares out variety and swing music, or informs the company in cultured tones of what is happening in China or Spain. Children no longer listen outside. There are very few who could listen, for the thirty or forty which throve there in those days have dwindled to about half a dozen, and these, happily, have books, wireless, and a good fire in their own homes. But, to one of an older generation, it seems that a faint echo of those songs must still linger round the inn doorway. The singers were rude and untaught and poor beyond modern imagining; but they deserve to be remembered, for they knew the now lost secret of being happy on little.

V

Survivals

There were three distinct types of home in the hamlet. Those of the old couples in comfortable circumstances, those of the married people with growing families, and the few new homes which had recently been established. The old people who were not in comfortable circumstances had no homes at all worth mentioning, for, as soon as they got past work, they had either to go to the workhouse or find accommodation in the already overcrowded cottages of their children. A father or a mother could usually be squeezed in, but there was never room for both, so one child would take one parent and another the other, and even then, as they used to say, there was always the in-law to be dealt with. It was a common thing to hear ageing people say that they hoped God would be pleased to take them before they got past work and became a trouble to anybody.

But the homes of the more fortunate aged were the most comfortable in the hamlet, and one of the most attractive of these was known as 'Old Sally's'. Never as 'Old Dick's', although Sally's husband, Dick, might have been seen at any hour of the day, digging and hoeing and watering and planting his garden, as much a part of the landscape as his own row of beehives.

He was a little, dry, withered old man, who always wore his smock-frock rolled up round his waist and the trousers on his thin legs gartered with buckled straps. Sally was tall and broad, not fat, but massive, and her large, beamingly good-natured face, with its well-defined moustache and tight, coal-black curls bobbing over each ear, was framed in a white cap frill; for Sally, though still strong and active, was over eighty, and had remained faithful to the fashions of her youth.

She was the dominating partner. If Dick was called upon to decide any question whatever, he would edge nervously aside and say, 'I'll just step indoors and see what Sally thinks about it,' or 'All depends upon what Sally says.' The house was hers and she carried the purse; but Dick was a willing subject and enjoyed her dominion over him. It saved him a lot of thinking, and left him free to give all his time and attention to the growing things in his garden.

Old Sally's was a long, low, thatched cottage with diamond-paned windows winking under the eaves and a rustic porch smothered in honeysuckle. Excepting the inn, it was the largest house in the hamlet, and of the two downstair rooms one was used as a kind of kitchen-storeroom, with pots and pans and a big red crockery water vessel at one end, and potatoes in sacks and peas and beans spread out to dry at the other. The apple crop was stored on racks suspended beneath the ceiling and bunches of herbs dangled below. In one corner stood the big brewing copper in which Sally still brewed with good malt and hops once a quarter. The scent of the last brewing hung over the place till the next and mingled with apple and onion and dried thyme and sage smells, with a dash of soapsuds thrown in, to compound the aroma which remained in the children's memories for life and caused a whiff of any two of the component parts in any part of the world to be recognized with an appreciative sniff and a mental ejaculation of 'Old Sally's!'

The inner room – 'the house', as it was called – was a perfect snuggery, with walls two feet thick and outside shutters to close at night and a padding of rag rugs, red curtains and feather cushions within. There was a good oak, gate-legged table, a dresser with pewter and willow-pattern plates, and a grandfather's clock that not only told the time, but the day of the week as well. It had even once told the changes of the moon; but the works belonging to that part had stopped and only the fat, full face, painted with eyes, nose and mouth, looked out from the square where the four quarters should have rotated. The clock portion kept such good time that half the hamlet set its own clocks by it. The other half preferred to follow the hooter at the brewery in the market town, which could be heard when the wind was in the right quarter. So there were two times in the hamlet and people would say when asking the hour, 'Is that hooter time, or Old Sally's?'

The garden was a large one, tailing off at the bottom into a little field where Dick grew his corn crop. Nearer the cottage were fruit trees, then the yew hedge, close and solid as a wall, which sheltered the beehives and enclosed the flower garden. Sally had such flowers, and so many of them, and nearly all of them sweet-scented! Wall-flowers and tulips, lavender and sweet william, and pinks and old-world roses with enchanting names – Seven Sisters. Maiden's Blush, moss rose, monthly rose, cabbage rose, blood rose, and, most thrilling of all to the children, a big bush of the York and Lancaster rose, in the blooms of which the rival roses mingled in a pied white and red. It seemed as though all the roses in Lark Rise had gathered together in that one garden. Most of the gardens had only one poor starveling bush or none; but, then, nobody else had so much of anything as Sally.

A continual subject for speculation was as to how Dick and Sally managed to live so comfortably with no visible means of support beyond their garden and beehives and the few shillings their two soldier sons might be supposed to send them, and Sally in her black silk on Sundays and Dick never without a few ha'pence for garden seeds or to fill his tobacco pouch. 'Wish they'd tell me how 'tis done,' somebody would grumble. 'I could do wi' a leaf out o' their book.'

But Dick and Sally did not talk about their affairs. All that was known of them was that the house belonged to Sally, and that it had been built by her grandfather before the open heath had been cut up into fenced fields and the newer houses had been built to accommodate the labourers who came to work in them. It was only when Laura was old enough to write their letters for them that she learned more. They could both read and Dick could write well enough to exchange letters with their own children; but one day they received a business letter that puzzled them, and Laura was called in, sworn to secrecy, and consulted. It was one of the nicest things that happened to her as a child, to be chosen out of the whole hamlet for their confidence and to know that Dick and Sally liked her, though so few other people did. After that, at twelve years old, she became their little woman of business, writing letters to seedsmen and fetching postal orders from the market town to put in them and helping Dick to calculate the interest due on their savings bank account. From them she learned a great deal about the past life of the hamlet.

Sally could just remember the Rise when it still stood in a wide expanse of open heath, with juniper bushes and furze thickets and close, springy, rabbit-bitten turf. There were only six houses then and they stood in a ring round an open green, all with large gardens and fruit trees and faggot piles. Laura could pick out most of the houses, still in a ring, but lost to sight of each other among the newer, meaner dwellings that had sprung up around and between them. Some of the houses had been built on and made into two, others had lost their lean-tos and outbuildings. Only Sally's remained the same, and Sally was eighty. Laura in her lifetime was to see a ploughed field where Sally's stood; but had she been told that she would not have believed it.

Country people had not been so poor when Sally was a girl, or their prospects so hopeless. Sally's father had kept a cow, geese, poultry, pigs, and a donkey-cart to carry his produce to the market town. He could do this because he had commoners' rights and could turn his animals out to graze, and cut furze for firing and even turf to make a lawn for one of his customers. Her mother made butter, for themselves and to sell, baked their own bread, and made candles for lighting. Not much of a light, Sally said, but it cost next to nothing, and, of course, they went to bed early.

Sometimes her father would do a day's work for wages, thatching a rick, cutting and laying a hedge, or helping with the shearing or the harvest. This provided them with ready money for boots and clothes; for food they relied almost entirely on home produce. Tea was a luxury seldom indulged in, for it cost five shillings a pound. But country people then had not acquired the taste for tea; they preferred home-brewed.

Everybody worked; the father and mother from daybreak to dark. Sally's job was to mind the cow and drive the geese to the best grass patches. It was strange to picture Sally, a little girl, running with her switch after the great hissing birds on the common, especially as both common and geese had vanished as completely as though they never had been.

Sally had never been to school, for, when she was a child, there was no dame school near enough for her to attend; but her brother had gone to a night school run by the vicar of an adjoining parish, walking the three miles each way after his day's work was done, and he had taught Sally to spell out a few words in her mother's Bible. After that, she had been left to tread the path of learning alone and had only managed to reach the point where she could write her own name and read the Bible or newspaper by skipping words of more than two syllables. Dick was a little more advanced, for he had had the benefit of the night-school education at first hand.

It was surprising to find how many of the old people in the hamlet who had had no regular schooling could yet read a little. A parent had taught some; others had attended a dame school or the night school, and a few had made their own children teach them in later life. Statistics of illiteracy of that period are often misleading, for many who could read and write sufficiently well for their own humble needs would modestly disclaim any pretensions to being what they called 'scholards'. Some who could write their own name quite well would make a cross as signature to a document out of nervousness or modesty.

After Sally's mother died, she became her father's right hand, indoors and out. When the old man became feeble, Dick used to come sometimes to do a bit of hard digging or to farm out the pigsties, and Sally had many tales to tell of the fun they had had carting their bit of hay or hunting for eggs in the loft. When, at a great age, the father died, he left the house and furniture and his seventy-five pounds in the savings bank to Sally, for, by that time, both her brothers were thriving and needed no share. So Dick and Sally were married and had lived there together for nearly sixty years. It had been a hard, frugal, but happy life. For most of the time Dick had worked as a farm labourer while Sally saw to things about home, for the cow, geese and other stock had long gone the way of the common. But when Dick retired from wage-earning the seventy-five pounds was not only intact, but had been added to. It had been their rule, Sally said, to save something every week, if only a penny or twopence, and the result of their hard work and self-denial was their present comfortable circumstances. 'But us couldn't've done it if us'd gone havin' a great tribe o' children,' Sally would say. 'I didn't never hold wi' havin' a lot o' poor brats and nothin' to put into their bellies. Took us all our time to bring up our two.' She was very bitter about the huge families around her and no doubt would have said more had she been talking to one of maturer age.

They had their little capital reckoned up and allotted: they could manage on so much a year in addition to the earnings of their garden, fowls, and beehives, and that much, and no more, was drawn every year from the bank. 'Reckon it'll about last our time,' they used to say, and it did, although both lived well on into the eighties.

After they had gone, their house stood empty for years. The population of the hamlet was falling and none of the young newly married couples cared for the thatched roof and stone floors. People who lived near used the well; it saved them many a journey. And many were not above taking the railings or the beehive bench or anything made of wood for firing, or gathering the apples or using the poor tattered remnant of the flower garden as a nursery. But nobody wanted to live there.

When Laura visited the hamlet just before the War, the roof had fallen in, the yew hedge had run wild and the flowers were gone, excepting one pink rose which was shedding its petals over the ruin. Today, all has gone, and only the limy whiteness of the soil in a corner of a ploughed field is left to show that a cottage once stood there.

Sally and Dick were survivals from the earliest hamlet days. Queenie represented another phase of its life which had also ended and been forgotten by most people. She lived in a tiny, thatched cottage at the back of the end house, which, although it was not in line, was always spoken of as 'next door'. She seemed very old to the children, for she was a little, wrinkled, yellow-faced old woman in a sunbonnet; but she cannot have been nearly as old as Sally. Queenie and her husband were not in such comfortable circumstances as Sally and Dick; but old Master Macey, commonly called 'Twister', was still able to work part of the time, and they managed to keep their home going.

It was a pleasant home, though bare, for Queenie kept it spotless, scrubbing her deal table and whitening her floor with hearthstone every morning and keeping the two brass candlesticks on her mantelpiece polished till they looked like gold. The cottage faced south and, in summer, the window and door stood open all day to the sunshine. When the children from the end house passed close by her doorway, as they had to do every time they went beyond their own garden, they would pause a moment to listen to Queenie's old sheep's-head clock ticking. There was no other sound; for, after she had finished her housework, Queenie was never indoors while the sun shone. If the children had a message for her, they were told to go round to the beehives, and there they would find her, sitting on a low stool with her lace-pillow on her lap, sometimes working and sometimes dozing with her lilac sunbonnet drawn down over her face to shield it from the sun.

Every fine day, throughout the summer, she sat there 'watching the bees'. She was combining duty and pleasure, for, if they swarmed, she was making sure of not losing the swarm; and, if they did not, it was still, as she said, 'a trate' to sit there, feeling the warmth of the sun, smelling the flowers, and watching 'the craturs' go in and out of the hives.

When, at last, the long-looked-for swarm rose into the air, Queenie would seize her coal shovel and iron spoon and follow it over cabbage beds and down pea-stick alleys, her own or, if necessary, other peoples', tanging the spoon on the shovel: *Tang tangtangety-tang!*

She said it was the law that, if they were not tanged, and they settled beyond her own garden bounds, she would have no further claim to them. Where they settled, they belonged. That would have been a serious loss, especially in early summer, for, as she reminded the children:

A swarm in May's worth a rick of hay;
And a swarm in June's worth a silver spoon; while
A swarm in July isn't worth a fly.

So she would follow and leave her shovel to mark her claim, then go back home for the straw skep and her long green veil and sheepskin gloves to protect her face and hands while she hived her swarm.

In winter she fed her bees with a mixture of sugar and water and might often have been seen at that time of the year with her ear pressed to one of the red pan roofs of the hives, listening. 'The craturs! The poor little craturs,' she would say, 'they must be a'most frozen. If I could have *my* way I'd take 'em all indoors and set 'em in rows in front of a good fire.'

Queenie at her lace-making was a constant attraction to the children. They loved to see the bobbins tossed hither and thither, at random it seemed to them, every bobbin weighted with its bunch of bright beads and every bunch with its own story, which they had heard so many times that they knew it by heart, how this bunch had been part of a blue bead necklace worn by her little sister who had died at five years old, and this other one had belonged to her mother, and that black one had been found, after she was dead, in a work-box belonging to a woman who was reputed to have been a witch.

There had been a time, it appeared, when lace-making was a regular industry in the hamlet. Queenie, in her childhood, had been 'brought up to the pillow', sitting among the women at eight years old and learning to fling her bobbins with the best of them. They would gather in one cottage in winter for warmth, she said, each one bringing her faggot or shovel of coals for the fire, and there they would sit all day, working, gossiping, singing old songs, and telling old tales till it was time to run home and put on the pots for their husbands' suppers. These were the older women and the young unmarried girls; the women with little children did what lace-making they could at home. In very cold winter weather the lace-makers would have a small earthen pot with a lid, called a 'pipkin', containing hot embers, at which they warmed their hands and feet and sometimes sat upon.

In the summer they would sit in the shade behind one of the 'housen', and, as they gossiped, the bobbins flew and the lovely, delicate pattern lengthened until the piece was completed and wrapped in blue paper and stored away to await the great day when the year's work was taken to Banbury Fair and sold to the dealer.

'Them wer' the days!' she would sigh. 'Money to spend.' And she would tell of the bargains she had bought with her earnings. Good brown calico and linsey-woolsey, and a certain chocolate print sprigged with white, her favourite gown, of which she could still show a pattern in her big patchwork quilt. Then there was a fairing to be bought for those at home – pipes and packets of shag tobacco for the men, rag dolls and ginger-bread for the 'little 'uns', and snuff for the old grannies. And the home-coming, loaded with treasure, and money in the pocket besides. Tripe. They always bought tripe; it was the only time in the year they could get it, and it was soon heated up, with onions and a nice bit of thickening; and after supper there was hot, spiced elderberry wine, and so to bed, everybody happy.

Now, of course, things were different. She didn't know what the world was coming to. This nasty machine-made stuff had killed the lace-making; the dealer had not been to the Fair for the last ten years; nobody knew a bit of good stuff when they saw it. Said they liked the Nottingham lace better; it was wider and had more pattern to it! She still did a bit to keep her hand in. One or two old ladies still used it to trim their shifts, and it was handy to give as presents to such as the children's mother; but, as for living by it, no, those days were over.

So it emerged from her talk that there had been a second period in the hamlet more prosperous than the present. Perhaps the women's earnings at lace-making had helped to tide them over the Hungry 'Forties, for no one seemed to remember that time of general hardship in country villages; but memories were short there, and it may have been that life had always been such a struggle they had noticed no difference in those lean years.

Queenie's ideal of happiness was to have a pound a week coming in. 'If I had a pound a week,' she would say, 'I 'udn't care if it rained hatchets and hammers.' Laura's mother longed for thirty shillings a week, and would say, 'If I could depend on thirty shillings, regular, I could keep you all so nice and tidy, and keep *such* a table!'

Queenie's income fell far short of even half of the pound a week she dreamed of, for her husband, Twister, was what was known in the hamlet as 'a slack-twisted sort o' chap', one who 'whatever he died on, 'udn't kill hisself wi' hard work'. He was fond of a bit of sport and always managed to get taken on as a beater at shoots, and took care never to have a job on hand when hounds were meeting in the neighbourhood. Best of all, he liked to go round with one of the brewers' travellers, perched precariously on the back seat of the high dogcart, to open and shut the gates they had to pass through and to hold the horse outside public houses. But, although he had retired from regular farm labour on account of age and chronic rheumatism, he still went to the farm and lent a hand when he had nothing more exciting to do. The farmer must have liked him, for he had given orders that whenever Twister was working about the farmstead he was to have a daily half-pint on demand. That half-pint was the salvation of Queenie's house-keeping, for, in spite of his varied interests, there were many days when Twister must either work or thirst.

He was a small, thin-legged, jackdaw-eyed old fellow, and dressed in an old velveteen coat that had once belonged to a gamekeeper, with a peacock's feather stuck in the band of his battered old bowler and a red-and-yellow neckerchief knotted under one ear. The neckerchief was a relic of the days when he had taken baskets of nuts to fairs, and, taking up his stand among the booths and roundabouts, had shouted: 'Bassalonies big as ponies!' until his throat felt dry. Then he had adjourned to the nearest public house and spent his takings and distributed the rest of his stock, gratis. That venture soon came to an end for want of capital.

To serve his own purposes, Twister would sometimes pose as a half-wit; but, as the children's father said, he was no fool where his own interests were concerned. He was ready at any time to clown in public for the sake of a pint of beer; but at home he was morose – one of those people who 'hang their fiddle up at the door when they go home', as the saying went there.

But in old age Queenie had him well in hand. He knew that he had to produce at least a few shillings on Saturday night, or, when Sunday dinner-time came, Queenie would spread the bare cloth on the table and they would just have to sit down and look at each other; there would be no food.

Forty-five years before she had served him with a dish even less to his taste. He had got drunk and beaten her cruelly with the strap with which he used to keep up his trousers. Poor Queenie had gone to bed sobbing; but she was not too overcome to think, and she decided to try an old country cure for such offences.

The next morning when he came to dress, his strap was missing. Probably already ashamed of himself, he said nothing, but hitched up his trousers with string and slunk off to work, leaving Queenie apparently still asleep.

At night, when he came home to tea, a handsome pie was placed before him, baked a beautiful golden-brown and with a pastry tulip on the top; such a pie as must have seemed to him to illustrate the old saying: '*A woman, a dog and a walnut tree, the more you beat 'em the better they be.*'

'You cut it, Tom,' said a smiling Queenie. 'I made it a-purpose for you. Come, don't 'ee be afraid on it. 'Tis all for you.' And she turned her back and pretended to be hunting for something in the cupboard.

Tom cut it; then recoiled, for, curled up inside, was the leather strap with which he had beaten his wife. 'A just went as white as a ghoo-ost, an' got up an' went out,' said Queenie all those years later. 'But it cured 'en, for's not so much as laid a finger on me from that day to this!'

Perhaps Twister's clowning was not all affected; for, in later years, he became a little mad and took to walking about talking to himself, with a large, open clasp-knife in his hand. Nobody thought of getting a doctor to examine him; but everybody in the hamlet suddenly became very polite to him.

It was at this time he gave the children's mother the fright of her life. She had gone out to hang out some clothes in the garden, leaving one of her younger children alone, asleep in his cradle. When she came back, Twister was stooping over the child with his head inside the hood of the cradle, completely hiding the babe from her sight. As she rushed forward, fearing the worst, the poor, silly old man looked up at her with his eyes full of tears. 'Ain't 'ee like little Jesus? Ain't 'ee just like little Jesus?' he said, and the little baby of two months woke up at that moment and smiled. It was the first time he had been known to smile.

But Twister's exploits did not always end as happily. He had begun to torture animals and was showing an inclination to turn nudist, and people were telling Queenie he ought to be 'put away' when the great snowstorm came. For days the hamlet was cut off from the outer world by great drifts which filled the narrow hamlet road to the tops of the hedges in places. In digging a way out they found a cart with the horse still between the shafts and still alive; but there was no trace of the boy who was known to have been in charge. Men, women, and children turned out to dig, expecting to find a dead body, and Twister was one of the foremost amongst them. They said he worked then as he had never worked before in his life; his strength and energy were marvellous. They did not find the boy, alive or dead, for the very good reason that he had, at the height of the storm, deserted the cart, forgotten the horse, and scrambled across country to his home in another village; but poor old Twister got pneumonia and was dead within a fortnight.

On the evening of the day he died, Edmund was round at the back of the end house banking up his rabbit-hutches with straw for the night, when he saw Queenie come out of her door and go towards her beehives. For some reason or other, Edmund followed her. She tapped on the roof of each hive in turn, like knocking at a door, and said, *'Bees, bees, your master's dead, an' now you must work for your missis.'* Then, seeing the little boy, she explained: 'I 'ad to tell 'em, you know, or they'd all've died, poor craturs.' So Edmund really heard bees seriously told of a death.

Afterwards, with parish relief and a little help here and there from her children and friends, Queenie managed to live. Her chief difficulty was to get her ounce of snuff a week, and that was the one thing she could not do without; it was as necessary to her as tobacco is to a smoker.

All the women over fifty took snuff. It was the one luxury in their hard lives. 'I couldn't do wi'out my pinch o' snuff,' they used to say. ''Tis meat an' drink to me,' and, tapping the sides of their snuffboxes, ''Ave a pinch, me dear.'

Most of the younger women pulled a face of disgust as they refused the invitation, for snuff-taking had gone out of fashion and was looked upon as a dirty habit; but Laura's mother would dip her thumb and forefinger into the box and sniff at them delicately, 'for manners' sake', as she said. Queenie's snuffbox had a picture of Queen Victoria and the Prince Consort on the lid. Sometimes, when every grain of the powder was gone, she would sniff at the empty box and say, 'Ah! That's better. The ghost o' good snuff 's better nor nothin'.'

She still had one great day every year, when, every autumn, the dealer came to purchase the produce of her beehives. Then, in her pantry doorway, a large muslin bag was suspended to drain the honey from the broken pieces of comb into a large, red pan which stood beneath, while, on her doorstep, the end house children waited to see 'the honeyman' carry out and weigh the whole combs. One year – one never-to-be-forgotten year – he had handed to each of them a rich, dripping fragment of comb. He never did it again; but they always waited, for the hope was almost as sweet as the honey.

There had been, when Laura was small, one bachelor's establishment near her home. This had belonged to 'the Major', who, as his nickname denoted, had been in the Army. He had served in many lands and then returned to his native place to set up house and do for himself in a neat, orderly, soldier-like manner. All went well until he became old and feeble. Even then, for some years, he struggled on alone in his little home, for he had a small pension. Then he was ill and spent some weeks in Oxford Infirmary. Before he went there, as he had no relatives or special friends, Laura's mother nursed him and helped him to get together the few necessities he had to take with him. She would have visited him at the hospital had it been possible; but money was scarce and her children were too young to be left, so she wrote him a few letters and sent him the newspaper every week. It was, as she said, 'the least anybody could do for the poor old fellow'. But the Major had seen the world and knew its ways and he did not take such small kindnesses as a matter of course.

He came home from the hospital late one Saturday night, after the children were in bed, and, next morning, Laura, waking at early dawn, thought she saw some strange object on her pillow. She dozed and woke again. It was still there. A small wooden box. She sat up in bed and opened it. Inside was a set of doll's dishes with painted wax food upon them – chops and green peas and new potatoes, and a jam tart with criss-cross pastry. Where could it have come from? It was not Christmas or her birthday. Then Edmund awoke and called out he had found an engine. It was a tiny tin engine, perhaps a penny one, but his delight was unbounded. Then Mother came into their room and said that the Major had brought the presents from Oxford. She had a little red silk handkerchief, such as were worn inside the coat-collar at that time for extra warmth. It was before fur collars were thought of. Father had a pipe and the baby a rattle. It was amazing. To be thought of! To be brought presents, and such presents, by one who was not even a relative! The good, kind Major was in no danger of being forgotten by the family at the end house. Mother made his bed and tidied his room, and Laura was sent with covered plates whenever there was anything special for dinner. She would knock at his door and go in and say in her demure little way, 'Please, Mr Sharman, Mother say could you fancy a little of so-and-so?'

But the Major was too old and ill to be able to live alone much longer, even with such help as the children's mother and other kind neighbours could give. The day came when the doctor called in the relieving officer. The old man was seriously ill; he had no relatives. There was only one place where he could be properly looked after, and that was the workhouse infirmary. They were right in their decision. He was not able to look after himself; he had no relatives or friends able to undertake the responsibility; the workhouse *was* the best place for him. But they made one terrible mistake. They were dealing with a man of intelligence and spirit, and they treated him as they might have done one in the extreme of senile decay. They did not consult him or tell him what they had decided; but ordered the carrier's cart to call at his house the next morning and wait at a short distance while they, in the doctor's gig, drove up to his door. When they entered, the Major had just dressed and dragged himself to his chair by the fire. 'It's a nice morning, and we've come to take you for a drive,' announced the doctor cheerfully, and, in spite of his protests, they hustled on his coat and had him out and in the carrier's cart in a very few minutes.

Laura saw the carrier touch up his horse with the whip and the cart turn, and she always wished afterwards she had not, for, as soon as he realized where he was being taken, the old soldier, the independent old bachelor, the kind family friend, collapsed and cried like a child. He was beaten. But not for long. Before six weeks were over he was back in the parish and all his troubles were over, for he came in his coffin.

As he had no relatives to be informed, the time appointed for his funeral was not known in the hamlet, or no doubt a few of his old neighbours would have gathered in the churchyard. As it was, Laura, standing back among the graves, a milk-can in her hand, was the only spectator, and that quite by chance. No mourner followed the coffin into the church, and she was far too shy to come forward; but when it was brought out and carried towards the open grave it was no longer unaccompanied, for the clergyman's middle-aged daughter walked behind it, an open prayer-book in her hand and an expression of gentle pity in her eyes. She could barely have known him in life, for he was not a churchgoer; but she had seen the solitary coffin arrive and had hurried across from her home to the church that he might at least have one fellow human being to say 'Farewell' to him. In after years, when Laura heard her spoken of slightingly, and, indeed, often felt irritated herself by her interfering ways, she thought of that graceful action.

The children's grandparents lived in a funny little house out in the fields. It was a round house, tapering off at the top, so there were two rooms downstairs and only one – and that a kind of a loft, with a sloping ceiling – above them. The garden did not adjoin the house, but was shut away between high hedges on the other side of the cart track which led to it. It was full of currant and gooseberry bushes, raspberry canes, and old hardy flowers run wild, almost solid with greenery, for, since the gardener had grown old and stiff in the joints, he had not been able to do much pruning or trimming. There Laura spent many happy hours, supposed to be picking fruit for jam, but for the better part of the time reading or dreaming. One corner, overhung by a damson tree and walled in with bushes and flowers, she called her 'green study'.

Laura's grandfather was a tall old man with snow-white hair and beard and the bluest eyes imaginable. He must at that time have been well on in the seventies, for her mother had been his youngest child and a late-comer. One of her outstanding distinctions in the eyes of her own children was that she had been born an aunt, and, as soon as she could talk, had insisted upon her two nieces, both older than herself, addressing her as 'Aunt Emma'.

Before he retired from active life, the grandfather had followed the old country calling of an eggler, travelling the countryside with a little horse and trap, buying up eggs from farms and cottages and selling them at markets and to shopkeepers. At the back of the round house stood the little lean-to stable in which his pony Dobbin had lived. The children loved to lie in the manger and climb about among the rafters. The death of Dobbin of old age had put an end to his master's eggling, for he had no capital with which to buy another horse. Far from it. Moreover, by that time he was himself suffering from Dobbin's complaint; so he settled down to doing what he could in his garden and making a private daily round on his own feet, from his home to the end house, from the end house to church, and back home again.

At the church he not only attended every service, Sunday and weekday, but, when there was no service, he would go there alone to pray and meditate, for he was a deeply religious man. At one time he had been a local preacher, and had walked miles on Sunday evenings to conduct, in turn with others, the services at the cottage meeting houses in the different villages. In old age he had returned to the Church of England, not because of any change of opinion, for creeds did not trouble him – his feet were too firmly planted on the Rock upon which they are all founded – but because the parish church was near enough for him to attend its services, was always open for his private devotions, and the music there, poor as it was, was all the music left to him.

Some members of his old meeting-house congregations still remembered what they considered his inspired preaching 'of the Word'. 'You did ought to be a better gal, wi' such a gran'fer,' said a Methodist woman to Laura one day when she saw her crawl through a gap in a hedge and tear her new pinafore. But Laura was not old enough to appreciate her grandfather, for he died when she was ten, and his loving care for her mother, his youngest and dearest child, led to many lectures and reproofs. Had he seen the torn pinafore, it would certainly have provoked both. However, she had just sufficient discrimination to know he was better than most people.

As has already been mentioned, he had at one time played the violin in one of the last instrumental church choirs in the district. He had also played it at gatherings at home and in neighbours' houses and, in his earlier, unregenerate days, at weddings and feasts and fairs. Laura, happening to think of this one day, said to her mother, 'Why doesn't Grandfather ever play his fiddle now! What's he done with it?'

'Oh,' said her mother in a matter-of-fact tone. 'He hasn't got it any longer. He sold it once when Granny was ill and they were a bit short of money. It was a good fiddle and he got five pounds for it.'

She spoke as though there was no more in selling your fiddle than in selling half a pig or a spare sack of potatoes in an emergency; but Laura, though so much younger, felt differently about it. Though devoid of the most rudimentary musical instinct herself, she had imagination enough to know that to a musician his musical instrument must be a most precious possession. So, when she was alone with her grandfather one day, she said, 'Didn't you miss your fiddle, Granda?'

The old man gave her a quick, searching look, then smiled sadly. 'I did, my maid, more than anything I've ever had to part with, and that's not a little, and I miss it still and always shall. But it went for a good cause, and we can't have everything we want in this world. It wouldn't be good for us.' But Laura did not agree. She thought it would have been good for him to have his dear old fiddle. That wretched money, or rather the lack of it, seemed the cause of everybody's troubles.

The fiddle was not the only thing he had had to give up. He had given up smoking when he retired and they had to live on their tiny savings and the small allowance from a brother who had prospered as a coal-merchant. Perhaps what he felt most keenly of all was that he had had to give up giving, for he loved to give.

One of Laura's earliest memories was of her grandfather coming through the gate and up the end house garden in his old-fashioned close-fitting black overcoat and bowler hat, his beard nicely trimmed and shining, with a huge vegetable marrow under his arm. He came every morning and seldom came empty-handed. He would bring a little basket of early raspberries or green peas, already shelled, or a tight little bunch of sweet williams and moss rosebuds, or a baby rabbit, which someone else had given him – always something. He would come indoors, and if anything in the house was broken, he would mend it, or he would take a stocking out of his pocket and sit down and knit, and all the time he was working he would talk in a kind, gentle voice to his daughter, calling her 'Emmie'. Sometimes she would cry as she told him of her troubles, and he would get up and smooth her hair and wipe her eyes and say, 'That's better! That's better! Now you're going to be my own brave little wench! And remember, my dear, there's One above who knows what's best for us, though we may not see it ourselves at the time.'

By the middle of the 'eighties the daily visits had ceased, for the chronic rheumatism against which he had fought was getting the better of him. First, the church was too far for him; then the end house; then his own garden across the road; and at last his world narrowed down to the bed upon which he was lying. That bed was not the four-poster with the silk-and-satin patchwork quilt in rich shades of red and brown and orange which stood in the best downstairs bedroom, but the plain white bed beneath the sloping ceiling in the little whitewashed room under the roof. He had slept there for years, leaving his wife the downstairs room, that she might not be disturbed by his fevered tossing during his rheumatic attacks, and also because, like many old people, he woke early, and liked to get up and light the fire and read his Bible before his wife was ready for her cup of tea to be taken to her.

Gradually, his limbs became so locked he could not turn over in bed without help. Giving to and doing for others was over for him. He would lie upon his back for hours, his tired old blue eyes fixed upon the picture nailed on the wall at the foot of his bed. It was the only coloured thing in the room; the rest was bare whiteness. It was of the Crucifixion, and, printed above the crown of thorns were the words:

This have I done for thee.

And underneath the pierced and bleeding feet:

What hast thou done for me?

His two years' uncomplaining endurance of excruciating pain answered for him.

When her husband was asleep, or lying, washed and tended, gazing at his picture, Laura's grandmother would sit among her feather cushions downstairs reading *Bow Bells* or the *Princess Novelettes* or the *Family Herald*. Except when engaged in housework, she was never seen without a book in her hand. It was always a novelette, and she had a large assortment of these which she kept tied up in flat parcels, ready to exchange with other novelette readers.

She had been very pretty when she was young. 'The Belle of Hornton', they had called her in her native village, and she often told Laura of the time when her hair had reached down to her knees, like a great yellow cape, she said, which covered her. Another of her favourite stories was of the day when she had danced with a real lord. It was at his coming-of-age celebrations, and a great honour, for he had passed over his own friends and the daughters of his tenants in favour of one who was but a gamekeeper's daughter. Before the evening was over he had whispered in her ear that she was the prettiest girl in the country, and she had cherished the compliment all her life. There were no further developments. My Lord was My Lord, and Hannah Pollard was Hannah Pollard, a poor girl, but the daughter of decent parents. No further developments were possible in real life, though such affairs ended differently in her novelettes. Perhaps that was why she enjoyed them.

It was difficult for Laura to connect the long, yellow hair and the white frock with blue ribbons worn at the coming-of-age fête with her grandmother, for she saw her only as a thin, frail old woman who wore her grey hair parted like curtains and looped at the ears with little combs. Still, there was something which made her worth looking at. Laura's mother said it was because her features were good. 'My mother,' she would say, 'will look handsome in her coffin. Colour goes and the hair turns grey, but the framework lasts.'

Laura's mother was greatly disappointed in her little daughter's looks. Her own mother had been an acknowledged belle, she herself had been charmingly pretty, and she naturally expected her children to carry on the tradition. But Laura was a plain, thin child: 'Like a moll heron, all legs and wings,' she was told in the hamlet, and her dark eyes and wide mouth looked too large for her small face. The only compliment ever paid her in childhood was that of a curate who said she was 'intelligent looking'. Those around her would have preferred curly hair and a rosebud mouth to all the intelligence in the world.

Laura's grandmother had never tramped ten miles on a Sunday night to hear her husband preach in a village chapel. She had gone to church once every Sunday, unless it rained or was too hot, or she had a cold, or some article of her attire was too shabby. She was particular about her clothes and liked to have everything handsome about her. In her bedroom there were pictures and ornaments, as well as the feather cushions and silk patchwork quilt.

When she came to the end house, the best chair was placed by the fire for her and the best possible tea put on the table, and Laura's mother did not whisper her troubles to her as she did to her father. If some little thing did leak out, she would only say, 'All men need a bit of humouring.'

Some women, too, thought Laura, for she could see that her grandmother had always been the one to be indulged and spared all trouble and unpleasantness. If the fiddle had belonged her, it would never have been sold; the whole family would have combined to buy a handsome new case for it.

After her husband died, she went away to live with her eldest son, and the round house shared the fate of Sally's. Where it stood is now a ploughed field. The husband's sacrifices, the wife's romance, are as though they had never been – 'melted into air, into thin air'.

Those were a few of the old men and women to whom the Rector referred as 'our old folks' and visiting townsmen lumped together as 'a lot of old yokels'. There were a few other homes of old people in the hamlet; that of Master Ashley, for instance, who, like Sally, had descended from one of the original squatters and still owned the ancestral cottage and strip of land. He must have been one of the last people to use a breast-plough, a primitive implement consisting of a ploughshare at one end of a stout stick and a cross-piece of shaped wood at the other which the user pressed to his breast to drive the share through the soil. On his land stood the only surviving specimen of the old furze and daub building which had once been common in the neighbourhood. The walls were of furze branches closely pressed together and daubed with a mixture of mud and mortar. It was said that the first settlers built their cottages of these materials with their own hands.

Then there were one or two poorer couples, just holding on to their homes, but in daily fear of the workhouse. The Poor Law authorities allowed old people past work a small weekly sum as outdoor relief; but it was not sufficient to live upon, and, unless they had more than usually prosperous children to help support them, there came a time when the home had to be broken up. When, twenty years later, the Old Age Pensions began, life was transformed for such aged cottagers. They were relieved of anxiety. They were suddenly rich. Independent for life! At first when they went to the Post Office to draw it, tears of gratitude would run down the cheeks of some, and they would say as they picked up their money, 'God bless that Lord George! [for they could not believe one so powerful and munificent could be a plain 'Mr'] and God bless *you*, miss!' and there were flowers from their gardens and apples from their trees for the girl who merely handed them the money.

VI

The Besieged Generation

To Laura, as a child, the hamlet once appeared as a fortress. She was coming home alone from school one wild, grey, March afternoon, and, looking up from her battling against the wind, got a swift new impression of the cluster of stark walls and slated roofs on the Rise, with rooks tumbling and clouds hurrying overhead, smoke beating down from the chimneys, and clothes on clothes-lines straining away in the wind.

'It's a fort! It's a fort!' she cried, and she went on up the road, singing in her flat, tuneless little voice the Salvation Army hymn of the day, 'Hold the fort, for I am coming'.

There was a deeper likeness than that of her childish vision. The hamlet was indeed in a state of siege, and its chief assailant was Want. Yet, like other citizens during a long, but not too desperate siege, its inhabitants had become accustomed to their hard conditions and were able to snatch at any small passing pleasure and even at times to turn their very straits to laughter.

To go from the homes of the older people to those of the besieged generation was to step into another chapter of the hamlet's history. All the graces and simple luxuries of the older style of living had disappeared. They were poor people's houses rich only in children, strong, healthy children, who, in a few years, would be ready to take their part in the work of the world and to provide good, healthy blood for the regeneration of city populations; but, in the meantime, their parents had to give their all in order to feed and clothe them.

In their houses the good, solid, hand-made furniture of their forefathers had given place to the cheap and ugly products of the early machine age. A deal table, the top ribbed and softened by much scrubbing; four or five windsor chairs with the varnish blistered and flaking; a side table for the family photographs and ornaments, and a few stools for fireside seats, together with the beds upstairs, made up the collection spoken of by its owners as 'our few sticks of furniture'.

If the father had a special chair in which to rest after his day's work was done, it would be but a rather larger replica of the hard windsors with wooden arms added. The clock, if any, was a cheap, foreign timepiece, standing on the mantelshelf – one which could seldom be relied upon to keep correct time for twelve hours together. Those who had no clock depended upon the husband's watch for getting up in the morning. The watch then went to work with him, an arrangement which must have been a great inconvenience to most wives; but was a boon to the gossips, who could then knock at a neighbour's door and ask the time when they felt inclined for a chat.

The few poor crocks were not good enough to keep on show and were hidden away in the pantry between mealtimes. Pewter plates and dishes as ornaments had gone. There were still plenty of them to be found, kicked about around gardens and pigsties. Sometimes a travelling tinker would spy one of these and beg or buy it for a few coppers, to melt down and use in his trade. Other casual callers at the cottages would buy a set of hand-wrought, brass drop-handles from an inherited chest of drawers for sixpence; or a corner cupboard, or a gate-legged table which had become slightly infirm, for half a crown. Other such articles of furniture were put out of doors and spoilt by the weather, for the newer generation did not value such things; it preferred the products of its own day, and, gradually, the hamlet was being stripped of such relics.

As ornaments for their mantelpieces and side tables the women liked gaudy glass vases, pottery images of animals, shell-covered boxes and plush photograph frames. The most valued ornaments of all were the white china mugs inscribed in gilt lettering 'A Present for a Good Child', or 'A Present from Brighton', or some other sea-side place. Those who had daughters in service to bring them would accumulate quite a collection of these, which were hung by the handles in rows from the edge of a shelf, and were a source of great pride in the owner and of envy in the neighbours.

Those who could find the necessary cash covered their walls with wall-paper in big, sprawling, brightly coloured flower designs. Those who could not, used whitewash or pasted up newspaper sheets. On the wall space near the hearth hung the flitch or flitches of bacon, and every house had a few pictures, mostly coloured ones given by grocers as almanacks and framed at home. These had to be in pairs, and lovers' meetings lovers' partings, brides in their wedding gowns, widows standing by newly made graves, children begging in the snow or playing with puppies or kittens in nurseries were the favourite subjects.

Yet, even out of these unpromising materials, in a room which was kitchen, living-room, nursery, and wash-house combined, some women would contrive to make a pleasant, attractive-looking home. A well-whitened hearth, a home-made rag rug in bright colours, and a few geraniums on the window-sill would cost nothing, but make a great difference to the general effect. Others despised these finishing touches. What was the good of breaking your back pegging rugs for the children to mess up when an old sack thrown down would serve the same purpose, they said. As to flowers in pots, they didn't hold with the nasty, messy things. But they did, at least, believe in cleaning up their houses once a day, for public opinion demanded that of them. There were plenty of bare, comfortless homes in the hamlet, but there was not one really dirty one.

Every morning, as soon as the men had been packed off to work, the older children to school, the smaller ones to play, and the baby had been bathed and put to sleep in its cradle, rugs and mats were carried out of doors and banged against walls, fireplaces were 'ridded up', and tables and floors were scrubbed. In wet weather, before scrubbing, the stone floor had often to be scraped with an old knife-blade to loosen the trodden-in mud; for, although there was a scraper for shoes beside every doorstep, some of the stiff, clayey mud would stick to the insteps and uppers of boots and be brought indoors.

To avoid bringing in more during the day, the women wore

pattens over their shoes to go to the well or the pigsty. The patten consisted of a wooden sole with a leather toepiece, raised about two inches from the ground on an iron ring. *Clack! Clack! Clack!* over the stones, and *Slush! Slush! Slush!* through the mud went the patten rings. You could not keep your movements secret if you wore pattens to keep yourself dry shod.

A pair of pattens only cost tenpence and lasted for years. But the patten was doomed. Vicarage ladies and farmers' wives no longer wore them to go to and fro between their dairies and poultry yards, and newly married cottagers no longer provided themselves with a pair. 'Too proud to wear pattens' was already becoming a proverb at the beginning of the decade, and by the end of it they had practically disappeared.

The morning cleaning proceeded to the accompaniment of neighbourly greetings and shouting across garden and fences, for the first sound of the banging of mats was a signal for others to bring out theirs, and it would be 'Have 'ee heard this?' and 'What d'ye think of that?' until industrious housewives declared that they would take to banging their mats overnight, for they never knew if it was going to take them two minutes or two hours.

Nicknames were not used among the women, and only the aged were spoken of by their Christian names, Old Sally or Old Queenie or sometimes Dame – Dame Mercer or Dame Morris. The other married women were Mrs This or Mrs That, even with those who had known them from their cradles. Old men were called Master, not Mister. Younger men were known by their nicknames or their Christian names, excepting a few who were more than usually respected. Children were carefully taught to address all as Mr or Mrs.

Cleaning began at about the same time in every house, but the time of finishing varied. Some housewives would have everything spick-and-span and themselves 'tidied up' by noon; others would still be at it at tea-time. 'A slut's work's never done' was a saying among the good housewives.

It puzzled Laura that, although everybody cleaned up every day, some houses looked what they called there 'a pictur' and others a muddle. She remarked on this to her mother.

'Come here,' was the answer. 'See this grate I'm cleaning? Looks done, doesn't it? But you wait.'

Up and down and round and round and between the bars went the brush; then: 'Now look. Looks different, doesn't it?' It did. It had been passably polished before; now it was resplendent. 'There!' said her mother. 'That's the secret; just that bit of extra elbow-grease after some folks would consider a thing done.'

But that final polish, the giving of which came naturally to Laura's mother, could not have been possible to all. Pregnancy and nursing and continual money worries must have worn down the strength and energy of many. Taking these drawbacks into account, together with the inconvenience and overcrowding of the cottages, the general standard of cleanliness was marvellous.

There was one postal delivery a day, and towards ten o'clock, the heads of the women beating their mats would be turned towards the allotment path to watch for 'Old Postie'. Some days there were two, or even three, letters for Lark Rise; quite as often there were none; but there were few women who did not gaze longingly. This longing for letters was called 'yearning' (pronounced 'yarnin''); 'No, I be-ant expectin' nothin', but I be so yarnin'' one woman would say to another as they watched the old postman dawdle over the stile and between the allotment plots. On wet days he carried an old green gig umbrella with whalebone ribs, and, beneath its immense circumference he seemed to make no more progress than an overgrown mushroom. But at last he would reach and usually pass the spot where the watchers were standing.

'No, I ain't got nothin' for you, Mrs Parish,' he would call. 'Your young Annie wrote to you only last week. She's got summat else to do besides sittin' down on her arse writing home all the time.' Or, waving his arm for some woman to meet him, for he did not intend to go a step further than he was obliged: 'One for you, Mrs Knowles, and, my! ain't it a thin-roed 'un! Not much time to write to her mother these days. I took a good fat 'un from her to young Chad Gubbins.'

So he went on, always leaving a sting behind, a gloomy, grumpy old man who seemed to resent having to serve such humble people.

He had been a postman forty years and had walked an incredible number of miles in all weathers, so perhaps the resulting flat feet and rheumaticky limbs were to blame; but the whole hamlet rejoiced when at last he was pensioned off and a smart, obliging young postman took his place on the Lark Rise round.

Delighted as the women were with the letters from their daughters, it was the occasional parcels of clothing they sent that caused the greatest excitement. As soon as a parcel was taken indoors, neighbours who had seen Old Postie arrive with it would drop in, as though by accident, and stay to admire, or sometimes to criticize, the contents.

All except the aged women, who wore what they had been accustomed to wearing and were satisfied, were very particular about their clothes. Anything did for everyday wear, as long as it was clean and whole and could be covered with a decent white apron; it was the 'Sunday best' that had to be just so. 'Better be out of the world than out of the fashion' was one of their sayings. To be appreciated, the hat or coat contained in the parcel had to be in the fashion, and the hamlet had a fashion of its own, a year or two behind outside standards, and strictly limited as to style and colour.

The daughter's or other kinswoman's clothes were sure to be appreciated, for they had usually already been seen and admired when the girl was at home for her holiday, and had indeed helped to set the standard of what was worn. The garments bestowed by the mistresses were unfamiliar and often somewhat in advance of the hamlet vogue, and so were often rejected for personal wear as 'a bit queer' and cut down for the children; though the mothers often wished a year or two later when that particular fashion arrived that they had kept them for themselves. Then they had colour prejudices. A red frock! Only a fast hussy would wear red. Or green – sure to bring any wearer bad luck! There was a positive taboo on green in the hamlet; nobody would wear it until it had been home-dyed navy or brown. Yellow ranked with red as immodest; but there was not much yellow worn anywhere in the 'eighties. On the whole, they preferred dark or neutral colours; but there was one exception;

blue had nothing against it. Marine and sky blue were the favourite shades, both very bright and crude.

Much prettier were the colours of the servant girls' print morning dresses – lilac, or pink, or buff, sprigged with white – which were cut down for the little girls to wear on May Day and for churchgoing throughout the summer.

To the mothers the cut was even more important than the colour. If sleeves were worn wide they liked them to be very wide; if narrow, skin tight. Skirts in those days did not vary in length; they were made to touch the ground. But they were sometimes trimmed with frills or flounces or bunched up at the back, and the women would spend days altering this trimming to make it just right, or turning gathers into pleats or pleats into gathers.

The hamlet's fashion lag was the salvation of its wardrobes, for a style became 'all the go' there just as the outer world was discarding it, and good, little-worn specimens came that way by means of the parcels. *The* Sunday garment at the beginning of the decade was the tippet, a little shoulder cape of black silk or satin with a long, dangling fringe. All the women and some of the girls had these, and they were worn proudly to church or Sunday school with a posy of roses or geraniums pinned in front.

Hats were of the chimney-pot variety, a tall cylinder of straw, with a very narrow brim and a spray of artificial flowers trained up the front. Later in the decade, the shape changed to wide brims and squashed crowns. The chimney-pot hat had had its day, and the women declared they would not be seen going to the privy in one.

Then there were the bustles, at first looked upon with horror, and no wonder! but after a year or two the most popular fashion ever known in the hamlet and the one which lasted longest. They cost nothing, as they could be made at home from any piece of old cloth rolled up into a cushion and worn under any frock. Soon all the women, excepting the aged, and all the girls, excepting the tiniest, were peacocking in their bustles, and they wore them so long that Edmund was old enough in the day of their decline to say that he had seen the last bustle on earth going round the Rise on a woman with a bucket of pig-wash.

This devotion to fashion gave a spice to life and helped to make bearable the underlying poverty. But the poverty was there; one might have a velvet tippet and no shoes worth mentioning; or a smart frock, but no coat; and the same applied to the children's clothes and the sheets and towels and cups and saucepans. There was never enough of anything, except food.

Monday was washing-day, and then the place fairly hummed with activity. 'What d'ye think of the weather?' 'Shall we get 'em dry?' were the questions shouted across gardens, or asked as the women met going to and from the well for water. There was no gossiping at corners that morning. It was before the days of patent soaps and washing powders, and much hard rubbing was involved. There were no washing coppers, and the clothes had to be boiled in the big cooking pots over the fire. Often these inadequate vessels would boil over and fill the house with ashes and steam. The small children would hang round their mothers' skirts and hinder them, and tempers grew short and nerves frayed long before the clothes, well blued, were hung on the lines or spread on the hedges. In wet weather they had to be dried indoors, and no one who has not experienced it can imagine the misery of living for several days with a firmament of drying clothes on lines overhead.

After their meagre midday meal, the women allowed themselves a little leisure. In summer, some of them would take out their sewing and do it in company with others in the shade of one of the houses. Others would sew or read indoors, or carry their babies out in the garden for an airing. A few who had no very young children liked to have what they called 'a bit of a lay down' on the bed. With their doors locked and window-blinds drawn, they, at least, escaped the gossips, who began to get busy at this hour.

One of the most dreaded of these was Mrs Mullins, a thin, pale, elderly woman who wore her iron-grey hair thrust into a black chenille net at the back of her head and wore a little black shawl over her shoulders, summer and winter alike. She was one of the most common sights of the hamlet, going round the Rise in her pattens, with her door-key dangling from her fingers.

That door-key was looked upon as a bad sign, for she only locked her door when she intended to be away some time. 'Where's she a prowlin' off to?' one woman would ask another as they rested with their water-buckets at a corner. 'God knows, an' He won't tell us,' was likely to be the reply. 'But, thanks be, she won't be a goin' to our place now she's seen me here.'

She visited every cottage in turn, knocking at the door and asking the correct time, or for the loan of a few matches, or the gift of a pin – anything to make an opening. Some housewives only opened the door a crack, hoping to get rid of her, but she usually managed to cross the threshold, and, once within, would stand just inside the door, twisting her door-key and talking.

She talked no scandal. Had she done so, her visits might have been less unwelcome. She just babbled on, about the weather, or her sons' last letters, or her pig, or something she had read in the Sunday newspaper. There was a saying in the hamlet: 'Standing gossipers stay longest', and Mrs Mullins was a standing example of this. 'Won't you sit down, Mrs Mullins?' Laura's mother would say if she happened herself to be seated. But it was always, 'No, oh no, thankee. I mustn't stop a minute'; but her minutes always mounted up to an hour or more, and at last her unwilling hostess would say 'Excuse me, I must just run round to the well,' or 'I'd nearly forgotten that I'd got to fetch a cabbage from the allotment,' and, even then, the chances were that Mrs Mullins would insist upon accompanying her, talking them both to a standstill every few yards.

Poor Mrs Mullins! With her children all out in the world, her home must have seemed to her unbearably silent, and, having no resources of her own and a great longing to hear her own voice, she was forced out in search of company. Nobody wanted her, for she had nothing interesting to say, and yet talked too much to allow her listener a fair share of the conversation. She was the worst of all bores, a melancholy bore, and at the sight of her door-key and little black shawl the pleasantest of little gossiping groups would scatter.

Mrs Andrews was an even greater talker; but, although most people objected to her visits on principle, they did not glance at the clock every two minutes while she was there or invent errands for themselves in order to get rid of her. Like Mrs Mullins, she had got her family off hand and so had unlimited leisure; but, unlike her, she had always something of interest to relate. If nothing had happened in the hamlet since her last call, she was quite capable of inventing something. More often, she would take up some stray, unimportant fact, blow it up like a balloon, tie it neatly with circumstantial detail and present it to her listener, ready to be launched on the air of the hamlet. She would watch the clothes-line of some expectant mother, and if no small garments appeared on it in what she considered due time, it would be: 'There's that Mrs Wren, only a month from her time, and not a stitch put into a rag yet.' If she saw a well-dressed stranger call at one of the cottages, she would know 'for a fac'' that he was the bailiff with a County Court summons, or that he had been to tell the parents that 'their young Jim', who was working up-country, had got into trouble with the police over some money. She 'sized up' every girl at home on holiday and thought that most of them looked pregnant. She took care to say 'thought' and 'looked' in those cases, because she knew that in ninety-nine cases out of a hundred time would prove her suspicions to have been groundless.

Sometimes she would widen her field and tell of the doings in high society. She 'knew for a fac'' that the then Prince of Wales had given one of his ladies a necklace with pearls the size of pigeon's eggs, and that the poor old Queen, with her crown on her head and tears streaming down her cheeks, had gone down on her knees to beg him to turn the whole lot of saucy hussies out of Windsor Castle. It was said in the hamlet that, when Mrs Andrews spoke, you could see the lies coming out of her mouth like steam, and nobody believed a word she said, even when, occasionally, she spoke the truth. Yet most of the women enjoyed a chat with her. As they said, it 'made a bit of a change'. Laura's mother was too hard on her when she called her a pest, or interrupted one of her stories at a crucial point to ask, 'Are you sure that is right, Mrs Andrews?' In a community without cinemas or wireless and with very little reading matter, she had her uses.

Borrowers were another nuisance. Most of the women borrowed at some time, and a few families lived entirely on borrowing the day before pay-day. There would come a shy, low-down, little knock at the door, and when it was opened, a child's voice would say, 'Oh, please Mrs So-and-So, could you oblige me mother with a spoonful of tea [or a cup of sugar, or half a loaf] till me Dad gets his money?' If the required article could not be spared at the first house, she would go from door to door repeating her request until she got what she wanted, for such were her instructions.

The borrowings were usually repaid, or there would soon have been nowhere to borrow from; but often an insufficient quantity or an inferior quality were returned, and the result was a smouldering resentment against the habitual borrowers. But no word of direct complaint was uttered. Had it been, the borrower might have taken offence, and the women wished above all things to be on good terms with their neighbours.

Laura's mother detested the borrowing habit. She said that when she had first set up housekeeping she had made it her rule when a borrower came to the door to say, 'Tell your mother I never borrow myself and I never lend. But here's the tea. I don't want it back again. Tell your mother she's welcome to it.' The plan did not work. The same borrower came again and again, until she had to say, 'Tell your mother I must have it back this time.' Again the plan did not work. Laura once heard her mother say to Queenie, 'Here's half a loaf, Queenie, if it's any good to you. But I won't deceive you about it; it's one that Mrs Knowles sent back that she'd borrowed from me, and I can't fancy it myself, out of her house. If you don't have it, it'll have to go in the pig-tub.'

'That's all right, me dear,' was Queenie's smiling response. 'It'll do fine for our Tom's tea. He won't know where it's been, an' 'ould'nt care if he did. All he cares about's a full belly.'

However, there were other friends and neighbours to whom it was a pleasure to lend, or to give on the rare occasions when that was possible. They seldom asked directly for a loan, but would say, 'My poor old tea-caddy's empty,' or 'I ain't got a mossel o' bread till the baker comes.' They spoke of this kind of approach as 'a nint' and said that if anybody liked to take it they could; if not, no harm was done, for they hadn't demeaned themselves by asking.

As well as the noted gossips, there were in Lark Rise, as elsewhere, women who, by means of a dropped hint or a subtle suggestion, could poison another's mind, and others who wished no harm to anybody, yet loved to discuss their neighbours' affairs and were apt to babble confidences. But, though few of the women were averse to a little scandal at times, most of them grew restive when it passed a certain point. 'Let's give it a rest,' they would say, or 'Well, I think we've plucked enough feathers out of her wings for one day,' and they would change the subject and talk about their children, or the rising prices, or the servant problem – from the maid's standpoint.

Those of the younger set who were what they called 'folks together', meaning friendly, would sometimes meet in the afternoon in one of their cottages to sip strong, sweet, milkless tea and talk things over. These tea-drinkings were never premeditated. One neighbour would drop in, then another, and another would be beckoned to from the doorway or fetched in to settle some disputed point. Then some one would say, 'How about a cup o' tay?' and they would all run home to fetch a spoonful, with a few leaves over to help make up the spoonful for the pot.

Those who assembled thus were those under forty. The older women did not care for the little tea-parties, nor for light, pleasant chit-chat; there was more of the salt of the earth in their conversation and they were apt to express things in terms which the others, who had all been in good service, considered coarse and countrified.

As they settled around the room to enjoy their cup of tea, some would have babies at the breast or toddlers playing 'bo-peep' with their aprons, and others would have sewing or knitting in their hands. They were pleasant to look at, with their large clean white aprons and smoothly plaited hair, parted in the middle. The best clothes were kept folded away in their boxes from Sunday to Sunday, and a clean apron was full dress on week-days.

It was not a countryside noted for feminine good looks and there were plenty of wide mouths, high cheekbones, and snub noses among them; but they nearly all had the country-bred woman's clear eyes, strong, white teeth and fresh colour. Their height was above that of the average working-class townswoman, and, when not obscured by pregnancy, their figures were straight and supple, though inclining to thickness.

This tea-drinking time was the women's hour. Soon the children would be rushing in from school; then would come the men, with their loud voices and coarse jokes and corduroys reeking of earth and sweat. In the meantime, the wives and mothers were free to crook their little fingers genteelly as they sipped from their tea-cups and talked about the, to them, latest fashion, or discussed the serial then running in the novelette they were reading.

Most of the younger women and some of the older ones were fond of what they called 'a bit of a read', and their mental fare consisted almost exclusively of the novelette. Several of the hamlet women took in one of these weekly, as published, for the price was but one penny, and these were handed round until the pages were thin and frayed with use. Copies of others found their way there from neighbouring villages, or from daughters in service, and there was always quite a library of them in circulation.

The novelette of the 'eighties was a romantic love story, in which the poor governess always married the duke, or the lady of title the gamekeeper, who always turned out to be a duke or an earl in disguise. Midway through the story there had to be a description of a ball, at which the heroine in her simple white gown attracted all the men in the room; or the gamekeeper, commandeered to help serve, made love to the daughter of the house in the conservatory. The stories were often prettily written and as innocent as sugared milk and water; but, although they devoured them, the women looked upon novelette reading as a vice, to be hidden from their menfolk and only discussed with fellow devotees.

The novelettes were as carefully kept out of the children's way as the advanced modern novel is, or should be, today; but children who wanted to read them knew where to find them, on the top shelf of the cupboard or under the bed, and managed to read them in secret. An ordinarily intelligent child of eight or nine found them cloying; but they did the women good, for, as they said, they took them out of themselves.

There had been a time when the hamlet readers had fed on

stronger food, and Biblical words and imagery still coloured the speech of some of the older people. Though unread, every well-kept cottage had still its little row of books, neatly arranged on the side table with the lamp, the clothes brush and the family photographs. Some of these collections consisted solely of the family Bible and a prayer-book or two; others had a few extra volumes which had either belonged to parents or been bought with other oddments for a few pence at a sale – *The Pilgrim's Progress*, *Drelincourt on Death*, Richardson's *Pamela*, *Anna Lee: The Maiden Wife and Mother*, and old books of travel and sermons. Laura's greatest find was a battered old copy of Belzoni's *Travels* propping open somebody's pantry window. When she asked for the loan of it, it was generously given to her, and she had the, to her, intense pleasure of exploring the burial chambers of the pyramids with her author.

Some of the imported books had their original owner's book-plate, or an inscription in faded copper-plate handwriting inside the covers, while the family ones, in a ruder hand, would proclaim:

> George Welby, his book:
> Give me grace therein to look,
> And not only to look, but to understand,
> For learning is better than houses and land
> When land is lost and money spent
> Then learning is most excellent.

Or:

> George Welby is my name,
>   England is my nation,
> Lark Rise is my dwelling place
>   And Christ is my salvation.
>
> When I am dead and in my grave
>   And all my bones are rotten,
> Take this book and think of me
>   And mind I'm not forgotten.

Another favourite inscription was the warning:

> Steal not this book for fear of shame,
> For in it doth stand the owner's name,
> And at the last day God will say
> 'Where is that book you stole away?'
> And if you say, 'I cannot tell,'
> He'll say, 'Thou cursed, go to hell.'

All or any of these books were freely lent, for none of the owners wanted to read them. The women had their novelettes, and it took the men all their time to get through their Sunday newspapers, one of which came into almost every house, either by purchase or borrowing. The *Weekly Despatch*, *Reynolds's News*, and *Lloyd's News* were their favourites, though a few remained faithful to that fine old local newspaper, the *Bicester Herald*.

Laura's father, as well as his *Weekly Despatch*, took the *Carpenter and Builder*, through which the children got their first instruction to Shakespeare, for there was a controversy in it as to Hamlet's words, 'I know a hawk from a handsaw'. It appeared that some scholar had suggested that it should read, 'I know a hawk from a heron, pshaw!' and the carpenters and builders were up in arms. *Of course*, the hawk was the mason's and plasterer's tool of that time, and the handsaw was *just* a handsaw. Although that line and a few extracts that she afterwards found in the school readers were all that Laura was to know of Shakespeare's works for some time, she sided warmly with the carpenters and builders, and her mother, when appealed to, agreed, for she said 'that heron, pshaw!' certainly sounded a bit left-handed.

While the novelette readers, who represented the genteel section of the community, were enjoying their tea, there would be livelier gatherings at another of the cottages. The hostess, Caroline Arless, was at that time about forty-five, and a tall, fine, upstanding woman with flashing dark eyes, hair like crinkled black wire, and cheeks the colour of a ripe apricot. She was not a native of the hamlet, but had come there as a bride, and it was said that she had gipsy blood in her.

Although she was herself a grandmother, she still produced a child of her own every eighteen months or so, a proceeding regarded as bad form in the hamlet, for the saying ran, 'When the young 'uns begin, 'tis time for the old 'uns to finish.' But Mrs Arless recognized no rules, excepting those of Nature. She welcomed each new arrival, cared for it tenderly while it was helpless, swept it out of doors to play as soon as it could toddle, to school at three, and to work at ten or eleven. Some of the girls married at seventeen and the boys at nineteen or twenty.

Ways and means did not trouble her. Husband and sons at work 'brassed up' on Friday nights, and daughters in service sent home at least half of their wages. One night she would fry steak and onions for supper and make the hamlet's mouth water; another night there would be nothing but bread and lard on her table. When she had money she spent it, and when she had none she got things on credit or went without. 'I shall feather the foam,' she used to say. 'I have before an' I shall again, and what's the good of worrying.' She always did manage to feather it, and usually to have a few coppers in her pocket as well, although she was known to be deeply in debt. When she received a postal order from one of her daughters she would say to any one who happened to be standing by when she opened the letter, 'I be-ant goin' to squander this bit o' money in paying me debts.'

Her idea of wise spending was to call in a few neighbours of like mind, seat them round a roaring fire, and dispatch one of her toddlers to the inn with the beer can. They none of them got drunk, or even fuddled, for there was not very much each, even when the can went round to the inn a second or a third time. But there was just enough to hearten them up and make them forget their troubles, and the talk and laughter and scraps of song which floated on the air from 'that there Mrs Arless's house' were shocking to the more sedate matrons. Nobody crooked their finger round the handle of a teacup or 'talked genteel' at Mrs Arless's gatherings, herself least of all. She was so charged with sex vitality that with her all subjects of conversation led to it – not in its filthy or furtive aspects, but as the one great central fact of life.

Yet no one could dislike Mrs Arless, however much she might offend their taste and sense of fitness. She was so full of life and vigour and so overflowing with good nature that she would force anything she had upon any one she thought needed it, regardless of the fact that it was not and never would be paid for. She knew the inside of a County Court well, and made no secret of her knowledge, for a County Court summons was to her but an invitation to a day's outing from which she would return victorious, having persuaded the judge that she was a model wife and mother who only got into debt because her family was so large and she herself was so generous. It was her creditor who retired discomfited.

Another woman who lived in the hamlet and yet stood somewhat aside from its ordinary life was Hannah Ashley. She was the daughter-in-law of the old Methodist who drove the breast plough, and she and her husband were also Methodists. She was a little brown mouse of a woman who took no part in the hamlet gossip or the hamlet disputes. Indeed, she was seldom seen on week-days, for her cottage stood somewhat apart from the others and had its own well in the garden. But on Sunday evenings her house was used as a Methodist meeting place, and then all her week-day reserve was put aside and all who cared to come were made welcome. As she listened to the preacher, or joined in the hymns and prayers, she would look round on the tiny congregation, and those whose eyes met hers would see such a glow of love in them that they could never again think, much less say, ill of her, beyond 'Well, she's a Methody', as though that explained and excused anything strange about her.

These younger Ashleys had one child, a son, about Edmund's age, and the children at the end house sometimes played with him. When Laura called at his home for him one Saturday morning she saw a picture which stamped itself upon her mind for life. It was the hour when every other house in the hamlet was being turned inside out for the Saturday cleaning. The older children, home from school, were running in and out of their homes, or quarrelling over their games outside. Mothers were scolding and babies were crying during the process of being rolled in their shawls for an outing on the arm of an older sister. It was the kind of day Laura detested, for there was no corner indoors for her and her book, and outside she was in danger of being dragged into games that either pulled her to pieces or bored her.

Inside Freddy Ashley's home all was peace and quiet and spotless purity. The walls were freshly whitewashed, the table and board floor were scrubbed to a pale straw colour, the beautifully polished grate glowed crimson, for the oven was being heated, and placed half-way over the table was a snowy cloth with paste-board and rolling-pin upon it. Freddy was helping his mother make biscuits, cutting the pastry she had rolled into shapes with a little tin cutter. Their two faces, both so plain and yet so pleasant, were close together above the paste-board, and their two voices as they bade Laura come in and sit by the fire sounded like angels' voices after the tumult outside.

It was a brief glimpse into a different world from the one she was accustomed to, but the picture remained with her as something quiet and pure and lovely. She thought that the home at Nazareth must have been something like Freddy's.

The women never worked in the vegetable gardens or on the allotments, even when they had their children off hand and had plenty of spare time, for there was a strict division of labour and that was 'men's work'. Victorian ideas, too, had penetrated to some extent, and any work outside the home was considered unwomanly. But even that code permitted a woman to cultivate a flower garden, and most of the houses had at least a narrow border beside the pathway. As no money could be spared for seeds or plants, they had to depend upon roots and cuttings given by their neighbours, and there was little variety; but they grew all the sweet old-fashioned cottage garden flowers, pinks and sweet williams and love-in-a-mist, wallflowers and forget-me-nots in spring and hollyhocks and Michaelmas daisies in autumn. Then there were lavender and sweet-briar bushes, and southern-wood, sometimes called 'lad's love', but known there as 'old man'.

Almost every garden had its rose bush; but there were no coloured roses amongst them. Only Old Sally had those; the other people had to be content with that meek, old-fashioned white rose with a pink flush at the heart known as the 'maiden's blush'. Laura used to wonder who had imported the first bush, for evidently slips of it had been handed round from house to house.

As well as their flower garden, the women cultivated a herb corner, stocked with thyme and parsley and sage for cooking, rosemary to flavour the home-made lard, lavender to scent the best clothes, and peppermint, pennyroyal, horehound, camomile, tansy, balm, and rue for physic. They made a good deal of camomile tea, which they drank freely to ward off colds, to soothe the nerves, and as a general tonic. A large jug of this was always prepared and stood ready for heating up after confinements. The horehound was used with honey in a preparation to be taken for sore throats and colds on the chest. Peppermint tea was made rather as a luxury than a medicine; it was brought out on special occasions and drunk from wine-glasses; and the women had a private use for the pennyroyal, though, judging from appearances, it was not very effective.

As well as the garden herbs, still in general use, some of the older women used wild ones, which they gathered in their seasons and dried. But the knowledge and use of these was dying out; most people depended upon their garden stock. Yarrow, or milleflower, was an exception; everybody still gathered that in large quantities to make 'yarb beer'. Gallons of this were brewed and taken to work in their tea cans by the men and stood aside in the pantry for the mother and children to drink whenever thirsty. The finest yarrow grew beside the turnpike, and in dry weather the whole plant became so saturated with white dust that the beer, when brewed, had a milky tinge. If the children remarked on this they were told, 'Us've all got to eat a peck o' dust before we dies, an' it'll slip down easy in this good yarb beer.'

The children at the end house used to wonder how they would ever obtain their peck of dust, for their mother was fastidiously particular. Such things as lettuce and watercress she washed in three waters, instead of giving them the dip and shake considered sufficient by most other people. Watercress had almost to be washed away, because of the story of the man who had swallowed a tadpole which had grown to a full-sized frog in his stomach. There was an abundance of watercress to be had for the picking, and a good deal of it was eaten in the spring, before it got tough and people got tired of it. Perhaps they owed much of their good health to such food.

All kinds of home-made wines were brewed by all but the poorest. Sloes and blackberries and elderberries could be picked from the hedgerows, dandelions and coltsfoot and cowslips from the fields, and the garden provided rhubarb, currants and gooseberries and parsnips. Jam was made from garden and hedgerow fruit. This had to be made over an open fire and needed great care in the making; but the result was generally good – too good, the women said, for the jam disappeared too soon. Some notable housewives made jelly. Crab-apple jelly was a speciality at the end house. Crab-apple trees abounded in the hedgerows and the children knew just where to go for red crabs, red-and-yellow streaked crabs, or crabs which hung like ropes of green onions on the branches.

It seemed to Laura a miracle when a basket of these, with nothing but sugar and water added, turned into jelly as clear and bright as a ruby. She did not take into account the long stewing, tedious straining, and careful measuring, boiling up and clarifying that went to the filling of the row of glass jars which cast a glow of red light on the whitewash at the back of the pantry shelf.

A quickly made delicacy was cowslip tea. This was made by picking the golden pips from a handful of cowslips, pouring boiling water over them, and letting the tea stand a few minutes to infuse. It could then be drunk either with or without sugar as preferred.

Cowslip balls were made for the children. These were fashioned by taking a great fragrant handful of the flowers, tying the stalks tightly with string, and pulling down the blooms to cover the stems. The bunch was then almost round, and made the loveliest ball imaginable.

Some of the older people who kept bees made mead, known there as 'metheglin'. It was a drink almost superstitiously esteemed, and the offer of a glass was regarded as a great compliment. Those who made it liked to make a little mystery of the process; but it was really very simple. Three pounds of honey were allowed to every

gallon of spring water. This had to be running spring water, and
was obtained from a place in the brook where the water bubbled
up; never from the well. The honey and water were boiled together,
and skimmed and strained and worked with a little yeast; then kept
in a barrel for six months, when the metheglin was ready for bottling.

Old Sally said that some folks messed up their metheglin with
lemons, bay leaves, and suchlike; but all she could say was that folks
who'd add anything to honey didn't deserve to have bees to work
for them.

Old metheglin was supposed to be the most intoxicating drink on
earth, and it was certainly potent, as a small girl once found when,
staying up to welcome home a soldier uncle from Egypt, she was
invited to take a sip from his glass and took a pull.

All the evening it had been 'Yes, please, Uncle Reuben', and 'Very
well, thank you, Uncle Reuben' with her; but as she went upstairs
to bed she astonished every one by calling pertly: 'Uncle Reuby is a
booby!' It was the mead speaking, not her. There was a dash in her
direction; but, fortunately for her, it was stayed by Sergeant Reuben
draining his glass, smacking his lips, and declaring: 'Well, I've tasted
some liquors in my time; but this beats all!' and under cover of the
fresh uncorking and pouring out, she tumbled sleepily into bed with
her white, starched finery still on her.

The hamlet people never invited each other to a meal; but when
it was necessary to offer tea to an important caller, or to friends
from a distance, the women had their resources. If, as often happened, there was no butter in the house, a child would be sent to
the shop at the inn for a quarter of the best fresh, even if it had to
'go down on the book' until pay-day. Thin bread and butter, cut
and arranged as in their old days in service, with a pot of homemade
jam, which had been hidden away for such an occasion, and a dish
of lettuce, fresh from the garden and garnished with little rosy
radishes, made an attractive little meal, fit, as they said, to put before
anybody.

In winter, salt butter would be sent for and toast would be
made and eaten with celery. Toast was a favourite dish for family
consumption. 'I've made 'em a stack o' toast as high as up to their

knees', a mother would say on a winter Sunday afternoon before her hungry brood came in from church. Another dish upon which they prided themselves was thin slices of cold, boiled streaky bacon on toast, a dish so delicious that it deserves to be more widely popular.

The few visitors from the outer world who came that way enjoyed such simple food, with a cup of tea; and a glass of homemade wine at their departure; and the women enjoyed entertaining them, and especially enjoyed the feeling that they, themselves, were equal to the occasion. 'You don't want to be poor and look poor, too,' they would say; and 'We've got our pride. Yes, we've got our pride.'

VII

Callers

Callers made a pleasant diversion in the hamlet women's day, and there were more of these than might have been expected. The first to arrive on Monday morning was old Jerry Parish with his cartload of fish and fruit. As he served some of the big houses on his round, Jerry carried quite a large stock; but the only goods he took round to the doors at Lark Rise were a box of bloaters and a basket of small, sour oranges. The bloaters were sold at a penny each and the oranges at three a penny. Even at these prices they were luxuries; but, as it was still only Monday and a few coppers might remain in a few purses, the women felt at liberty to crowd round his cart to examine and criticize his wares, even if they bought nothing.

Two or three of them would be tempted to buy a bloater for their midday meal, but it had to be a soft-roed one, for, in nearly every house there were children under school age at home; so the bloater had to be shared, and the soft roes spread upon bread for the smallest ones.

'Lor' blime me!' Jerry used to say. 'Never knowed such a lot in me life for soft roes. Good job I ain't a soft-roed 'un or I should've got aten up meself before now.' And he pinched the bloaters between his great red fingers, pretended to consider the matter with his head on one side, then declared each separate fish had the softest of soft roes, whether it had or not. 'Oozin', simply oozin' with goodness, I tell ye!' and oozing it certainly was when released from his grip. 'But what's the good of one bloater amongst the lot of ye? Tell ye what I'll do,' he would urge. 'I'll put ye in these three whoppers for tuppence-ha'penny.'

It was no good. The twopence-halfpenny was never forthcoming;

even the penny could so ill be spared that the purchaser often felt selfish and greedy after she had parted with it; but, after a morning at the washtub, she needed a treat so badly, and a bloater made a tasty change from her usually monotonous diet.

The oranges were tempting, too, for the children loved them. It was one of their greatest treats to find oranges on the mantelshelf when they came home from school in winter. Sour they might be and hard and skinny within; but without how rich and glowing! and what a strange foreign scent pervaded the room when their mother divided each one into quarters and distributed them. Even when the pulp had been eaten, the peel remained, to be dried on the hob and taken to school to chew in class or 'swopped' for conkers or string or some other desirable object.

Jerry's cart had a great attraction for Laura. At the sound of his wheels she would run out to feast her eyes on the lovely rich colours of grapes and pears and peaches. She loved to see the fish, too, with their cool colours and queer shapes, and would imagine them swimming about in the sea or resting among the seaweed. 'What is that one called?' she asked one day, pointing to a particularly queer-looking one.

'That's a John Dory, me dear. See them black marks? Look like finger-marks, don't 'em? An' they do say that they be finger-marks. *He* made 'em, that night, ye know, when they was fishin', ye know, an' *He* took some an' cooked 'em all ready for 'em, an' ever since, they say, that ivery John Dory as comes out o' th' sea have got *His* finger-marks on 'un.'

Laura was puzzled, for Jerry had mentioned no name and he was, moreover, a drinking, swearing old man, little likely, as she thought, to repeat a sacred legend.

'Do you mean the Sea of Galilee?' she asked timidly.

'That's it, me dear. That's what they say, whether true or not, of course, I *don't* know; but there be the finger-marks, right enough, an' that's what they say in our trade.'

It was on Jerry's cart tomatoes first appeared in the hamlet. They had not long been introduced into this country and were slowly making their way into favour. The fruit was flatter in shape then than now and deeply grooved and indented from the stem, giving it an almost starlike appearance. There were bright yellow ones, too, as well as the scarlet; but, after a few years, the yellow ones disappeared from the market and the red ones became rounder and smoother, as we see them now.

At first sight, the basket of red and yellow fruit attracted Laura's colour-loving eye. 'What are those?' she asked old Jerry.

'Love-apples, me dear. Love-apples, they be; though some hignorant folks be a callin' 'em tommytoes. But you don't want any o' they – nasty sour things, they be, as only gentry can eat. You have a nice sweet orange wi' your penny.' But Laura felt she must taste the love-apples and insisted upon having one.

Such daring created quite a sensation among the onlookers. 'Don't 'ee go tryin' to eat it, now,' one woman urged. 'It'll only make 'ee sick. I know because I had one of the nasty horrid things at our Minnie's.' And nasty, horrid things tomatoes remained in the popular estimation for years; though most people today would prefer them as they were then, with the real tomato flavour pronounced, to the watery insipidity of our larger, smoother tomato.

Mr Wilkins, the baker, came three times a week. His long, lank figure, girded by a white apron which always seemed about to slip down over his hips, was a familiar one at the end house. He always stayed there for a cup of tea, for which he propped himself up against the end of the dresser. He would never sit down; he said he had not time, and that was why he did not stop to change his flour-dusty bakehouse clothes before he started on his round.

He was no ordinary baker, but a ship's carpenter by trade who had come to the neighbouring village on a visit to relatives, met his present wife, married her, and cast anchor inland. Her father was old, she was the only child, and the family business had to be attended to; so, partly for love and partly for future gain he had given up the sea, but he still remained a sailor at heart.

He would stand in the doorway of Laura's home and look out at the wheatfields billowing in the breeze and the white clouds hurrying over them, and say: 'All very fine; but it seems a bit dead to me, right away from the sea, like this.' And he would tell the children how the waves pile up in a storm, 'like the wall of a house coming down on your ship', and about other seas, calm and bright as a looking-glass, with little islands and palm trees – but treacherous, too – and treacherous little men living in palm leaf huts, 'their faces as brown as your frock, Laura.' Once he had been shipwrecked and spent nine days in an open boat, the last two without water. His tongue had stuck to the roof of his mouth and he had spent weeks after rescue in hospital.

'And yet,' he would say, 'I'd dearly love just one more trip; but my dear wife would cry her eyes out if I mentioned it, and the business, of course, couldn't be left. No. I've swallowed the anchor, all right. I've swallowed the anchor.'

Mr Wilkins brought the image of the real living sea to the end house; otherwise the children would have only known it in pictures. True, their mother in her nursing days had been to the seaside with her charges and had many pleasant stories to tell of walks on piers, digging on sands, gathering seaweed, and shrimping with nets. But the seaside was different – delightful in its way, no doubt, but nothing like the wide tumbling ocean with ships on it.

The only portion of the sea which came their way was contained in a medicine bottle which a hamlet girl in service at Brighton brought home as a curiosity. In time the bottle of seawater became the property of a younger sister, a school-fellow of Laura's, who was persuaded to barter it for a hunch of cake and a blue-bead necklace. Laura treasured it for years.

Many casual callers passed through the hamlet. Travelling tinkers with their barrows, braziers, and twirling grindstones turned aside from the main road and came singing:

> Any razors or scissors to grind?
>   Or anything else in the tinker's line?
> Any old pots or kettles to mend?

After squinting into any leaking vessel against the light, or trying the edges of razors or scissors upon the hard skin of their palms, they would squat by the side of the road to work, or start their emery wheel whizzing, to the delight of the hamlet children, who always formed a ring around any such operations.

Gipsy women with cabbage-nets and clothes-pegs to sell were more frequent callers for they had a camping-place only a mile away and no place was too poor to yield them a harvest. When a door was opened to them, if the housewife appeared to be under forty, they would ask in a wheedling voice: 'Is your mother at home, my dear?' Then, when the position was explained, they would exclaim in astonished tones: 'You don't mean to tell me you *be* the mother? Look at that, now. I shouldn't have taken you to be a day over twenty.'

No matter how often repeated, this compliment was swallowed whole, and made a favourable opening for a long conversation, in the course of which the wily 'Egyptian' not only learned the full history of the woman's own family, but also a good deal about those of her neighbours, which was duly noted for future use. Then would come a request for 'handful of little 'taters, or an onion or two for the pot', and, if these were given, as they usually were, 'My pretty lady' would be asked for an old shift of her own or an old shirt of her husband's, or anything that the children might have left off, and, poverty-stricken though the hamlet was, a few worn-out garments would be secured to swell the size of the bundle which, afterwards, would be sold to the rag merchant.

Sometimes the gipsies would offer to tell fortunes; but this offer was always refused, not out of scepticism or lack of curiosity about the future, but because the necessary silver coin was not available. 'No, thank 'ee,' the women would say. 'I don't want nothink of that sort. My fortune's already told.'

'Ah, my lady! you med think so; but them as has got childern never knows. You be born, but you ain't dead yet, an' you may dress in silks and ride in your own carriage yet. You wait till that fine strappin' boy o' yourn gets rich. He won't forget his mother, I'll bet!' and after this free prognostication, they would trail off to the next house, leaving behind a scent as strong as a vixen's.

The gipsies paid in entertainment for what they received. Their calls made a welcome break in the day. Those of the tramps only harrowed the feelings and left the depressed in spirit even more depressed.

There must have been hundreds of tramps on the roads at that time. It was a common sight, when out for a walk, to see a dirty, unshaven man, his rags topped with a battered bowler, lighting a fire of sticks by the roadside to boil his tea-can. Sometimes he would have a poor bedraggled woman with him and she would be lighting the fire while he lolled at ease on the turf or picked out the best pieces from the bag of food they had collected at their last place of call.

Some of them carried small, worthless things to sell – matches, shoe-laces, or dried-lavender bags. The children's mother often bought from these out of pity; but never from the man who sold oranges, for they had seen him on one of their walks, spitting on his oranges and polishing them with a filthy rag. Then there was the woman who, very early one morning, knocked at the door with small slabs of tree-bark in her apron. She was cleaner and better dressed than the ordinary tramp and brought with her a strong scent of lavender. The bark appeared to be such as could have been hacked with a clasp-knife from the nearest pine tree; but she claimed for it a very different origin. It was the famous lavender bark, she said, brought from foreign parts by her sailor son. One fragment kept among clothes was not only an everlasting perfume, but it was also death to moths. 'You just smell it, my dears,' she said, handing pieces to the mother and the children, who had crowded to the door.

It certainly smelt strongly of lavender. The children handled it lovingly, fascinated by a substance which had travelled so far and smelt so sweetly.

She asked sixpence a slab; but obligingly came down to twopence, and three pieces were purchased and placed in a fancy bowl on the side table to perfume the room and to be exhibited as a rarity.

Alas! the vendor had barely time to clear out of the hamlet before all the perfume had evaporated and the bark became what it had been before she sprinkled it with oil of lavender – just ordinary bark from a pine trunk!

Such brilliance was exceptional. Most of the tramps were plain beggars. 'Please could you give me a morsel of bread, for I be so hungry. I'm telling God I haven't put a bite between my lips since yesterday morning' was a regular formula with them when they knocked at the door of a cottage; and, although many of them looked well-nourished, they were never turned away. Thick slices, which could ill be spared, were plastered with lard; the cold potatoes which the housewife had intended to fry for her own dinner were wrapped in newspaper, and by the time they left the hamlet they were insured against starvation for at least a week. The only reward for such generosity, beyond the whining professional 'God bless ye', was the cheering reflection that however badly off one might be oneself, there were others poorer.

Where all these wayfarers came from or how they had fallen so low in the social scale was uncertain. According to their own account, they had been ordinary decent working people with homes 'just such another as yourn, mum'; but their houses had been burned down or flooded, or they had fallen out of work, or spent a long time in hospital and had never been able to start again. Many of the women pleaded that their husbands were dead, and several men came begging with the plea that, having lost their wives, they had the children to look after and could not leave them to work for their living.

Sometimes whole families took to the road with their bags and bundles and tea-cans, begging their food as they went and sleeping in casual wards or under ricks or in ditches. Laura's father, coming home from work at dusk one night, thought he heard a rustling in the ditch by the roadside. When he looked down into it, a row of white faces looked up at him, belonging to a mother, a father, and three or four children. He said that in the half light only their faces were visible and that they looked like a set of silver coins, ranging from a florin to a threepenny bit. Though late in the summer, the night was not cold. 'Thank God for that!' said the children's mother when she heard about them, for, had it been cold, he might have brought them all home with him. He had brought home tramps before and had them sit at table with the family, to his wife's disgust, for he had what she considered peculiar ideas on hospitality and the brotherhood of man.

There was no tallyman, or Johnny Fortnight, in those parts; but once, for a few months, a man who kept a small furniture shop in a neighbouring town came round selling his wares on the instalment plan. On his first visit to Lark Rise he got no order at all; but on his second one of the women, more daring than the rest, ordered a small wooden washstand and a zinc bath for washing day. Immediately washstands and zinc baths became the rage. None of the women could think how they had managed to exist so long without a washstand in their bedroom. They were quite satisfied with the buckets and basins of water in the pantry or by the fireside or out of doors for their own use; but supposing someone fell ill and the doctor had to wash his hands in a basin placed on a clean towel on the kitchen table! or supposing some of their town relatives came on a visit, those with a real sink and water laid on! They felt they would die with mortification if they had to apologize for having no washstand. As to the zinc bath, that seemed even more necessary. That wooden tub their mother had used was 'a girt okkard old thing'. Although they had not noticed its weight much before, it seemed almost to break their backs when they could see a bright, shining new bath hanging under the eaves of the next-door barn.

It was not long before practically every house had a new bath and washstand. A few mothers of young children went farther and ordered a fireguard as well. Then the fortnightly payments began. One-and-six was the specified instalment, and, for the first few fortnights, this was forthcoming. But it was so difficult to get that eighteenpence together. A few pence had always to be used out of the first week's ninepence, then in the second week some urgent need for cash would occur. The instalments fell to a shilling. Then to sixpence. A few gave up the struggle and defaulted.

Month after month the salesman came round and collected what he could; but he did not try to tempt them to buy anything more, for he could see that he would never be paid for it. He was a good-hearted man who listened to their tales of woe and never bullied or threatened to County Court them. Perhaps the debts were not as important to him as they appeared to his customers; or he may have felt he was to blame for tempting them to order things they could not afford. He continued calling until he had collected as much as he thought possible, then disappeared from the scene.

A more amusing episode was that of the barrels of beer. At that time in that part of the country, brewers' travellers, known locally as 'outriders', called for orders at farm-houses and superior cottages, as well as at inns. No experienced outrider visited farm labourers' cottages; but the time came when a beginner, full of youthful enthusiasm and burning to fill up his order book, had the brilliant idea of canvassing the hamlet for orders.

Wouldn't it be splendid, he asked the women, to have their own nine-gallon cask of good ale in for Christmas, and only have to go into the pantry and turn the tap to get a glass for their husband and friends. The ale cost far less by the barrel than when bought at the inn. It would be an economy in the long run, and how well it would look to bring out a jug of foaming ale from their own barrel for their friends. As to payment, they sent in their bills quarterly, so there would be plenty of time to save up.

The women agreed that it would, indeed, be splendid to have their own barrel, and even the men, when told of the project at night, were impressed by the difference in price when buying by the nine-gallon cask. Some of them worked it out on paper and were satisfied that, considering that they would be spending a few shillings extra at Christmas in any case, and that the missus had been looking rather peaked lately and a glass of good beer cost less than doctor's physic, and that maybe a daughter in service would be sending a postal order, they might venture to order the cask.

Others did not trouble to work it out; but, enchanted with the idea, gave the order lightheartedly. After all, as the outrider said, Christmas came but once a year, and this year they would have a jolly one. Of course there were kill-joys, like Laura's father, who said sardonically. 'They'll laugh the other side of their faces when it comes to paying for it.'

The barrels came and were tapped and the beer was handed around. The barrels were empty and the brewer's carter in his leather apron heaved them into the van behind his steaming, stamping horses; but none of the mustard or cocoa tins hidden away in secret places contained more than a few coppers towards paying the bill. When the day of reckoning came only three of the purchasers had the money ready. But time was allowed. Next month would do; but, mind! it must be forthcoming then. Most of the women tried hard to get that money together; but, of course, they could not. The traveller called again and again, each time growing more threatening, and, after some months, the brewer took the matter to the County Court, where the judge, after hearing the circumstances of sale and the income of the purchasers, ordered them all to pay twopence weekly off the debt. So ended the great excitement of having one's own barrel of beer on tap.

The packman, or pedlar, once a familiar figure in that part of the country, was seldom seen in the 'eighties. People had taken to buying their clothes at the shops in the market town, where fashions were newer and prices lower. But one last survivor of the once numerous clan still visited the hamlet at long and irregular intervals.

He would turn aside from the turnpike and come plodding down the narrow hamlet road, an old white-headed, white-bearded man, still hale and rosy, although almost bent double under the heavy, black canvas-covered pack he carried strapped on his shoulders. 'Anything out of the pack today?' he would ask at each house, and, at the least encouragement, fling down his load and open it on the doorstep. He carried a tempting variety of goods: dress-lengths and shirt-lengths and remnants to make up for the children; aprons and pinafores, plain and fancy; corduroys for the men, and coloured scarves and ribbons for Sunday wear.

'That's a bit of right good stuff, ma'am, that is,' he would say, holding up some dress-length to exhibit it. 'A gown made of this piece'd last anybody for ever and then make 'em a good petticoat afterwards.' Few of the hamlet women could afford to test the quality of his piece goods; cottons or tapes, or a paper of pins, were their usual purchases; but his dress-lengths and other fabrics were of excellent quality and wore much longer than anyone would wish anything to wear in these days of rapidly changing fashions. It was from his pack the soft, warm woollen, grey with a white fleck in it, came to make the frock Laura wore with a little black satin apron and a bunch of snow-drops pinned to the breast when she went to sell stamps in the post office.

Once every summer a German band passed through the hamlet and halted outside the inn to play. It was composed of an entire family, a father and his six sons, the latter graded in size like a set of jugs, from the tall young man who played the cornet to the chubby pink-faced little boy who beat the drum.

Drawn up in the semicircle in their neat, green uniforms, they would blow away at their instruments until their chubby German cheeks seemed near to bursting point. Most of the music they played was above the heads of the hamlet folks, who said they liked something with a bit more 'chune' in it; but when, at the end of the performance, they gave *God Save the Queen* the standers-by joined with gusto in singing it.

That was the sign for the landlord to come out in his shirt-sleeves with three frothing beer mugs. One for the father, who poured the beer down his throat like water down a sink, and the other two to be passed politely from son to son. Unless a farmer's gig or a tradesman's trap happened to pull up at the inn gate during the performance, the beer was their only reward for the entertainment. They did not take their collecting bag round to the women and children who had gathered to listen, for they knew from experience there were no stray half-pence for German bands in a farm labourer's wife's pocket. So after shaking the saliva from their brass instruments, they bowed, clicked their heels, and marched off up the dusty road to the mother village. It was good beer and they were hot and thirsty, so perhaps the reward was sufficient.

The only other travelling entertainment which came there was known as the dancing dolls. These, alas! did not dance in the open, but in a cottage to which a penny admission was charged, and, as the cottage was not of the cleanest, Laura was never allowed to witness this performance. Those who had seen them said the dolls were on wires and that the man who exhibited them said the words for them, so it must have been some kind of marionette show.

Once, very early in their school life, the end house children met a man with a dancing bear. The man, apparently a foreigner, saw that the children were afraid to pass, and, to reassure them, set his bear dancing. With a long pole balanced across its front paws, it waltzed heavily to the tune hummed by its master, then shouldered the pole and did exercises at his word of command. The elders of the hamlet said the bear had appeared there at long intervals for many years; but that was its last appearance. Poor Bruin, with his mangy fur and hot, tainted breath, was never seen in those parts again. Perhaps he died of old age.

The greatest thrill of all and the one longest remembered in the hamlet, was provided by the visit of a cheap-jack about half-way through the decade. One autumn evening, just before dusk, he arrived with his cartload of crockery and tinware and set out his stock on the grass by the roadside before a back-cloth painted with icebergs and penguins and polar bears. Soon he had his naphtha lamps flaring and was clashing his basins together like bells and calling: 'Come buy! Come buy!'

It was the first visit of a cheap-jack to the hamlet and there was great excitement. Men, women, and children rushed from the houses and crowded around in the circle of light to listen to his patter and admire his wares. And what bargains he had! The tea-service decorated with fat, full-blown pink roses: twenty-one pieces and not a flaw in any one of them. The Queen had purchased its fellow set for Buckingham Palace it appeared. The teapots, the trays, the nests of dishes and basins, and the set of bedroom china which made everyone blush when he selected the most intimate utensil to rap with his knuckles to show it rang true.

'Two bob!' he shouted. 'Only two bob for this handsome set of jugs. Here's one for your beer and one for your milk and another in case you break one of the other two. Nobody willing to speculate? Then what about this here set of trays, straight from Japan and the peonies hand-painted; or this lot of basins, exact replicas of the one the Princess of Wales supped her gruel from when Prince George was born. Why damme, they cost me more n'r that. I could get twice the price I'm asking in Banbury tomorrow; but I'll give 'em to you, for you can't call it selling, because I like your faces and me load's heavy for me 'oss. Alarming bargains! Tremendous sacrifices! Come buy! Come buy!'

But there were scarcely any offers. A woman here and there would give threepence for a large pudding-basin or sixpence for a tin saucepan. The children's mother bought a penny nutmeg-grater and a set of wooden spoons for cooking; the innkeeper's wife ran to a dozen tumblers and a ball of string; then there was a long pause during which the vendor kept up a continual stream of jokes and anecdotes which sent his audience into fits of laughter. Once he broke into song:

> There was a man in his garden walked
> And cut his throat with a lump of chalk;
> His wife, she knew not what she did,
> She strangled herself with the saucepan lid.
> There was a man and a fine young fellow
> Who poisoned himself with an umbrella.
> Even Joey in his cradle shot himself dead with a silver ladle.
> When you hear this horrible tale
> It makes your faces all turn pale,
> Your eyes go green, you're overcome,
> So tweedle, tweedle, tweedle twum.

All very fine entertainment; but it brought him no money and he began to suspect that he would draw a blank at Lark Rise.

'Never let it be said,' he implored, 'that this is the poverty-strickenist place on God's earth. Buy something, if only for your own credit's sake. Here!' snatching up a pile of odd plates. 'Good dinner-plates for you. Everyone a left-over from a first-class service. Buy one of these and you'll have the satisfaction of knowing you're eating off the same ware as lords and dukes. Only three-halfpence each. Who'll buy? Who'll buy?'

There was a scramble for the plates, for nearly every one could muster three-halfpence; but every time anything more costly was produced there was dead silence. Some of the women began to feel uncomfortable. 'Don't be poor and look poor, too' was their motto, and here they were looking poor indeed, for who, with money in their pockets, could have resisted such wonderful bargains.

Then the glorious unexpected happened. The man had brought the pink rose tea-service forward again and was handing one of the cups round. 'You just look at the light through it – and you, ma'am – and you. Ain't it lovely china, thin as an eggshell, practically transparent, and with every one of them roses hand-painted with a brush? You can't let a set like that go out of the place, now can you? I can see all your mouths a-watering. You run home, my dears, and bring out them stockings from under the mattress and the first one to get back shall have it for twelve bob.'

Each woman in turn handled the cup lovingly, then shook her head and passed it on. None of them had stockings of savings hidden away. But, just as the man was receiving back the cup, a little roughly, for he was getting discouraged, a voice spoke up in the background.

'How much did you say, mister? Twelve bob? I'll give you ten.' It was John Price, who, only the night before, had returned from his soldiering in India. A very ordinary sort of chap at most times, for he was a teetotaller and stood no drinks at the inn, as a returned soldier should have done; but now, suddenly, he became important. All eyes were upon him. The credit of the hamlet was at stake.

'I'll give you ten bob.'

'Can't be done, matey. Cost me more nor that. But, look see, tell you what I will do. You give me eleven and six and I'll throw in this handsome silver-gilt vase for your mantelpiece.'

'Done!' The bargain was concluded; the money changed hands, and the reputation of the hamlet was rehabilitated. Willing hands helped John carry the tea-service to his home. Indeed, it was considered an honour to be trusted with a cup. His bride-to-be was still away in service and little knew how many were envying her that night. To have such a lovely service awaiting her return, no cracked or odd pieces, every piece alike and all so lovely; lucky, lucky, Lucy! But though they could not help envying her a little, they shared in her triumph, for surely such a purchase must shed a glow of reflected prosperity on the whole hamlet. Though it might not be convenient to all of them to buy very much on that particular night, the man must see there *was* a bit of money in the place and folks who knew how to spend it.

What came after was anti-climax, and yet very pleasant from the end house children's point of view. A set of pretty little dishes, suitable for holding jam, butter or fruit, according to size, was being exhibited. The price had gone down from half a crown to a shilling without response, when once more a voice spoke up in the background. 'Pass them over, please. I expect my wife can find a use for them,' and, behold, it was the children's father who had halted on his way home from work to see what the lights and the crowd meant.

Perhaps in all the man took a pound that night, which was fifteen shillings more than any one could have foretold; but it was not sufficient to tempt him to come again, and thenceforth the year was dated as 'that time the cheap-jack came'.

VIII

'The Box'

A familiar sight at Lark Rise was that of a young girl – any young girl between ten and thirteen – pushing one of the two perambulators in the hamlet round the Rise with a smallish-sized, oak clothes box with black handles lashed to the seat. Those not already informed who met her would read the signs and inquire: 'How is your mother' – or your sister or your aunt – 'getting on?' and she, well-primed, would answer demurely, 'As well as can be expected under the circumstances, thank you, Mrs So-and-So.'

She had been to the Rectory for THE BOX, which appeared almost simultaneously with every new baby, and a gruelling time she would have had pushing her load the mile and a half and, at the same time, keeping it from slipping from its narrow perch. But, very soon, such small drawbacks would be forgotten in the pleasure of seeing it unpacked. It contained half a dozen of everything – tiny shirts, swathes, long flannel barrows, nighties, and napkins, made, kept in repair, and lent for every confinement by the clergyman's daughter. In addition to the loaned clothes, it would contain, as a gift, packets of tea and sugar and a tin of patent groats for making gruel.

The box was a popular institution. Any farm labourer's wife, whether she attended church or not, was made welcome to the loan of it. It appeared in most of the cottages at regular intervals and seemed to the children as much a feature of family life as the new babies. It was so constantly in demand that it had to have an understudy, known as 'the second-best box', altogether inferior, which fell to the lot of those careless matrons who had neglected to bespeak the loan the moment they 'knew their luck again'.

The boxes were supposed to be returned at the end of a month with the clothes freshly laundered; but, if no one else required them, an extension could be had, and many mothers were allowed to keep their box until, at six or seven weeks old, the baby was big enough to be put into short clothes; so saving them the cost of preparing a layette other than the one set of clothes got ready for the infant's arrival. Even that might be borrowed. The stock at the end house was several times called for in what, by a polite fiction, passed as an emergency. Other women had their own baby clothes, beautifully sewn and laundered; but there was scarcely one who did not require the clothes in the box to supplement them. For some reason or other, the box was never allowed to go out until the baby had arrived.

The little garments on loan were all good quality and nicely trimmed with embroidery and hand tucking. The clergyman's daughter also kept two christening robes to lend to the mothers, and made a new frock, as a gift, for every baby's 'shortening'. Summer or winter, these little frocks were made of flowered print, blue for the boys and pink for the girls, and every one of the tiny, strong stitches in them were done by her own hands. She got little credit for this. The mothers, like the children, looked upon the small garments, both loaned and given, as a provision of Nature. Indeed, they were rather inclined to criticize. One woman ripped off the deep flounce of old Buckinghamshire lace from the second-best christening robe and substituted a frill of coarse, machine-made embroidery, saying she was not going to take her child to church 'trigged out' in that old-fashioned trash. As she had not troubled to unpick the stitches, the lace was torn beyond repair, and the gown ever after was decidedly second-best, for the best one was the old Rectory family christening robe and made of the finest lawn, tucked and inserted all over with real Valenciennes.

When the hamlet babies arrived, they found good clothes awaiting them, and the best of all nourishment – Nature's own. The mothers did not fare so well. It was the fashion at that time to keep maternity patients on low diet for the first three days, and the hamlet women found no difficulty in following this régime; water gruel, dry toast, and weak tea was their menu. When the time came for more nourishing diet, the parson's daughter made for every patient one large sago pudding, followed up by a jug of veal broth. After these were consumed they returned to their ordinary food, with a half-pint of stout a day for those who could afford it. No milk was taken, and yet their own milk supply was abundant. Once, when a bottle-fed baby was brought on a visit to the hamlet, its bottle was held up as a curiosity. It had a long, thin rubber tube for the baby to suck through which must have been impossible to clean.

The only cash outlay in an ordinary confinement was half a crown, the fee of the old woman who, as she said, saw the beginning and end of everybody. She was, of course, not a certified midwife; but she was a decent, intelligent old body, clean in her person and methods and very kind. For the half-crown she officiated at the birth and came every morning for ten days to bath the baby and make the mother comfortable. She also tried hard to keep the patient in bed for the ten days; but with little success. Some mothers refused to stay there because they knew they were needed downstairs; others because they felt so strong and fit they saw no reason to lie there. Some women actually got up on the third day, and, as far as could be seen at the time, suffered no ill effects.

Complications at birth were rare; but in the two or three cases where they did occur during her practice, old Mrs Quinton had sufficient skill to recognize the symptoms and send post haste for the doctor. No mother lost her life in childbed during the decade.

In these more enlightened days the mere mention of the old, untrained village midwife raises a vision of some dirty, drink-sodden old hag without skill or conscience. But not all of them were Sairey Gamps. The great majority were clean, knowledgeable old women who took a pride in their office. Nor had many of them been entirely without instruction. The country doctor of that day valued a good midwife in an outlying village and did not begrudge time and trouble in training her. Such a one would save him many a six or eight mile drive over bad roads at night, and, if a summons did come, he would know that his presence was necessary.

The trained district nurses, when they came a few years later, were a great blessing in country districts; but the old midwife also had her good points, for which she now receives no credit. She was no superior person coming into the house to strain its resources to the utmost and shame the patient by forced confessions that she did not possess this or that; but a neighbour, poor like herself, who could make do with what there was, or, if not, knew where to send to borrow it. This Mrs Quinton possessed quite a stock of the things she knew she would not find in every house, and might often be met with a baby's little round bath in her hand, or a clothes-horse, for airing, slung over her arm.

Other days, other ways; and, although they have now been greatly improved upon, the old country midwives did at least succeed in bringing into the world many generations of our forefathers, or where should we be now?

The general health of the hamlet was excellent. The healthy, open-air life and the abundance of coarse but wholesome food must have been largely responsible for that; but lack of imagination may also have played a part. Such people at that time did not look for or expect illness, and there were not as many patent medicine advertisements then as now to teach them to search for symptoms of minor ailments in themselves. Beecham's and Holloway's Pills were already familiar to all newspaper readers, and a booklet advertising Mother Siegel's Syrup arrived by post at every house once a year. But only Beecham's Pills were patronized, and those only by a few; the majority relied upon an occasional dose of Epsom salts to cure all ills. One old man, then nearly eighty, had for years drunk a teacupful of frothing soap-suds every Sunday morning. 'Them cleans the outers,' he would say, 'an' stands to reason they must clean th' innards, too.' His dose did not appear to do him any harm; but he made no converts.

Although only babies and very small children had baths, the hamlet folks were cleanly in their persons. The women would lock their cottage doors for a whole afternoon once a week to have what they called 'a good clean up'. This consisted of stripping to the waist and washing downward; then stepping into a footbath and washing upward. 'Well, I feels all the better for that,' some woman would say complacently. 'I've washed up as far as possible and down as far as possible,' and the ribald would inquire what poor 'possible' had done that that should not be included.

Toothbrushes were not in general use; few could afford to buy such luxuries; but the women took a pride in their strong white teeth and cleaned them with a scrap of clean, wet rag dipped in salt. Some of the men used soot as a tooth-powder.

After a confinement, if the eldest girl was too young and there was no other relative available, the housework, cooking, and washing would be shared among the neighbours, who would be repaid in kind when they themselves were in like case.

Babies, especially young babies, were adored by their parents and loved and petted and often spoilt by the whole family until another arrived; then, as they used to say, its 'nose was put out of joint'; all the adoration was centred on the newcomer and the ex-baby was fortunate if it had a still devoted elder sister to stand by it.

In the production of their large families the parents appeared reckless. One obvious method of birth control, culled from the Old Testament, was known in the hamlet and practised by one couple, which had managed to keep their family down to four. The wife told their secret to another woman, thinking to help her; but it only brought scorn down on her own head. 'Did you ever! Fancy begrudging a little child a bit o' food, the nasty greedy selfish hussy, her!' was the general verdict. But, although they protested so volubly, and bore their own frequent confinements with courage and cheerfulness, they must have sometimes rebelled in secret, for there was great bitterness in the tone in which in another mood they would say: 'The wife ought to have the first child and the husband the second, then there wouldn't ever be any more.'

That showed how the land lay, as Laura's mother said to her in later life. She herself lived to see the decline in the birth-rate, and, when she discussed it with her daughter in the early 1930s, laughed heartily at some of the explanations advanced by the learned, and said: 'If they knew what it meant to carry and bear and bring up a child themselves, they wouldn't expect the women to be in a hurry to have a second or third now they've got a say in the matter. Now, if they made it a bit easier for people, dividing it out a bit, so to speak, by taking over some of the money worry. It's never seemed fair to my mind that the one who's got to go through all a confinement means should have to scrape and pinch beforehand to save a bit as well. Then there's the other child or children. What mother wants to rob those she's already got by bringing in another to share what there's too little of already?'

None of the unmarried hamlet girls had babies in the 'eighties, although there must have been quite a crop of illegitimate births a few years earlier, for when the attendance register was called out at school the eldest children of several families answered to another surname than that borne by their brothers and sisters and by which they themselves were commonly known. These would be the children of couples who had married after the birth of their first child, a common happening at that time and little thought of.

In the 'eighties a young woman of thirty came from Birmingham to have her illegitimate baby at her sister's home in the hamlet, and a widow who had already three legitimate children and afterwards married again managed to produce two children between her two marriages. These births passed without much comment; but when a young girl of sixteen whose home was out in the fields near the hamlet was known to be 'in trouble' public feeling was stirred.

One evening, a few weeks before the birth, Emily passed through the hamlet with her father on their way to interview the young man she had named as responsible for her condition. It was a sad little sight. Emily, who had so recently been romping with the other children, going slowly, unwillingly, and red-eyed from crying, her tell-tale figure enveloped in her mother's plaid shawl, and her respectable, grey-headed father in his Sunday suit urging her to 'Come on!' as though longing to be through with a disagreeable business. Women came to their cottage gates and children left their play to watch them pass by, for every one knew or guessed their errand, and much sympathy was felt towards them on account of Emily's youth and her parents' respectability.

The interview turned out even more mortifying than the father could have expected, for Emily had named the young son of the house where she had been in service, and he not only repudiated the charge, but was able to prove that he had been away from home for some time before and after the crucial date. Yet, in spite of the evidence, the neighbours still believed Emily's version of the story and treated her as a wronged heroine, to be petted and made much of. Perhaps they made too much of her, for what should have been an episode turned into a habit, and, although she never married, Emily had quite a good-sized family.

The hamlet women's attitude towards the unmarried mother was contradictory. If one of them brought her baby on a visit to the hamlet they all went out of their way to pet and fuss over them. 'The pretty dear!' they would cry. 'How ever can anybody say such a one as him ought not to be born. Ain't he a beauty! Ain't he a size! They always say, you know, that that sort of child is the finest. An' don't you go mindin' what folks says about you, me dear. It's only the good girls, like you, that has 'em; the others is too artful!'

But they did not want their own daughters to have babies before they were married. 'I allus tells my gals,' one woman would say confidentially to another, 'that if they goes getting theirselves into trouble they'll have to go to th' work'us, for I won't have 'em at home.' And the other would agree, saying, 'So I tells mine, an' I allus think that's why I've had no trouble with 'em.'

To those who knew the girls, the pity was that their own mothers should so misjudge their motives for keeping chaste; but there was little room for their finer feelings in the hamlet mother's life. All her strength, invention and understanding were absorbed in caring for her children's bodies; their mental and spiritual qualities were outside her range. At the same time, if one of the girls had got into trouble, as they called it, the mother would almost certainly have had her home and cared for her. There was more than one home in the hamlet where the mother was bringing up a grandchild with her own younger children, the grandchild calling the grandmother 'Mother'.

If, as sometimes happened, a girl had to be married in haste, she was thought none the worse of on that account. She had secured her man. All was well. ' 'Tis but Nature' was the general verdict.

But though they were lenient with such slips, especially when not in their own families, anything in the way of what they called 'loose living' was detested by them. Only once in the history of the hamlet had a case of adultery been known to the general public, and, although that had occurred ten or twelve years before, it was still talked of in the 'eighties. The guilty couple had been treated to 'rough music'. Effigies of the pair had been made and carried aloft on poles by torchlight to the house of the woman, to the accompaniment of the banging of pots, pans, and coal-shovels, the screeching of tin whistles and mouth-organs, and cat-calls, hoots, and jeers. The man, who was a lodger at the woman's house, disappeared before daybreak the next morning, and soon afterwards the woman and her husband followed him.

About the middle of the decade, the memory of that historic night was revived when an unmarried woman with four illegitimate children moved into a vacant house in the hamlet. Her coming raised a fury of indignation. Words hitherto only heard by the children when the Lessons were read in church were flung about freely: 'harlot' was one of the mildest. The more ardent moralists were for stoning her or driving her out of the place with rough music. The more moderate proposed getting her landlord to turn her out as a bad character. However, upon closer acquaintance, she turned out to be so clean, quiet, and well-spoken, that her sins, which she had apparently abandoned, were forgiven her, and one after another of the neighbours began 'passing the time of day' with her when they met. Then, as though willing to do anything in reason to conform to their standard, she got married to a man who had been navvying on a stretch of new railway line and then settled down to farm labour. So there were wedding bells instead of rough music and the family gradually merged into ordinary hamlet life.

It was the hamlet's gain. One of the boys was musical, an aunt had bought him a good melodeon, and, every light evening, he played it for hours on the youths' gathering round in front of the 'Wagon and Horses'.

Before his arrival there had been no musical instrument of any kind at Lark Rise, and, in those days before gramophones or wireless, any one who liked 'a bit of a tune' had to go to church to hear it, and then it would only be a hymn tune wheezed out by an ancient harmonium. Now they could have all the old favourites – 'Home Sweet Home', 'Annie Laurie', 'Barbara Allen', and 'Silver Threads Among the Gold' – they had only to ask for what they fancied. Alf played well and had a marvellous ear. If the baker or any other caller hummed the tune of a new popular song in his hearing, Alf would be playing it that night on his melodeon.

Women stood at their cottage gates, men leaned out of the inn window, and children left their play and gathered around him to listen. Often he played dance tunes, and the youths would foot it with each other as partners, for there was seldom a grown-up girl at home and the little ones they despised. So the little girls, too, had to dance with each other. One stout old woman, who was said to have been gay in her time, would come out and give them hints, or she would take a turn herself, gliding around alone, her feet hidden by her long skirts, massively graceful.

Sometimes they would sing to the dance music, and the standers-by would join in:

> I have a bonnet, trimmed with blue.
> Why don't you wear it? So I do.
> When do you wear it? When I can,
> When I go out with my young man.
>
> My young man is gone to sea
> With silver buckles on his knee,
> With his blue coat and yellow hose,
> And that's the way the polka goes.

Or perhaps it would be:

> Step and fetch her, step and fetch her,
>   Step and fetch her, pretty little dear.
> Do not tease her, try and please her,
>   Step and fetch her, pretty little dear.

And so they would dance and sing through the long summer evenings, until dusk fell and the stars came out and they all went laughing and panting home, a community simple enough to be made happy by one little boy with a melodeon.

IX

Country Playtime

'Shall we dance tonight or shall we have a game?' was a frequent question among the girls after Alf's arrival. Until the novelty of the dancing wore off, the old country games were eclipsed; but their day was not over. Some of the quieter girls always preferred the games, and, later, on those evenings when Alf was away, playing for dancers in other villages, they all went back to the games.

Then, beneath the long summer sunsets, the girls would gather on one of the green open spaces between the houses and bow and curtsey and sweep to and fro in their ankle-length frocks as they went through the game movements and sang the game rhymes as their mothers and grandmothers had done before them.

How long the games had been played and how they originated no one knew, for they had been handed down for a time long before living memory and accepted by each succeeding generation as a natural part of its childhood. No one inquired the meaning of the words of the game rhymes; many of the girls, indeed, barely mastered them, but went through the movements to the accompaniment of an indistinct babbling. But the rhymes had been preserved; breaking down into doggerel in places; but still sufficiently intact to have spoken to the discerning, had any such been present, of an older, sweeter country civilization than had survived, excepting in a few such fragments.

Of all the generations that had played the games, that of the 'eighties was to be the last. Already those children had one foot in the national school and one on the village green. Their children and grandchildren would have left the village green behind them; new and as yet undreamed-of pleasures and excitements would be theirs.

In ten years' time the games would be neglected, and in twenty forgotten. But all through the 'eighties the games went on and seemed to the children themselves and to onlookers part of a life that always had been and always would be.

The Lark Rise children had a large repertoire, including the well-known games still met with at children's parties, such as 'Oranges and Lemons', 'London Bridge', and 'Here We Go Round the Mulberry Bush'; but also including others which appear to have been peculiar to that part of the country. Some of these were played by forming a ring, others by taking sides, and all had distinctive rhymes, which were chanted rather than sung.

The boys of the hamlet did not join in them, for the amusement was too formal and restrained for their taste, and even some of the rougher girls when playing would spoil a game, for the movements were stately and all was done by rule. Only at the end of some of the games, where the verse had deteriorated into doggerel, did the play break down into a romp. Most of the girls when playing revealed graces unsuspected in them at other times; their movements became dignified and their voices softer and sweeter than ordinarily, and when hauteur was demanded by the part, they became, as they would have said, 'regular duchesses'. It is probable that carriage and voice inflexion had been handed down with the words.

One old favourite was 'Here Come Three Tinkers'. For this all but two of the players, a big girl and a little one, joined hands in a row, and the bigger girl out took up her stand about a dozen paces in front of the row with the smaller one lying on the turf behind her feigning sleep. Then three of the line of players detached themselves and, hand in hand, tripped forward, singing:

> Here come three tinkers, three by three,
> To court your daughter, fair ladye,
> Oh, can we have a lodging here, here, here?
> Oh, can we have a lodging here?

Upon which the fair lady (pronounced 'far-la-dee') admonished her sleeping daughter:

> Sleep, sleep, my daughter. Do not wake.
> Here come three tinkers you can't take.

Then, severely, to the tinkers:

> You cannot have a lodging here, here, here.
> You cannot have a lodging here.

And the tinkers returned to the line, and three others came forward, calling themselves tailors, soldiers, sailors, gardeners, bricklayers, or policemen, according to fancy, the rhymes being sung for each three, until it was time for the climax, and, putting fresh spirit into their tones, the conquering candidates came forward, singing:

> Here come three princes, three by three,
> To court your daughter fair ladye,
> Oh, can we have a lodging here, here, here?
> Oh, can we have a lodging here?

At the mere mention of the rank of the princes the scene changed. The fair lady became all becks and nods and smiles, and, lifting up her supposedly sleeping daughter, sang:

> Oh, wake, my daughter, wake, wake, wake.
> Here come three princes you can take.

And, turning to the princes:

> Oh, you can have a lodging here, here, here.
> Oh, you can have a lodging here.

Then, finally, leading forward and presenting her daughter, she said:

> Here is my daughter, safe and sound,
> And in her pocket five thousand pound,

And on her finger a gay gold ring,
And I'm sure she's fit to walk with a king.

For 'Isabella' a ring was formed with one of the players standing alone in the centre. Then circling slowly, the girls sang:

Isabella, Isabella, Isabella, farewell.
  Last night when we parted
  I left you broken-hearted,
And on the green gravel there stands a young man.

Isabella, Isabella, Isabella, farewell.
Take your choice, love, take your choice, love,
Take your choice, love. Farewell.

The girl in the middle of the ring then chose another who took up her position inside with her, while the singers continued:

Put the banns up, put the banns up,
Put the banns up. Farewell.
Come to church, love, come to church, love. Farewell.

Put the ring on, put the ring on,
Put the ring on, Farewell.

Come to supper, love, come to supper, love,
Come to supper, love. Farewell.

Now to bed, love, now to bed, love,
Now to bed, love. Farewell.

With other instructions, all of which were carried out in dumb show by the couple in the middle of the ring. Having got the pair wedded and bedded, the spirit of the piece changed. The stately game became a romp. Jumping up and down, still with joined hands, round the two in the middle, the girls shouted:

Now they're married we wish them joy,
First a girl and then a boy,
Sixpence married sevenpence's daughter,
Kiss the couple over and over.

In that game the Isabella of the sad farewell to whom the sweet plaintive tune of the rhyme originally belonged had somehow got mixed up in a country courtship and wedding.

A pretty, graceful game to watch was 'Thread the Tailor's Needle'. For this two girls joined both hands and elevated them to form an arch or bridge, and the other players, in single file and holding on to each other's skirts, passed under, singing:

Thread the tailor's needle,
Thread the tailor's needle.
The tailor's blind and he can't see,
So thread the tailor's needle.

As the end of the file passed under the arch the last two girls detached themselves, took up their stand by the original two and joined their hands and elevated them, thus widening the arch, and this was repeated until the arch became a tunnel. As the file passing under grew shorter, the tune was quickened, until, towards the end, the game became a merry whirl.

A grim little game often played by the younger children was called 'Daddy'. For this a ring was formed, one of the players remaining outside it, and the outside player stalked stealthily round the silent and motionless ring and chose another girl by striking her on the shoulder. The chosen one burst from the ring and rushed round it, closely pursued by the first player, the others chanting meanwhile:

Round a ring to catch a king,
Round a ring to catch a king,
Round a ring to catch a king –

and, as the pursuer caught up with the pursued and struck her neck
with the edge of her hand:

Down falls Daddy!

At the stroke on the neck the second player fell flat on the turf,
beheaded, and the game continued until all were stretched on the
turf.

Round *what* ring, to catch *what* king? And who was Daddy? Was
the game founded on some tale dished up for the commonality of
the end of one who 'nothing common did or mean'? The players
did not know or care, and we can only guess.

'Honeypots' was another small children's game. For this the
children squatted down with their hands clasped tightly under their
buttocks and two taller girls approached them, singing:

Honeypots, honeypots, all in a row!
Who will buy my honeypots, O?

One on each side of a squatting child, they 'tried' it by swinging
by the arms, the child's hands still being clasped under its buttocks.
If the hands gave way, the honeypot was cast away as broken; if
they held, it was adjudged a good pot.

A homely game was 'The Old Woman from Cumberland'. For
this a row of girls stood hand in hand with a bigger one in the
middle to represent the old woman from Cumberland. Another
bigger girl stood alone a few paces in front. She was known as the
'mistress'. Then the row of girls tripped forward, singing:

Here comes an old woman from Cumberland
With all her children in her hand.
And please do you want a servant to-day?

'What can they do?' demanded the mistress as they drew up before
her. Then the old woman of Cumberland detached herself and

walked down the row, placing a hand on the heads of one after another of her children as she said:

> This can brew, and this can bake,
> This can make a wedding cake,
> This can wear a gay gold ring,
> This can sit in the barn and sing,
> This can go to bed with a king,
> And this one can do everything.

'Oh! I will have that one,' said the mistress, pointing to the one who could do everything, who then went over to her. The proceedings were repeated until half the girls had gone over, when the two sides had a tug-of-war.

'The Old Woman from Cumberland' was a brisk, business-like game; but most of the rhymes of the others were long-drawn-out and sad, and saddest of all was 'Poor Mary is A-weeping', which went:

> Poor Mary is a-weeping, a-weeping, a-weeping,
> Poor Mary is a-weeping on a bright summer's day.
>
> And what's poor Mary a-weeping for, a-weeping for, a-weeping
>   for?
> Oh, what's poor Mary a-weeping for on a bright summer's day?
>
> She's weeping for her own true love on a bright summer's own
>   true love.
> She's weeping for her own true love on a bright summer's day.
>
> Then let her choose another love, another love, another love.
> Then let her choose another love on a bright summer's day.

'Waly, Waly, Wallflower' ran 'Poor Mary' close in gentle melancholy; but the original verse in this seems to have broken down after the fourth line. The Lark Rise version ran:

Waly, waly, wallflower, growing up so high.
We're all maidens, we must all die,
Excepting So-and-So [*naming one of the players*]
And she's the youngest maid.

Then, the tune changing to a livelier air:

She can hop and she can skip,
She can play the candlestick,
Fie! Fie! Fie!
Turn your face to the wall again.

All clasping hands and jumping up and down:

All the boys in this town
    Lead a happy life,
Excepting So-and-So [*naming some hamlet boy, not necessarily present*]
    And he wants a wife.
A wife he shall have and a-courting he shall go,
Along with So-and-So; because he loves her so.

He kissed her, he cuddled her, he sat her on his knee,
And he said 'My dearest So-and-So, how happy we shall be.'
First he bought the frying-pan and then he bought the cradle
And then he bought the knives and forks and set them on the table.

So-and-So made a pudding, she made it very sweet,
She daren't stick the knife in till So-and-So came home at night.
Taste, So-and-So, taste, and do not be afraid,
Next Monday morning the wedding day shall be,
And the cat shall sing and the bells shall ring
And we'll all clap hands together.

Evidently in the course of the centuries 'Waly, Waly, Wallflower' had become mixed with something else. The youngest maid of the first verse would never have played the candlestick or been courted by such a lover. Her destiny was very different. But what?

'Green Gravel' was another ring game. The words were:

> Green gravel, green gravel, the grass is so green,
> The fairest young damsel that ever was seen,
> Sweet So-and-So, sweet So-and-So, your true love is dead,
> I send you a letter, so turn round your head.

And as each name was mentioned the bearer turned outwards from the middle of the ring and, still holding hands with the others, went on revolving. When all had turned, the girls jigged up and down, shouting:

> Bunch o' rags! Bunch o' rags! Bunch o' rags!

until all fell down.

Then there was 'Sally, Sally Waters', who 'sprinkled in the pan'; and 'Queen Anne, Queen Anne', who 'sat in the sun'. The local version of the first verse of the latter ran:

> Queen Anne, Queen Anne, she sat in the sun,
> She had a pair of ringlets on.
> She shook them off, she shook them on,
> She shook them into Scotland.

Which seems to suggest that the Queen Anne intended was Anne of Denmark, consort of our James the First, and not the last of our Stuart monarchs, as sometimes supposed. When the founders of the new royal house first arrived in England, there would certainly be gossip about them, and Queen Anne would most probably be supposed to favour Scotland, Scots, and things Scottish.

The brisk and rather disagreeable little game known as 'Queen Caroline' must have been of comparatively recent date. For this two lines of girls stood facing each other, while one other one ran the gauntlet. As she dashed between the lines the girls on both sides 'buffeted' her with hands, pinafores and handkerchiefs, singing:

Queen, Queen Caroline,
Dipped her head in turpentine.
Why did she look so fine?
Because she wore a crinoline.

An echo of the coronation scene of George IV?
Contemporary with that was 'The Sheepfold', which began:

Who's that going round my sheepfold?
Oh, it's only your poor neighbour Dick.
Do not steal my sheep while I am fast asleep.

But that was not a favourite and no one seemed to know the whole of it. Then there were 'How Many Miles to Banbury Town?', 'Blind Man's Buff', and many other games. The children could play for hours without repeating a game.

As well as the country games, a few others, probably as old, but better known, were played by the hamlet children. Marbles, peg-tops, and skipping-ropes appeared in their season, and when there happened to be a ball available a game called 'Tip-it' was played. There was not always a ball to be had; for the smallest rubber one cost a penny, and pennies were scarce. Even marbles, at twenty a penny, were seldom bought, although there were a good many in circulation, for the hamlet boys were champion marble players and thought nothing of walking five or six miles on a Saturday to play with the boys of other villages and replenish their own store with their winnings. Some of them owned as trophies the scarce and valued glass marbles, called 'alleys'. These were of clear glass enclosing bright, wavy, multi-coloured threads, and they looked very handsome among the dingy-coloured clay ones. The girls skipped with any odd length of rope, usually a piece of their mothers' old clothes-lines.

A simple form of hopscotch was played, for which three lines, or steps, enclosed in an oblong were scratched in the dust. The elaborate hopscotch diagrams, resembling an astrological horoscope, still to be seen chalked on the roads in the West Country were unknown there.

'Dibs' was a girls' game, played with five small, smooth pebbles, which had to be kept in the air at the same time and caught on the back of the hand. Laura, who was clumsy with her hands, never mastered this game; nor could she play marbles or spin tops or catch balls, or play hopscotch. She was by common consent 'a duffer'. Skipping and running were her only accomplishments.

Sometimes in the summer the 'pin-a-sight' was all the rage, and no girl would feel herself properly equipped unless she had one secreted about her. To make a 'pin-a-sight' two small sheets of glass, a piece of brown paper, and plenty of flowers were required. Then the petals were stripped from the flowers and arranged on one of the sheets of glass with the other sheet placed over it to form a kind of floral sandwich, and the whole was enveloped in brown paper, in which a little square window was cut, with a flap left hanging to act as a drop-scene. Within the opening then appeared a multi-coloured medley of flower petals, and that was the 'pin-a-sight'. No design was aimed at; the object being to show as many and as brightly coloured petals as possible; but Laura, when alone, loved to arrange her petals as little pictures, building up a geranium or a rose, or even a little house, against a background of green leaves.

Usually the girls only showed their 'pin-a-sights' to each other; but sometimes they would approach one of the women, or knock at a door, singing:

A pin to see a pin-a-sight,
All the ladies dressed in white.
A pin behind and a pin before,
And a pin to knock at the lady's door.

They would then lift the flap and show the 'pin-a-sight', for which they expected to be rewarded with a pin. When this was forthcoming, it was stuck with any others that might be received on the front of the pinafore. There was always a competition as to who should get the longest row of pins.

After they reached school-going age, the boys no longer played with the girls, but found themselves a separate pitch on which to play marbles or spin tops or kick an old tin about by way of a football. Or they would hunt in couples along the hedgerows, shooting at birds with their catapults, climbing trees, or looking for birds' nests, mushrooms, or chestnuts, according to the season.

The birds'-nesting was a cruel sport, for not only was every egg taken from every nest they found, but the nests themselves were demolished and all the soft moss and lining feathers were left torn and scattered around on the grass and bushes.

'Oh, dear! What must the poor bird have felt when she saw that!' was Laura's cry when she came upon that, to her, saddest of all sad sights, and once she even dared to remonstrate with some boys she had found in the act. They only laughed and pushed her aside. To them, the idea that anything so small as a mother chaffinch could feel was ridiculous. They were thinking of the lovely long string of threaded eggshells, blue and speckled and pearly white, they hoped to collect and hang up at home as an ornament. The tiny whites and yolks which would come from the eggs when blown they would make their mothers whip up and stir into their own cup of tea as a delicacy, and their mothers would be pleased and say what kind, thoughtful boys they had, for they, like the boys, did not consider the birds' point of view.

No one in authority told them that such wholesale robbery of birds' nests was cruel. Even the Rector, when he called at the cottages, would admire the collections and sometimes even condescend to accept a rare specimen. Ordinary country people at that time, though not actively cruel to animals, were indifferent to their sufferings. 'Where there's no sense there's no feeling,' they would say when they had hurt some creature by accident or through carelessness. By sense they meant wits or understanding, and these they imagined purely human attributes.

A few birds were sacred. No boy would rob a robin's or a wren's nest; nor would they have wrecked a swallow's nest if they could have reached one, for they believed that:

The robin and the wrens
Be God Almighty's friends.
And the martin and the swallow
Be God Almighty's birds to follow.

And those four were safe from molestation. Their cruelty to the other birds and to some other animals was due to an utter lack of imagination, not to bad-heartedness. When, a little later, country boys were taught in school to show mercy to animals and especially to birds, one egg only from a clutch became the general rule. Then came the splendid Boy Scout movement, which has done more than all the Preservation of Wild Birds Acts to prevent the wholesale raiding of nests, by teaching the boys mercy and kindness.

In winter in the 'eighties the youths and big boys of the hamlet would go out on dark nights 'spadgering'. For this a large net upon four poles was carried; two bearers going on one side of a hedge and two on the other. When they came to a spot where a flock of sparrows or other small birds was roosting, the net was dropped over the hedge and drawn tight and the birds enclosed were slaughtered by lantern light. One boy would often bring home as many as twenty sparrows, which his mother would pluck and make into a pudding. A small number of birds, or a single bird, would be toasted in front of the fire. Many of the children and some of the women set traps for birds in their gardens. This was done by strewing crumbs or corn around and beneath a sieve or a shallow box set up endways. To the top of the trap as it stood, one end of a length of fine twine was attached and the other end was held by someone lurking in a barn doorway or behind a hedge or wall. When a bird was in a favourable position, the trap was jerked down upon it. One old woman in particular excelled as a bird-trapper, and, even in snowy weather, she might often have been seen sitting in her barn doorway with the string of a trap in her hand. Had a kindly disposed stranger seen her, his heart would have bled with pity for the poor old soul, so starving that she spent hours in the snow snaring a sparrow for her supper. His pity would have been wasted. She was quite comfortably off according to hamlet standards, and often did not trouble to pluck and cook her bag. She was out for the sport.

In one way and another a bird, or a few birds, were a regular feature of the hamlet menu. But there were birds and birds. 'Do you think you could fancy a bird, me dear?' a man would say to his ailing wife or child, and if they thought they would the bird would appear; but it would not be a sparrow, or even a thrush or a lark. It would be a much bigger bird with a plump breast; but it would never be named and no feathers would be left lying about by which to identify it. The hamlet men were not habitual poachers. They called poaching 'a mug's game' and laughed at those who practised it. 'One month in quod and one out,' as they said. But, when the necessity arose, they knew where the game birds were and how to get them.

Edmund and Laura once witnessed a neat bit of poaching. They had climbed a ladder they had found set against the side of a haystack which had been unthatched, ready for removal, and, after an exciting hour of sticking out their heads and making faces to represent gargoyles on a tower, they were lying, hidden from below, while the men on their way home from work passed along the footpath beneath the rick.

It was near sunset and the low, level light searched the path and the stubble and aftermath on either side of it. The men sauntered along in twos and threes, smoking and talking, then disappeared, group by group, over the stile at the farther side of the field. Just as the last group was nearing the stile and the children were breathing a sigh of relief at not having been seen and scolded, a hare broke from one of the hedges and went bounding and capering across the field in the headlong way hares have. It looked for a moment as if it would land under the feet of the last group of men, who were nearing the stile; but, suddenly, it scented danger and drew up and squatted motionless behind a tuft of green clover a few feet from the pathway. Just then one of the men fell behind to tie his bootlace: the others passed over the stile. The moment they were out of sight, in one movement, the man left behind rose and flung himself sideways over the clover clump where the hare was hiding. There was a short scuffle, a slight raising of dust; then the limp form was pressed into a dinner-basket, and, after a good look round to make sure his action had not been observed, the man followed his workmates.

X

Daughters of the Hamlet

A stranger coming to Lark Rise would have looked in vain for the sweet country girl of tradition, with her sunbonnet, hay-rake, and air of rustic coquetry. If he had, by chance, seen a girl well on in her teens, she would be dressed in town clothes, complete with gloves and veil, for she would be home from service for her fortnight's holiday, and her mother would insist upon her wearing her best every time she went out of doors, in order to impress the neighbours.

There was no girl over twelve or thirteen living permanently at home. Some were sent out to their first place at eleven. The way they were pushed out into the world at that tender age might have seemed heartless to a casual observer. As soon as a little girl approached school-leaving age, her mother would say, 'About time you was earnin' your own livin', me gal,' or, to a neighbour, 'I shan't be sorry when our young So-and-So gets her knees under somebody else's table. Five slices for breakfast this mornin', if you please!' From that time onward the child was made to feel herself one too many in the overcrowded home; while her brothers, when they left school and began to bring home a few shillings weekly, were treated with a new consideration and made much of. The parents did not want the boys to leave home. Later on, if they wished to strike out for themselves, they might even meet with opposition, for their money, though barely sufficient to keep them in food, made a little more in the family purse, and every shilling was precious. The girls, while at home, could earn nothing.

Then there was the sleeping problem. None of the cottages had more than two bedrooms, and when children of both sexes were entering their teens it was difficult to arrange matters, and the departure of even one small girl of twelve made a little more room for those remaining.

When the older boys of a family began to grow up, the second bedroom became the boys' room. Boys, big and little were packed into it, and the girls still at home had to sleep in the parents' room. They had their own standard of decency; a screen was placed or a curtain was drawn to form a partition between the parents' and children's beds; but it was, at best, a poor makeshift arrangement, irritating, cramped, and inconvenient. If there happened to be one big boy, with several girls following him in age, he would sleep downstairs on a bed made up every night and the second bedroom would be the girls' room. When the girls came home from service for their summer holiday, it was the custom for the father to sleep downstairs that the girl might share her mother's bed. It is common now to hear people say, when looking at some little old cottage, 'And they brought up ten children there. Where on earth did they sleep?' And the answer is, or should be, that they did not all sleep there at the same time. Obviously they could not. By the time the youngest of such a family was born, the eldest would probably be twenty and have been out in the world for years, as would those who came immediately after in age. The overcrowding was bad enough; but not quite as bad as people imagine.

Then, again, as the children grew up, they required more and more food, and the mother was often at her wits' end to provide it. It was no wonder her thoughts and hopes sprang ahead to the time when one, at least, of her brood would be self-supporting. She should not have spoken her thoughts aloud, for many a poor, sensitive, little girl must have suffered. But the same mother would often at mealtimes slip the morsel of meat from her own to her child's plate, with a 'I don't seem to feel peckish tonight. You have it. You're growing.'

After the girls left school at ten or eleven, they were usually kept at home for a year to help with the younger children, then places were found for them locally in the households of tradesmen, school-masters, stud grooms, or farm bailiffs. Employment in a public house was looked upon with horror by the hamlet mothers, and farm-house servants were a class apart. 'Once a farm-house servant, always a farm-house servant' they used to say, and they were more ambitious for their daughters.

The first places were called 'petty places' and looked upon as stepping-stones to better things. It was considered unwise to allow a girl to remain in her petty place more than a year; but a year she must stay whether she liked it or not, for that was the custom. The food in such places was good and abundant, and in a year a girl of thirteen would grow tall and strong enough for the desired 'gentlemen's service', her wages would buy her a few clothes, and she would be learning.

The employers were usually very kind to these small maids. In some houses they were treated as one of the family; in others they were put into caps and aprons and ate in the kitchen, often with one or two of the younger children of the house to keep them company. The wages were small, often only a shilling a week; but the remuneration did not end with the money payment. Material, already cut out and placed, was given them to make their underwear, and the Christmas gift of a best frock or a winter coat was common. Caps and aprons and morning print dresses, if worn, were provided by the employer. 'She shan't want for anything while she is with me' was a promise frequently made by a shopkeeper's wife when engaging a girl, and many were even better than their word in that respect. They worked with the girls themselves and trained them; then as they said, just as they were becoming useful they left to 'better themselves'.

The mothers' attitude towards these mistresses of small households was peculiar. If one of them had formerly been in service herself, her situation was avoided, for 'a good servant makes a bad missis' they said. In any case they considered it a favour to allow their small untrained daughters to 'oblige' (it was always spoke of as 'obliging') in a small household. They were jealous of their children's rights, and ready to rush in and cause an upset if anything happened of which they did not approve; and they did not like it if the small maid became fond of her employer or her family, or wished to remain in her petty place after her year was up. One girl who had been sent out at eleven as maid to an elderly couple and had insisted upon remaining there through her teens, was always spoken of by her mother as 'our poor Em'. 'When I sees t'other girls and how they keeps on improvin' an' think of our poor Em wastin' her life in a petty place, I could sit down an' howl like a dog, that I could', she would say, long after Em had been adopted as a daughter by the people to whom she had become attached.

Of course there were queer places and a few definitely bad places; but these were the exception and soon became known and avoided. Laura once accompanied a schoolfellow to interview a mistress who was said to require a maid. At ordinary times a mother took her daughter to such interviews; but Mrs Beamish was near her time, and it was not thought safe for her to venture so far from home. So Martha and Laura set out, accompanied by a younger brother of Martha's, aged about ten. Martha in her mother's best coat with the sleeves turned back to the elbows and with her hair, done up for the first time that morning, plaited into an inverted saucer at the back of her head and bristling with black hairpins. Laura in a chimney-pot hat, a short brown cape, and buttoned boots reaching nearly to her knees. The little brother wore a pale grey astrakan coat, many sizes too small, a huge red knitted scarf, and carried no pocket-handkerchief.

It was a mild, grey November day with wisps of mist floating over the ploughed fields and water drops hanging on every twig and thorn of the hedgerows. The lonely country house they were bound for was said to be four miles from the hamlet; but, long before they reached it, the distance seemed to them more like forty. It was all cross-country going; over field-paths and stiles, through spinneys and past villages. They asked the way of everybody they met or saw working in the fields and were always directed to some short cut or other, which seemed to bring them out at the same place as before. Then there were delays. Martha's newly done-up hair kept tumbling down and Laura had to take out all the hairpins and adjust it. The little brother got stones in his shoes, and all their feet felt tired from the rough travelling and the stiff mud which caked their insteps. The mud was a special source of worry to Laura, because she had put on her best boots without asking permission, and knew she would get into trouble about it when she returned.

Still, such small vexations and hindrances could not quite spoil her pleasure in the veiled grey day and the new fields and woods and villages, of which she did not even know the names.

It was late afternoon when, coming out of a deep, narrow lane with a stream trickling down the middle, they saw before them a grey-stone mansion with twisted chimney-stacks and a sundial standing in long grass before the front door. Martha and Laura were appalled at the size of the house. Gentry must live there. Which door should they go to and what should they say?

In a paved yard a man was brushing down a horse, hissing so loudly as he did so that he did not hear their first timid inquiry. When it was repeated he raised his head and smiled. 'Ho! Ho!' he said. 'Yes, yes, it's Missis at the house there you'll be wanting, I'll warrant.'

'Please does she want a maid?'

'I dare say she do. She generally do. But where's the maid? Goin' to roll yourselves up into one, all three of ye? You go on round by that harness-room and across the lawn by the big pear trees and you'll find the back door. Go on; don't be afraid. She's not agoin' to eat ye.'

In response to their timid knock, the door was opened by a youngish woman. She was like no one Laura had ever seen. Very slight – she would have been called 'scraggy' in the hamlet – with a dead white face, dark, arched brows, and black hair brushed straight back from her forehead, and with all this black and whiteness set off by a little scarlet jacket that, when Laura described it to her mother later, was identified as a garibaldi. She seemed glad to see the children, though she looked doubtful when she heard their errand and saw Martha's size.

'So you want a place?' she asked as she conducted them into a kitchen as large as a church and not unlike one with its stone-paved floor and central pillar. Yes, she wanted a maid, and she thought Martha might do. How old was she? Twelve? And what could she do? Anything she was told? Well, that was right. It was not a hard place, for, although there were sixteen rooms, only three or four of them were in use. Could she get up at six without being called? There would be the kitchen range to light and the flues to be swept once a week, and the dining-room to be swept and dusted and the fire lighted before breakfast. She herself would be down in time to cook breakfast. No cooking was required, beyond preparing vegetables. After breakfast Martha would help her with the beds, turning out the rooms, paring the potatoes and so on; and after dinner there was plenty to do – washing up, cleaning knives and boots and polishing silver. And so she went on, mapping out Martha's day, until at nine o'clock she would be free to go to bed, after placing hot water in her mistress's bedroom.

Laura could see that Martha was bewildered. She stood, twisting her scarf, curtseying, and saying 'Yes, mum' to everything.

'Then, as wages, I can offer you two pounds ten a year. It is not a great wage, but you are very small, and you'll have an easy place and a comfortable home. How do you like your kitchen?'

Martha's gaze wandered round the huge place, and once more she said, 'Yes, mum.'

'You'll find it nice and cosy here, eating your meals by the fire. You won't feel lonely, will you?'

This time Martha said, 'No, mum.'

'Tell your mother I shall expect her to fit you out well. You will want caps and aprons. I like my maids to look neat. And tell her to let you bring plenty of changes, for we only wash once in six weeks. I have a woman in to do it all up,' and although Martha knew her mother had not a penny to spend on her outfit, and that she had been told the last thing before she left home that morning to ask her prospective employer to send her mother her first month's wages in advance to buy necessaries, once again she said, 'Yes, mum.'

'Well, I shall expect you next Monday, then. And, now, are you hungry?' and for the first time there was feeling in Martha's tone as she answered, 'Yes, mum.'

Soon a huge sirloin of cold beef was placed on the table and liberal helpings were being carved for the three children. It was such a joint of beef as one only sees in old pictures with an abbot carving; immense, and so rich in flavour and so tender that it seemed to melt in the mouth. The three plates were clean in a twinkling.

'Would any of you like another helping?'

Laura, conscious that she was no principal in the affair, and only invited to partake out of courtesy, declined wistfully but firmly; Martha said she would like a little more if 'mum' pleased, and the little brother merely pushed his plate forward. Martha, mindful of her manners, refused a third helping. But the little brother had no such scruples; he was famishing, and accepted a third and a fourth plateful, the mistress of the house standing by with an amused smile on her face. She must have remembered him for the rest of her life as the little boy with the large appetite.

It was dark before they reached home, and Laura got into trouble, not only for spoiling her best boots, but still more for telling a lie, for she had led her mother to believe they were going into the market town shopping. But even when she lay in bed supperless she felt the experience was worth the punishment, for she had been where she had never been before and seen the old house and the lady in the scarlet jacket and tasted the beef and seen Tommy Beamish eat four large helpings.

After all, Martha did not go to live there. Her mother was not satisfied with her account of the place and her father heard the next day that the house was haunted. 'She shan't goo there while we've got a crust for her,' said her Dad. 'Not as I believes in Ghostesses – lot o' rubbish I calls 'em – but the child might think she seed summat and be scared out of her wits an' maybe catch her death o' cold in that girt, draughty, old kitchen.'

So Martha waited until two sisters, milliners in the market town, wanted a maid; and, once there, grew strong and rosy and, according to their report, learned to say a great deal more than 'Yes, mum'; for their only complaint against her was that she was inclined to be saucy and sang so loudly about her work that the customers in the shop could hear her.

When the girls had been in their petty places a year, their mothers began to say it was time they 'bettered themselves' and the clergyman's daughter was consulted. Did she know if a scullery-maid or a tweeny was required at any of the big country houses around? If not, she would wait until she had two or three such candidates for promotion on her list, then advertise in the *Morning Post* or the *Church Times* for situations for them. Other girls secured places through sisters or friends already serving in large establishments.

When the place was found, the girl set out alone on what was usually her first train journey, with her yellow tin trunk tied up with thick cord, her bunch of flowers and brown paper parcel bursting with left-overs.

The tin trunk would be sent on to the railway station by the carrier and the mother would walk the three miles to the station with her daughter. They would leave Lark Rise, perhaps before it was quite light on a winter morning, the girl in her best, would-be fashionable clothes and the mother carrying the baby of the family, rolled in its shawl. Neighbours would come to their garden gates to see them off and call after them 'Pleasant journey! Hope you'll have a good place!' or 'Mind you be a good gal, now, an' does just as you be told!' or, more comfortingly, 'You'll be back for y'r holidays before you knows where you are and then there won't be no holdin' you, you'll have got that London proud!' and the two would go off in good spirits, turning and waving repeatedly.

Laura once saw the departure of such a couple, the mother enveloped in a large plaid shawl, with her baby's face looking out from its folds, and the girl in a bright blue, poplin frock which had been bought at the second-hand clothes shop in the town – a frock made in the extreme fashion of three years before, but by that time ridiculously obsolete. Laura's mother, foreseeing the impression it would make at the journey's end, shook her head and clicked her tongue and said, 'Why ever couldn't they spend the money on a bit of good navy serge!' But they, poor innocents, were delighted with it.

They went off cheerfully, even proudly; but, some hours later, Laura met the mother returning alone. She was limping, for the sole of one of her old boots had parted company with the upper, and the eighteen-months-old child must have hung heavily on her arm. When asked if Aggie had gone off all right, she nodded, but could not answer; her heart was too full. After all, she was just a mother who had sent her young daughter into the unknown and was tormented with doubts and fears for her.

What the girl, bound for a strange and distant part of the country to live a new, strange life among strangers, felt when the train moved off with her can only be imagined. Probably those who saw her round, stolid little face and found her slow in learning her new duties for the next few days would have been surprised and even a little touched if they could have read her thoughts.

The girls who 'went into the kitchen' began as scullerymaids, washing up stacks of dishes, cleaning saucepans and dish covers, preparing vegetables, and doing the kitchen scrubbing and other rough work. After a year or two of this, they became under kitchen-maids and worked up gradually until they were second in command to the cook. When they reached that point, they did much of the actual cooking under supervision; sometimes they did it without any, for there were stories of cooks who never put hand to a dish, but, having taught the kitchen-maid, left all the cooking to her, expecting some spectacular dish for a dinner party. This pleased the ambitious kitchen-maid, for she was gaining experience and would soon be a professional cook herself; then, if she attained the summit of her ambition, cook-housekeeper.

Some girls preferred house to kitchen work, and they would be found a place in some mansion as third or fourth house-maid and work upward. Troops of men and maid-servants were kept in large town and country houses in those days.

The maids on the lower rungs of the ladder seldom saw their employers. If they happened to meet one or other of them about the house, her ladyship would ask kindly how they were getting on and how their parents were; or his lordship would smile and make some mild joke if he happened to be in a good humour. The upper servants were their mistresses, and they treated beginners as a sergeant treated recruits, drilling them well in their duties by dint of much scolding; but the girl who was anxious to learn and did not mind hard work or hard words and could keep a respectful tongue in her head had nothing to fear from them.

The food of the maids in those large establishments was whole-some and abundant, though far from dainty. In some houses they would be given cold beef or mutton, or even hot Irish stew for breakfast, and the midday meal was always a heavy one, with suet pudding following a cut from a hot joint. Their bedrooms were poor according to modern standards; but, sleeping in a large attic, shared with two or three others, was not then looked upon as a hardship, provided they had a bed each and their own chest of drawers and washstands. The maids had no bathroom. Often their employers had none either. Some families had installed one for their own use; others preferred the individual tub in the bedroom. A hip-bath was part of the furniture of the maids' room. Like the children of the family, they had no evenings out, unless they had somewhere definite to go and obtained special leave. They had to go to church on Sunday, whether they wanted to or not, and had to leave their best hats with the red roses and ostrich tips in the boxes under their beds and 'make frights of themselves' in funny little flat bonnets. When the Princess of Wales, afterwards Queen Alexandra, set the fashion of wearing the hair in a curled fringe over the forehead, and the fashion spread until it became universal, a fringe was forbidden to maids. They must wear their hair brushed straight back from their brows. A great hardship.

The wages paid would amuse the young housekeepers of today. At her petty place, a girl was paid from one to two shillings a week. A grown-up servant in a tradesman's family received seven pounds a year, and that was about the wage of a farm-house servant. The Rectory cook had sixteen pounds a year; the Rectory house-maid twelve; both excellent servants. The under-servants in big houses began at seven pounds a year, which was increased at each advance-ment, until, as head housemaid, they might receive as much as thirty. A good cook could ask fifty, and even obtain another five by threatening to leave. 'Everybody who was anything,' as they used to say, kept a maid in those days – stud grooms' wives, village schoolmasters' wives, and, of course, inn-keepers' and shopkeepers' wives. Even the wives of carpenters and masons paid a girl sixpence to clean the knives and boots and take out the children on Saturday.

As soon as a mother had even one daughter in service, the strain upon herself slackened a little. Not only was there one mouth less to feed, one pair of feet less to be shod, and a tiny space left free in the cramped sleeping quarters; but, every month, when the girl received her wages, a shilling or more would be sent to 'our Mum', and, as the wages increased, the mother's portion grew larger. In addition to presents, some of the older girls undertook to pay their parents' rent; others to give them a ton of coal for the winter; and all sent Christmas and birthday presents and parcels of left-off clothing.

The unselfish generosity of these poor girls was astonishing. It was said in the hamlet that some of them stripped themselves to help those at home. One girl did so literally. She had come for her holidays in her new best frock – a pale grey cashmere with white lace collar and cuffs. It had been much admired and she had obviously enjoyed wearing it during her fortnight at home; but when Laura said, 'I do like your new frock, Clem,' she replied in what was meant for an off-hand tone, 'Oh, that! I'm leaving that for our young Sally. She hasn't got hardly anything, and it don't matter what I wear when I'm away. There's nobody I care about to see it,' and Clem went back in her second-best navy serge and Sally wore the pale grey to church the next Sunday.

Many of them must have kept themselves very short of money, for they would send half or even more of their wages home. Laura's mother used to say that she would rather have starved than allow a child of hers to be placed at such a disadvantage among other girls at their places in service, not to mention the temptations to which they might be exposed through poverty. But the mothers were so poor, so barely able to feed their families and keep out of debt, that it was only human of them to take what their children sent and sometimes even pressed upon them.

Strange to say, although they were grateful to and fond of their daughters, their boys, who were always at home and whose money barely paid for their keep, seemed always to come first with them. If there was any inconvenience, it must not fall on the boys; if there was a limited quantity of anything, the boys must still have their full share; the boys' best clothes must be brushed and put away for them; their shirts must be specially well ironed, and tit-bits must always be saved for their luncheon afield. No wonder the fathers were jealous at times and exclaimed, 'Our Mum, she do make a reg'lar fool o' that boo-oy!'

A few of the girls were engaged to youths at home, and, after several years of courtship, mostly conducted by letter, for they seldom met except during the girl's summer holiday, they would marry and settle in or near the hamlet. Others married and settled away. Butchers and milkmen were favoured as husbands, perhaps because these were frequent callers at the houses where the girls were employed. A hamlet girl would marry a milkman or a butcher's roundsman in London, or some other distant part of the country, and, after a few years, the couple would acquire a business of their own and become quite prosperous. One married a butler and with him set up an apartment house on the East Coast; another married a shopkeeper and, with astonishing want to tact, brought a nurse-maid to help look after her children when she visited her parents. The nursemaid was invited into most of the cottages and well pumped for information about the home life; but Susie herself was eyed coldly: she had departed from the normal. The girls who had married away remained faithful to the old custom of spending a summer fortnight with their parents, and the outward and visible signs of their prosperity must have been trying to those who had married farm labourers and returned to the old style of living.

With the girls away, the young men of the hamlet would have had a dull time had there not been other girls from other homes in service within walking distance. On Sunday afternoons, those who were free would be off, dressed in their best, with their boots well polished and a flower stuck in the band of their Sunday hats, to court the dairy-maids at neighbouring farms or the under-servants at the big country houses. Those who were pledged would go upstairs to write their weekly love-letter, and a face might often be seen at an upper window, chewing a pen-holder and gazing sadly out at what must have appeared an empty world.

There were then no dances at village halls and no cinemas or cheap excursions to lead to the picking up of casual acquaintances; but, from time to time, one or other of the engaged youths would shock public opinion by walking out with another girl while his sweetheart was away. When taxed with not being 'true to Nell', he would declare it was only friendship or only a bit of fun; but Nell's mother and his mother would think otherwise and upbraid him until the meetings were dropped or grew furtive.

But such sideslips were never mentioned when, at last, Nellie herself came home for her holiday. Then, every evening, neighbours peeping from behind window-curtains would see the couple come out of their respective homes and stroll in the same direction, but not together as yet, for that would have been thought too brazen. As soon as they were out of sight of the windows, they would link up, arm in arm, and saunter along field-paths between the ripening corn, or stand at stiles, whispering and kissing and making love until the dusk deepened and it was time for the girl to go home, for no respectable girl was supposed to be out after ten. Only fourteen nights of such bliss, and all the other nights of the year blank, and this not for one year, but for six or seven or eight. Poor lovers!

Mistresses used to say – and probably those who are fortunate enough to keep their maids from year to year still say – that the girls are sullen and absent-minded for the first few days after they return to their duties. No doubt they are, for their thoughts must still be with the dear ones left behind and the coming months must stretch out, an endless seeming blank, before they will see them again. That is the time for a little extra patience and a little human sympathy to help them to adjust themselves, and if this is forthcoming, as it still is in many homes, in spite of newspaper correspondence, the young mind will soon turn from memories of the past to hopes for the future.

The hamlet children saw little of such love-making. Had they attempted to follow or watch such couples, the young man would have threatened them with what he would have called 'a good sock on the ear'ole'; but there was always a country courtship on view if they felt curious to witness it. This was that of an elderly pair called Chokey and Bess, who had at that time been walking out together for ten or twelve years and still had another five or six to go before they were married. Bessie, then about forty, was supposed not to be strong enough for service and lived at home, doing the housework for her mother, who was the last of the lacemakers. Chokey was a farm labourer, a great lumbering fellow who could lift a sack of wheat with ease, but was supposed to be 'a bit soft in the upper storey'. He lived in a neighbouring village and came over every Sunday.

Bessie's mother sat at the window with her lace-pillow all day long; but her earnings must have been small, for, although her husband received the same wages as the men who had families and they had only Bess, they were terribly poor. It was said that when the two women fried a rasher for their midday meal, the father being away at work, they took it in turn to have the rasher, the other one dipping her bread in the fat, day and day about. When they went out, they wore clothes of a bygone fashion, shawls and bonnets, instead of coats and hats, and short skirts and white stockings, when the rest of the hamlet world wore black stockings and skirts touching the ground. To see them set off to the market town for their Saturday shopping always raised a smile among the beholders; the mother carrying an old green gig umbrella and Bessie a double-lidded marketing basket over her arm. They were both long-faced and pale, and the mother lifted her feet high and touched earth with her umbrella at every step, while Bess trailed along a little in the rear with the point of her shawl dangling below her skirt at the back. 'For all the world like an old white mare an' her foal,' as the hamlet funny man said.

Every Sunday evening, Chokey and Bess would appear, he in his best pale grey suit and pink tie, with a geranium, rose, or dahlia stuck in his hat. She in her Paisley shawl and little black bonnet with velvet strings tied in a bow under her chin. They were not shy. It was arm in arm with them from the door, and often a pale grey arm round the Paisley shawl before they were out of sight of the windows; although, to be sure, nobody took the trouble to watch, the sight was too familiar.

They always made for the turnpike and strolled a certain distance along it, then turned back and went to Bessie's home. They seldom walked unattended; a little band of hamlet children usually accompanied them, walking about a dozen paces behind, stopping when they stopped and walking on when they walked on. 'Going with Chokey and Bess' was a favourite Sunday evening diversion. As one batch of children grew up, another took its place; though what amusement they found in following them was a mystery, for the lovers would walk a mile without exchanging a remark, and when they did it would only be: 'Seems to me there's rain in the air', or 'My! ain't it hot!' They did not seem to resent being followed. They would sometimes address a friendly remark to one of the children, or Chokey would say as he shut the garden gate on setting out, 'Comin' our way tonight?'

At last came their funny little wedding, with Bess still in the Paisley shawl, and only her father and mother to follow them on foot through the allotments and over the stile to church. After a wedding breakfast of sausages, they went to live in a funny little house with a thatched roof and a magpie in a wicker cage hanging beside the door.

The up-to-date lovers asked more of life than did Chokey and his Bess. More than their own parents had done.

There was a local saying, 'Nobody ever dies at Lark Rise and nobody goes away.' Had this been exact, there would have been no new homes in the hamlet; but, although no building had been done there for many years and there was no migration of families, a few aged people died, and from time to time a cottage was left vacant. It did not stand empty long, for there was always at least one young man waiting to get married and the joyful news of a house to let brought his bride-to-be home from service as soon as the requisite month's notice to her employer had expired.

The homes of these newly married couples illustrated a new phase in the hamlet's history. The furniture to be found in them might lack the solidity and comeliness of that belonging to their grandparents; but it showed a marked improvement on their parents' possessions.

It had become the custom for the bride to buy the bulk of the furniture with her savings in service, while the bridegroom redecorated the interior of the house, planted the vegetable garden and put a pig, or a couple of pigs, in the sty. When the bride bought the furniture, she would try to obtain things as nearly as possible like those in the houses in which she had been employed. Instead of the hard windsor chairs of her childhood's home, she would have small 'parlour' chairs with round backs and seats covered with horsehair or American cloth. The deal centre table would be covered with a brightly coloured woollen cloth between meals and cookery operations. On the chest of drawers which served as a sideboard, her wedding presents from her employers and fellow servants would be displayed – a best tea-service, a shaded lamp, a case of silver tea-spoons with the lid propped open, or a pair of owl pepper-boxes with green-glass eyes and holes at the top of the head for the pepper to come through. Somewhere in the room would be seen a few books and a vase or two of flowers. The two wicker arm-chairs by the hearth would have cushions and antimacassars of the bride's own working.

Except in a few cases, and those growing fewer, where the first child of a marriage followed immediately on the ceremony, the babies did not pour so quickly into these new homes as into the older ones. Often more than a year would elapse before the first child appeared, to be followed at reasonable intervals by four or five more. Families were beginning to be reckoned in half-dozens rather than dozens.

Those belonging to this new generation of housewives were well-trained in household work. Many of them were highly skilled in one or other of its branches. The young woman laying her own simple dinner table with knives and forks only could have told just how many knives, forks, spoons, and glasses were proper to each place at a dinner party and the order in which they should be placed. Another, blowing on her finger-tips to cool them as she unswathed the inevitable roly-poly, must have thought of the seven-course dinners she had cooked and dished up in other days. But, except for a few small innovations, such as a regular Sunday joint, roasted before the fire if no oven were available, and an Irish stew once in the week, they mostly reverted to the old hamlet dishes and style of cooking them. The square of bacon was cut, the roly-poly made, and the black cooking-pot was slung over the fire at four o'clock; for wages still stood at ten shillings a week and they knew that their mothers' way was the only way to nourish their husbands and children on so small a sum.

In decorating their homes and managing their housework, they were able to let themselves go a little more. There were fancy touches, hitherto unknown in the hamlet. Cosy corners were built of old boxes and covered with cretonne; gridirons were covered with pink wool and tinsel and hung up to serve as letter racks; Japanese fans appeared above picture frames and window curtains were tied back with ribbon bows. Blue or pink ribbon bows figured largely in these new decorative schemes. There were bows on the curtains, on the corners of cushion covers, on the cloth that covered the chest of drawers, and sometimes even on photograph frames. Some of the older men used to say that one bride, an outstanding example of the new refinement, had actually put the blue ribbon bows on the handle of her bedroom utensil. Another joke concerned the vase of flowers the same girl placed on her table at mealtimes. Her father-in-law, it was said, being entertained to tea at the new home, exclaimed, 'Hemmed if I've ever heard of eatin' flowers before!' and the mother-in-law passed the vase to her son, saying, 'Here, Georgie. Have a mouthful of sweet peas.' But the brides only laughed and tossed their heads at such ignorance. The old hamlet ways were all very well, some of them; but they had seen the world and knew how things were done. It was their day now.

Changing ideas in the outer world were also reflected in the relationship between husband and wife. Marriage was becoming more of a partnership. The man of the house was no longer absolved of all further responsibility when he had brought his week's wages home; he was made to feel that he had an interest in the management of the home and the bringing up of the children. A good, steady husband who could be depended upon was encouraged to keep part of his wages, out of which he paid the rent, bought the pig's food, and often the family footwear. He would chop the wood, sweep the path and fetch water from the well.

'So you be takin' a turn at 'ooman's work?' the older men would say teasingly, and the older women had plenty to say about the lazy, good-for-nothing wenches of these days; but the good example was not lost; the better-natured among the older men began to do odd jobs about their homes, and though, at first, their wives would tell them to 'keep out o' th' road', and say that they could do it themselves in half the time, they soon learned to appreciate, then to expect it.

Then the young wives, unused to never having a penny of their own and sorely tried by their straitened housekeeping, began to look round for some way of adding to the family income. One, with the remains of her savings, bought a few fowls and fowl-houses and sold the eggs to the grocer in the market town. Another who was clever with her needle made frocks for the servants at the neighbouring farm-houses; another left her only child with her mother and did the Rectory charring twice a week. The old country tradition of self-help was reviving; but, although there was a little extra money and there were fewer mouths to feed, the income was still woefully inadequate. Whichever way the young housewife turned, she was, as she said, 'up against it'. 'If only we had more money!' was still the cry.

Early in the 'nineties some measure of relief came, for then the weekly wage was raised to fifteen shillings; but rising prices and new requirements soon absorbed this rise and it took a world war to obtain for them anything like a living wage.

XI

School

School began at nine o'clock, but the hamlet children set out on their mile-and-a-half walk there as soon as possible after their seven o'clock breakfast, partly because they liked plenty of time to play on the road and partly because their mothers wanted them out of the way before house-cleaning began.

Up the long, straight road they straggled, in twos and threes and in gangs, their flat, rush dinner-baskets over their shoulders and their shabby little coats on their arms against rain. In cold weather some of them carried two hot potatoes which had been in the oven, or in the ashes, all night, to warm their hands on the way and to serve as a light lunch on arrival.

They were strong, lusty children, let loose from control, and there was plenty of shouting, quarrelling, and often fighting among them. In more peaceful moments they would squat in the dust of the road and play marbles, or sit on a stone heap and play dibs with pebbles, or climb into the hedges after birds' nests or blackberries, or to pull long trails of bryony to wreathe round their hats. In winter they would slide on the ice on the puddles, or make snowballs – soft ones for their friends, and hard ones with a stone inside for their enemies.

After the first mile or so the dinner-baskets would be raided; or they would creep through the bars of the padlocked field gates for turnips to pare with the teeth and munch, or for handfuls of green pea shucks, or ears of wheat, to rub out the sweet, milky grain between the hands and devour. In spring they ate the young green from the hawthorn hedges, which they called 'bread and cheese', and sorrel leaves from the wayside, which they called 'sour grass', and in autumn there was an abundance of haws and blackberries and sloes and crab-apples for them to feast upon. There was always something to eat, and they ate, not so much because they were hungry as from habit and relish of the wild food.

At that early hour there was little traffic upon the road. Sometimes, in winter, the children would hear the pounding of galloping hoofs and a string of hunters, blanketed up to the ears and ridden and led by grooms, would loom up out of the mist and thunder past on the grass verges. At other times the steady tramp and jingle of the teams going afield would approach, and, as they passed, fathers would pretend to flick their offspring with whips, saying, 'There! that's for that time you deserved it an' didn't get it'; while elder brothers, themselves at school only a few months before, would look patronizingly down from the horses' backs and call: 'Get out o' th' way, you kids!'

Going home in the afternoon there was more to be seen. A farmer's gig, on the way home from market, would stir up the dust; or the miller's van or the brewer's dray, drawn by four immense, hairy-legged, satin-backed carthorses. More exciting was the rare sight of Squire Harrison's four-in-hand, with ladies in bright, summer dresses, like a garden of flowers, on the top of the coach, and Squire himself, pink-cheeked and white-hatted, handling the four greys. When the four-in-hand passed, the children drew back and saluted, the Squire would gravely touch the brim of his hat with his whip, and the ladies would lean from their high seats to smile on the curtseying children.

A more familiar sight was the lady on a white horse who rode slowly on the same grass verge in the same direction every Monday and Thursday. It was whispered among the children that she was engaged to a farmer living at a distance, and that they met half-way between their two homes. If so, it must have been a long engagement, for she rode past at exactly the same hour twice a week throughout Laura's schooldays, her face getting whiter and her figure getting fuller and her old white horse also putting on weight.

It has been said that every child is born a little savage and has to be civilized. The process of civilization had not gone very far with some of the hamlet children; although one civilization had them in hand at home and another at school, they were able to throw off both on the road between the two places and revert to a state of Nature. A favourite amusement with these was to fall in a body upon some unoffending companion, usually a small girl in a clean frock, and to 'run her', as they called it. This meant chasing her until they caught her, then dragging her down and sitting upon her, tearing her clothes, smudging her face, and tousling her hair in the process. She might scream and cry and say she would 'tell on' them; they took no notice until, tiring of the sport, they would run whooping off, leaving her sobbing and exhausted.

The persecuted one never 'told on' them, even when reproved by the schoolmistress for her dishevelled condition, for she knew that, if she had, there would have been a worse 'running' to endure on the way home, and one that went to the tune of:

> Tell-tale tit!
> Cut her tongue a-slit,
> And every little puppy-dog shall have a little bit!

It was no good telling the mothers either, for it was the rule of the hamlet never to interfere in the children's quarrels. 'Let 'em fight it out among theirselves,' the woman would say; and if a child complained the only response would be: 'You must've been doin' summat to them. If you'd've left them alone, they'd've left you alone; so don't come bringing your tales home to me!' It was harsh schooling; but the majority seemed to thrive upon it, and the few quieter and more sensitive children soon learned either to start early and get to school first, or to linger behind, dipping under bushes and lurking inside field gates until the main body had passed.

When Edmund was about to start school, Laura was afraid for him. He was such a quiet, gentle little boy, inclined to sit gazing into space, thinking his own thoughts and dreaming his own dreams. What would he do among the rough, noisy crowd? In imagination she saw him struggling in the dust with the runners sitting on his small, slender body, while she stood by, powerless to help.

At first she took him to school by a field path, a mile or more round; but bad weather and growing crops soon put an end to that and the day came when they had to take the road with the other children. But, beyond snatching his cap and flinging it into the hedge as they passed, the bigger boys paid no attention to him, while the younger ones were definitely friendly, especially when he invited them to have a blow each on the whistle which hung on a white cord from the neck of his sailor suit. They accepted him, in fact, as one of themselves, allowing him to join in their games and saluting him with a grunted 'Hello, Ted,' when they passed.

When the clash came at last and a quarrel arose, and Laura, looking back, saw Edmund in the thick of a struggling group and heard his voice shouting loudly and rudely, not gentle at all, 'I shan't! I won't! Stop it, I tell you!' and rushed back, if not to rescue, to be near him, she found Edmund, her gentle little Edmund, with face as red as a turkey-cock, hitting out with clenched fists at such a rate that some of the bigger boys, standing near, started applauding.

So Edmund was not a coward, like she was! Edmund could fight! Though where and how he had learned to do so was a mystery. Perhaps, being a boy, it came to him naturally. At any rate, fight he did, so often and so well that soon no one near his own age risked offending him. His elders gave him an occasional cuff, just to keep him in his place; but in scuffles with others they took his part, perhaps because they knew he was likely to win. So all was well with Edmund. He was accepted inside the circle, and the only drawback, from Laura's point of view, was that she was still outside.

Although they started to school so early, the hamlet children took so much time on the way that the last quarter of a mile was always a race, and they would rush, panting and dishevelled, into school just as the bell stopped, and the other children, spick and span, fresh from their mothers' hands, would eye them sourly. 'That gipsy lot from Lark Rise!' they would murmur.

Fordlow National School was a small grey one-storied building, standing at the cross-roads at the entrance to the village. The one large classroom which served all purposes was well lighted with several windows, including the large one which filled the end of the building which faced the road. Beside, and joined on to the school, was a tiny two-roomed cottage for the schoolmistress, and beyond that a playground with birch trees and turf, bald in places, the whole being enclosed within pointed, white-painted palings.

The only other building in sight was a row of model cottages occupied by the shepherd, the blacksmith, and other superior farm-workers. The school had probably been built at the same time as the houses and by the same model landlord; for, though it would seem a hovel compared to a modern council school, it must at that time have been fairly up-to-date. It had a lobby with pegs for clothes, boys' and girls' earth-closets, and a backyard with fixed wash-basins, although there was no water laid on. The water supply was con-tained in a small bucket, filled every morning by the old woman who cleaned the schoolroom, and every morning she grumbled because the children had been so extravagant that she had to 'fill 'un again'.

The average attendance was about forty-five. Ten or twelve of the children lived near the school, a few others came from cottages in the fields, and the rest were the Lark Rise children. Even then, to an outsider, it would have appeared a quaint, old-fashioned little gathering; the girls in their ankle-length frocks and long, straight pinafores, with their hair strained back from their brows and secured on their crowns by a ribbon or black tape or a bootlace; the bigger boys in corduroys and hobnailed boots, and the smaller ones in home-made sailor suits or, until they were six or seven, in petticoats.

Baptismal names were such as the children's parents and grand-parents had borne. The fashion in Christian names was changing; babies were being christened Mabel and Gladys and Doreen and Percy and Stanley; but the change was too recent to have affected the names of the older children. Mary Ann, Sarah Ann, Eliza, Martha, Annie, Jane, Amy, and Rose were favourite girls' names. There was a Mary Ann in almost every family, and Eliza was nearly as popular. But none of them were called by their proper names. Mary Ann and Sarah Ann were contracted to Mar'ann and Sar'ann. Mary, apart from Ann, had, by stages, descended through Molly and Polly to Poll. Eliza had become Liza, then Tiza, then Tize; Martha was Mat or Pat; Jane was Jin; and every Amy had at least one 'Aim' in life, of which she had constant reminder. The few more uncommon names were also distorted. Two sisters named at the font Beatrice and Agnes, went through life as Beat and Agg, Laura was Lor, or Low, and Edmund was Ned or Ted.

Laura's mother disliked this cheapening of names and named her third child May, thinking it would not lend itself to a diminutive. However, while still in her cradle, the child became Mayie among the neighbours.

There was no Victoria in the school, nor was there a Miss Victoria or a Lady Victoria in any of the farm-houses, rectories, or mansions in the district, nor did Laura ever meet a Victoria in later life. That great name was sacred to the Queen and was not copied by her subjects to the extent imagined by period novelists of today.

The schoolmistress in charge of the Fordlow school at the beginning of the 'eighties had held that position for fifteen years and seemed to her pupils as much a fixture as the school building; but for most of that time she had been engaged to the squire's head gardener and her long reign was drawing to a close.

She was, at that time, about forty, and was a small, neat little body with a pale, slightly pock-marked face, snaky black curls hanging down to her shoulders, and eyebrows arched into a perpetual inquiry. She wore in school stiffly starched, holland aprons with bibs, one embroidered with red one week, and one with blue the next, and was seldom seen without a posy of flowers pinned on her breast and another tucked into her hair.

Every morning, when school had assembled, and Governess, with her starched apron and bobbing curls appeared in the doorway, there was a great rustling and scraping of curtseying and pulling of forelocks. 'Good morning, children,' 'Good morning, ma'am,' were the formal, old-fashioned greetings. Then, under her determined fingers the harmonium wheezed out 'Once in Royal', or 'We are but little children weak', prayers followed, and the day's work began.

Reading, writing, and arithmetic were the principal subjects, with a Scripture lesson every morning, and needlework every afternoon for the girls. There was no assistant mistress; Governess taught all the classes simultaneously, assisted only by two monitors – ex-scholars, aged about twelve, who were paid a shilling a week each for their services.

Every morning at ten o'clock the Rector arrived to take the older children for Scripture. He was a parson of the old school; a commanding figure, tall and stout, with white hair, ruddy cheeks and an aristocratically beaked nose, and he was as far as possible removed by birth, education, and worldly circumstances from the lambs of his flock. He spoke to them from a great height, physical, mental, and spiritual. 'To order myself lowly and reverently before my betters' was the clause he underlined in the Church Catechism, for had he not been divinely appointed pastor and master to those little rustics and was it not one of his chief duties to teach them to realize this? As a man, he was kindly disposed – a giver of blankets and coals at Christmas, and of soup and milk puddings to the sick.

His lesson consisted of Bible reading, turn and turn about round the class, of reciting from memory the names of the kings of Israel and repeating the Church Catechism. After that, he would deliver a little lecture on morals and behaviour. The children must not lie or steal or be discontented or envious. God had placed them just where they were in the social order and given them their own special work to do; to envy others or to try to change their own lot in life was a sin of which he hoped they would never be guilty. From his lips the children heard nothing of that God who is Truth and Beauty and Love; but they learned for him and repeated to him long passages from the Authorized Version, thus laying up treasure for themselves; so the lessons, in spite of much aridity, were valuable.

Scripture over and the Rector bowed and curtsied out of the door, ordinary lessons began. Arithmetic was considered the most important of the subjects taught, and those who were good at figures ranked high in their classes. It was very simple arithmetic, extending only to the first four rules, with the money sums, known as 'bills of parcels', for the most advanced pupils.

The writing lesson consisted of the copying of copperplate maxims: 'A fool and his money are soon parted'; 'Waste not, want not'; 'Count ten before you speak', and so on. Once a week composition would be set, usually in the form of writing a letter describing some recent event. This was regarded chiefly as a spelling test.

History was not taught formally; but history readers were in use containing such picturesque stories as those of King Alfred and the cakes, King Canute commanding the waves, the loss of the White Ship, and Raleigh spreading his cloak for Queen Elizabeth.

There were no geography readers and, excepting what could be gleaned from the descriptions of different parts of the world in the ordinary readers, no geography was taught. But, for some reason or other, on the walls of the schoolroom were hung splendid maps: The World, Europe, North America, South America, England, Ireland, and Scotland. During long waits in class for her turn to read, or to have her copy or sewing examined, Laura would gaze on these maps until the shapes of the countries with their islands and inlets became photographed on her brain. Baffin Bay and the land around the poles were especially fascinating to her.

Once a day, at whatever hour the poor, overworked mistress could find time, a class would be called out to toe the chalked semicircle on the floor for a reading lesson. This lesson, which should have been pleasant, for the reading matter was good, was tedious in the extreme. Many of the children read so slowly and haltingly that Laura, who was impatient by nature, longed to take hold of their words and drag them out of their mouths, and it often seemed to her that her own turn to read would never come. As often as she could do so without being detected, she would turn over and peep between the pages of her own *Royal Reader*, and, studiously holding the book to her nose, pretend to be following the lesson while she was pages ahead.

There was plenty there to enthral any child: 'The Skater Chased by Wolves'; 'The Siege of Torquilstone', from *Ivanhoe*; Fenimore Cooper's *Prairie on Fire*; and Washington Irving's *Capture of Wild Horses*.

Then there were fascinating descriptions of such far-apart places as Greenland and the Amazon; of the Pacific Ocean with its fairy islands and coral reefs; the snows of Hudson Bay Territory and the sterile heights of the Andes. Best of all she loved the description of the Himalayas, which began: 'Northward of the great plain of India, and along its whole extent, towers the sublime mountain region of the Himalayas, ascending gradually until it terminates in a long range of summits wrapped in perpetual snow.'

Interspersed between the prose readings were poems: 'The Slave's Dream'; 'Young Lochinvar'; 'The Parting of Douglas and Marmion'; Tennyson's 'Brook' and 'Ring out, Wild Bells'; Byron's 'Shipwreck'; Hogg's 'Skylark', and many more. 'Lochiel's Warning' was a favourite with Edmund, who often, in bed at night, might be heard declaiming: 'Lochiel! Lochiel! beware of the day!' while Laura, at any time, with or without encouragement, was ready to 'look back into other years' with Henry Glassford Bell, and recite his scenes from the life of Mary Queen of Scots, reserving her most impressive tone for the concluding couplet:

> Lapped by a dog. Go think of it in silence and alone,
> Then weigh against a grain of sand the glories of a throne.

But long before their schooldays were over they knew every piece in the books by heart and it was one of their greatest pleasures in life to recite them to each other. By that time Edmund had appropriated Scott and could repeat hundreds of lines, always showing a preference for scenes of single combat between warrior chiefs. The selection in the *Royal Readers*, then, was an education in itself for those who took to it kindly; but the majority of the children would have none of it; saying that the prose was 'dry old stuff' and that they hated 'portry'.

Those children who read fluently, and there were several of them in every class, read in monotonous sing-song, without expression, and apparently without interest. Yet there were very few really stupid children in the school, as is proved by the success of many of them in after life, and though few were interested in their lessons, they nearly all showed an intelligent interest in other things – the boys in field work and crops and cattle and agricultural machinery; the girls in dress, other people's love affairs and domestic details.

It is easy to imagine the education authorities of that day, when drawing up the scheme for that simple but sound education, saying, 'Once teach them to read and they will hold the key to all knowledge.' But the scheme did not work out. If the children, by the time they left school, could read well enough to read the newspaper and perhaps an occasional book for amusement, and write well enough to write their own letters, they had no wish to go farther. Their interest was not in books, but in life, and especially the life that lay immediately about them. At school they worked unwillingly, upon compulsion, and the life of the schoolmistress was a hard one.

As Miss Holmes went from class to class, she carried the cane and laid it upon the desk before her; not necessarily for use, but as a reminder, for some of the bigger boys were very unruly. She punished by a smart stroke on each hand. 'Put out your hand,' she would say, and some boys would openly spit on each hand before proffering it. Others murmured and muttered before and after a caning and threatened to 'tell me feyther'; but she remained calm and cool, and after the punishment had been inflicted there was a marked improvement – for a time.

It must be remembered that in those days a boy of eleven was nearing the end of his school life. Soon he would be at work; already he felt himself nearly a man and too old for petticoat government. Moreover, those were country boys, wild and rough, and many of them as tall as she was. Those who had failed to pass Standard IV and so could not leave school until they were eleven, looked upon that last year as a punishment inflicted upon them by the school authorities and behaved accordingly. In this they were encouraged by their parents, for a certain section of these resented their boys being kept at school when they might be earning. 'What do our young Alf want wi' a lot o' book-larnin'?' they would say. 'He can read and write and add up as much money as he's ever likely to get. What more do he want?' Then a neighbour of more advanced views would tell them: 'A good education's everything in these days. You can't get on in the world if you ain't had one,' for they read their newspapers and new ideas were percolating, though slowly. It was only the second generation to be forcibly fed with the fruit of the tree of knowledge: what wonder if it did not always agree with it.

Meanwhile, Miss Holmes carried her cane about with her. A poor method of enforcing discipline, according to modern educational ideas: but it served. It may be that she and her like all over the country at that time were breaking up the ground that other, later comers to the field, with a knowledge of child psychology and with tradition and experiment behind them, might sow the good seed.

She seldom used the cane on the girls and still more seldom on the infants. Standing in a corner with their hands on their heads was their punishment. She gave little treats and encouragements, too, and, although the children called her 'Susie' behind her back, they really liked and respected her. Many times there came a knock at the door and a smartly dressed girl on holidays, or a tall young soldier on leave, in his scarlet tunic and pill-box cap, looked in 'to see Governess'.

That Laura could already read when she went to school was never discovered. 'Do you know your ABC?' the mistress asked her on the first morning. 'Come, let me hear you say it: A – B – C –'

'A – B – C –' Laura began; but when she got to F she stumbled, for she had never memorized the letters in order. So she was placed in the class known as 'the babies' and joined in chanting the alphabet from A to Z. Alternatively they recited it backward, and Laura soon had that version by heart, for it rhymed:

> Z–Y–X and W–V
> U–T–S and R–Q–P
> O–N–M and L–K–J
> I–H–G and F–E–D
> And C–B–A!

Once started, they were like a watch wound up, and went on alone for hours. The mistress, with all the other classes on her hands, had no time to teach the babies, although she always had a smile for them when she passed and any disturbance or cessation of the chanting would bring her down to them at once. Even the monitors were usually engaged in giving out dictation to the older children, or in hearing tables or spelling repeated; but, in the afternoon, one of the bigger girls, usually the one who was the poorest needlewoman (it was always Laura in later years) would come down from her own form to point to and name each letter on a wall-sheet, the little ones repeating them after her. Then she would teach them to form pot-hooks and hangers, and, afterwards, letters, on their slates, and this went on for years, as it seemed to Laura, but perhaps it was only one year.

At the end of that time the class was examined and those who knew and could form their letters were moved up into the official 'Infants'. Laura, who by this time was reading *Old St Paul's* at home, simply romped through this Little-Go; but without credit, for it was said she 'gabbled' her letters, and her writing was certainly poor.

It was not until she reached Standard I that her troubles really began. Arithmetic was the subject by which the pupils were placed, and as Laura could not grasp the simplest rule with such small help as the mistress had time to give, she did not even know how to begin working out the sums and was permanently at the bottom of the class. At needlework in the afternoon she was no better. The girls around her in class were making pinafores for themselves, putting in tiny stitches and biting off their cotton like grown women, while she was still struggling with her first hemming strip. And a dingy, crumpled strip it was before she had done with it, punctuated throughout its length with blood spots where she had pricked her fingers.

'Oh, Laura! What a dunce you are!' Miss Holmes used to say every time she examined it, and Laura really was the dunce of the school in those two subjects. However, as time went on, she improved a little, and managed to pass her standard every year with moderate success until she came to Standard V and could go no farther, for that was the highest in the school. By that time the other children she had worked with had left, excepting one girl named Emily Rose, who was an only child and lived in a lonely cottage far out in the fields. For two years Standard V consisted of Laura and Emily Rose. They did few lessons and those few mostly those they could learn from books by themselves, and much of their time was spent in teaching the babies and assisting the schoolmistress generally.

That mistress was not Miss Holmes. She had married her head gardener while Laura was still in the Infants and gone to live in a pretty old cottage which she had renamed 'Malvern Villa'. Immediately after her had come a young teacher, fresh from her training college, with all the latest educational ideas. She was a bright, breezy girl, keen on reform and anxious to be a friend as well as a teacher to her charges.

She came too early. The human material she had to work on was not ready for such methods. On the first morning she began a little speech, meaning to take the children into her confidence:

'Good morning, children. My name is Matilda Annie Higgs, and I want us all to be friends –' A giggling murmur ran round the school. 'Matilda Annie! Matilda Annie! Did she say Higgs or pigs?' The name made direct appeal to their crude sense of humour, and, as to the offer of friendship, they scented weakness in that, coming from one whose office it was to rule. Thenceforth, Miss Higgs might drive her pigs in the rhyme they shouted in her hearing; but she could neither drive nor lead her pupils. They hid her cane, filled her inkpot with water, put young frogs in her desk, and asked her silly, unnecessary questions about their work. When she answered them, they all coughed in chorus.

The girls were as bad as the boys. Twenty times in one afternoon a hand would shoot upward and it would be: 'Please, miss, can I have this or that from the needlework box?' and poor Miss Higgs, trying to teach a class at the other end of the room, would come and unlock and search the box for something they had already and had hidden.

Several times she appealed to them to show more consideration. Once she burst into tears before the whole school. She told the woman who cleaned that she had never dreamed there were such children anywhere. They were little savages.

One afternoon, when a pitched battle was raging among the big boys in class and the mistress was calling imploringly for order, the Rector appeared in the doorway.

'Silence!' he roared.

The silence was immediate and profound, for they knew he was not one to be trifled with. Like Gulliver among the Lilliputians, he strode into the midst of them, his face flushed with anger, his eyes flashing blue fire. 'Now, what is the meaning of this disgraceful uproar?'

Some of the younger children began to cry; but one look in their direction froze them into silence and they sat, wide-eyed and horrified, while he had the whole class out and caned each boy soundly, including those who had taken no part in the fray. Then, after a heated discourse in which he reminded the children of their lowly position in life and the twin duties of gratitude to and respect towards their superiors, school was dismissed. Trembling hands seized coats and dinner-baskets and frightened little figures made a dash for the gate. But the big boys who had caused the trouble showed a different spirit. 'Who cares for him?' they muttered, 'Who cares? Who cares? He's only an old parson!' Then, when safely out of the playground, one voice shouted:

> Old Charley-wag! Old Charley-wag!
> Ate the pudden and gnawed the bag!

The other children expected the heavens to fall; for Mr Ellison's Christian name was Charles. The shout was meant for him and was one of defiance. He did not recognize it as such. There were several Charleses in the school, and it must have been inconceivable to him that his own Christian name should be intended. Nothing happened, and, after a few moments of tense silence, the rebels trooped off to get their own account of the affair in first at home.

After that, it was not long before the station fly stood at the school gate and Miss Higgs's trunk and bundles and easy-chair were hauled on top. Back came the married Miss Holmes, now Mrs Tenby. Girls curtsied again and boys pulled their forelocks. It was 'Yes, ma'am', and 'No, ma'am', and 'What did you please to say, ma'am?' once more. But either she did not wish to teach again permanently or the education authorities already had a rule against employing married-women teachers, for she only remained a few weeks until a new mistress was engaged.

This turned out to be a sweet, frail-looking, grey-haired, elderly lady named Miss Shepherd, and a gentle shepherd she proved to her flock. Unfortunately, she was but a poor disciplinarian, and the struggle to maintain some degree of order wore her almost to shreds. Again there was always a buzz of whispering in class; stupid and unnecessary questions were asked, and too long intervals elapsed between the word of command and the response. But, unlike Miss Higgs, she did not give up. Perhaps she could not afford to do so at her age and with an invalid sister living with and dependent upon her. She ruled, if she can be said to have ruled at all, by love and patience and ready forgiveness. In time, even the blackest of her sheep realized this and kept within certain limits; just sufficient order was maintained to avoid scandal, and the school settled down under her mild rule for five or six years.

Perhaps these upheavals were a necessary part of the transition which was going on. Under Miss Holmes, the children had been weaned from the old free life; they had become accustomed to regular attendance, to sitting at a desk and concentrating, however imperfectly. Although they had not learned much, they had been learning to learn. But Miss Holmes's ideas belonged to an age that was rapidly passing. She believed in the established order of society, with clear divisions, and had done her best to train the children to accept their lowly lot with gratitude to and humility before their betters. She belonged to the past; the children's lives lay in the future, and they needed a guide with at least some inkling of the changing spirit of the times. The new mistresses, who came from the outside world, brought something of this spirit with them. Even the transient and unappreciated Miss Higgs, having given as a subject for composition one day 'Write a letter to Miss Ellison, telling her what you did at Christmas', when she read over one girl's shoulder the hitherto conventional beginning 'Dear and Honoured Miss', exclaimed 'Oh, no! That's a *very* old-fashioned beginning. Why not say, "Dear Miss Ellison"?' An amendment which was almost revolutionary.

Miss Shepherd went further. She taught the children that it was not what a man or woman had, but what they were which mattered.

That poor people's souls are as valuable and that their hearts may be as good and their minds as capable of cultivation as those of the rich. She even hinted that on the material plane people need not necessarily remain always upon one level. Some boys, born of poor parents, had struck out for themselves and become great men, and everybody had respected them for rising upon their own merits. She would read them the lives of some of these so-called self-made men (there were no women, Laura noticed!) and though their circumstances were too far removed from those of her hearers for them to inspire the ambition she hoped to awaken, they must have done something to widen their outlook on life.

Meanwhile the ordinary lessons went on. Reading, writing, arithmetic, all a little less rather than more well taught and mastered than formerly. In needlework there was a definite falling off. Miss Shepherd was not a great needle-woman herself and was inclined to cut down the sewing time to make way for other work. Infinitesimal stitches no longer provoked delighted exclamations, but more often a 'Child! You will ruin your eyes!' As the bigger girls left who in their time had won county prizes, the standard of the output declined, until, from being known as one of the first needlework schools in the district, Fordlow became one of the last.

XII

Her Majesty's Inspector

Her Majesty's Inspector of Schools came once a year on a date of which previous notice had been given. There was no singing or quarrelling on the way to school that morning. The children, in clean pinafores and well blackened boots, walked deep in thought; or, with open spelling or table books in hand, tried to make up in an hour for all their wasted yesterdays.

Although the date of 'Inspector's' visit had been notified, the time had not. Some years he would come to Fordlow in the morning; other years in the afternoon, having examined another school earlier. So, after prayers, copybooks were given out and the children settled down for a long wait. A few of the more stolid, leaning forward with tongues slightly protruding, would copy laboriously, 'Lightly on the up-strokes, heavy on the down', but most of the children were too apprehensive even to attempt to work and the mistress did not urge them, for she felt even more apprehensive herself and did not want nervously executed copies to witness against her.

Ten – eleven – the hands of the clock dragged on, and forty-odd hearts might almost be heard thumping when at last came the sound of wheels crunching on gravel and two top hats and the top of a whip appeared outside the upper panes of the large end window.

Her Majesty's Inspector was an elderly clergyman, a little man with an immense paunch and tiny grey eyes like gimlets. He had the reputation of being 'strict', but that was a mild way of describing his autocratic demeanour and scathing judgement. His voice was an exasperated roar and his criticism was a blend of outraged learning and sarcasm. Fortunately, nine out of ten of his examinees were proof against the latter. He looked at the rows of children as if he hated them and at the mistress as if he despised her. The Assistant Inspector was also a clergyman, but younger, and, in comparison, almost human. Black eyes and very red lips shone through the bushiness of the whiskers which almost covered his face. The children in the lower classes, which he examined, were considered fortunate.

The mistress did not have to teach a class in front of the great man, as later; her part was to put out the books required and to see that the pupils had the pens and paper they needed. Most of the time she hovered about the Inspector, replying in low tones to his scathing remarks, or, with twitching lips, smiling encouragement at any child who happened to catch her eye.

What kind of a man the Inspector really was it is impossible to say. He may have been a great scholar, a good parish priest, and a good friend and neighbour to people of his own class. One thing, however, is certain, he did not care for or understand children, at least not national school children. In homely language, he was the wrong man for the job. The very sound of his voice scattered the few wits of the less gifted, and even those who could have done better were too terrified in his presence to be able to collect their thoughts or keep their hands from trembling.

But, slowly as the hands of the clock seemed to move, the afternoon wore on. Classes came out and toed the chalk line to read; other classes bent over their sums, or wrote letters to grandmothers describing imaginary summer holidays. Some wrote to the great man's dictation pieces full of hard spelling words. One year he made the confusion of their minds doubly confused by adopting the, to them, new method of giving out the stops by name: 'Water-fowl and other aquatic birds dwell on their banks semicolon while on the surface of the placid water float the wide-spreading leaves of the *Victoria regia* comma and other lilies and water dash plants full stop.'

Of course, they all wrote the names of the stops, which, together with their spelling, would have made their papers rich reading had there been any one there capable of enjoying it.

The composition class made a sad hash of their letters. The children had been told beforehand that they must fill at least one page, so they wrote in a very large hand and spaced their lines well; but what to say was the difficulty! One year the Inspector, observing a small boy sitting bolt upright gazing before him, called savagely: 'Why are you not writing – you at the end of the row? You have your pen and your paper, have you not?'

'Yes, thank you, sir.'

'Then why are you idling?'

'Please, sir, I was only thinking what to say.'

A grunt was the only answer. What other was possible from one who must have known well that pen, ink, and paper were no good without at least a little thinking.

Once he gave out to Laura's class two verses of *The Ancient Mariner*, reading them through first, then dictating them very slowly, with an air of aloof disdain, and yet rolling the lines on his tongue as if he relished them:

'All in a hot and copper sky,' he bawled. Then his voice softened. So perhaps there was another side to his nature.

At last the ordeal was over. No one would know who had passed and who had not for a fortnight; but that did not trouble the children at all. They crept like mice from the presence, and then, what shouting and skipping and tumbling each other in the dust as soon as they were out of sight and hearing!

When the papers arrived and the examination results were read out it was surprising to find what a number had passed. The standard must have been very low, for the children had never been taught some of the work set, and in what they had learned nervous dread had prevented them from reaching their usual poor level.

Another Inspector, also a clergyman, came to examine the school in Scripture. But that was a different matter. On those days the Rector was present, and the mistress, in her best frock, had nothing to do beyond presiding at the harmonium for hymn singing. The examination consisted of Scripture questions, put to a class as a whole and answered by any one who was able to shoot up a hand to show they had the requisite knowledge; or portions of the Church Catechism, repeated from memory in order round the class; and of a written paper on some set Biblical subject. There was little nervous tension on that day, for 'Scripture Inspector' beamed upon and encouraged the children, even to the extent of prompting those who were not word-perfect. While the writing was going on, he and the Rector talked in undertones, laughing aloud at the doings of 'old So-and-So', and, at one point, the mistress slipped away into her cottage and brought them cups of tea on a tray.

The children did reasonably well, for Scripture was the one subject they were thoroughly taught; even the dullest knew most of the Church Catechism by heart. The written paper was the stumbling-block to many; but this was Laura and Edmund's best subject and both succeeded in different years in carrying off the large, calf-bound, gilt-edged 'Book of Common Prayer' which was given as a prize – the only prize given at that school.

Laura won hers by means of a minor miracle. That day, for the first and last time in her life, the gift of words descended upon her. The subject set was 'The Life of Moses', and although up to that moment she had felt no special affection for the great law-giver, a sudden wave of hero-worship surged over her. While her classmates were still wrinkling their brows and biting their pens, she was well away with the baby in the bulrushes scene. Her pen flew over her paper as she filled sheet after sheet, and she had got the Children of Israel through the Red Sea, across the desert, and was well in sight of Pisgah when the little bell on the mistress's table tinkled that time was up.

The Inspector, who had been watching her, was much amused by her verbosity and began reading her paper at once, although, as a rule, he carried the essay away to read. After three or four pages he laughingly declared that he must have more tea as 'that desert' made him feel thirsty.

Such inspiration never visited her again. She returned to her usual pedestrian style of essay writing, in which there were so many alterations and erasures that, although she wrote a fair amount, she got no more marks than those who got stuck at 'My dear Grandmother'.

There was a good deal of jealousy and unkindness among the parents over the passes and still more over the one annual prize for Scripture. Those whose children had not done well in examinations would never believe that the success of others was due to merit. The successful ones were spoken of as 'favourites' and disliked. 'You ain't a-goin' to tell me that that young So-and-So did any better n'r our Jim,' some disappointed mother would say. 'Stands to reason that what he could do our Jimmy could do, *and* better, too. Examinations are all a lot of humbug, if you asks me.' The parents of those who had passed were almost apologetic. ' 'Tis all luck,' they would say. 'Our Tize happened to hit it this time; next year it'll be your Alice's turn.' They showed no pleasure in any small success their own children might have. Indeed, it is doubtful if they felt any, except in the case of a boy who, having passed the fourth standard, could leave school and start work. Their ideal for themselves and their children was to keep to the level of the normal. To them outstanding ability was no better than outstanding stupidity.

Boys who had been morose or rebellious during their later school-days were often transformed when they got upon a horse's back or were promoted to driving a dung-cart afield. For the first time in their lives, they felt themselves persons of importance. They bandied lively words with the men and gave themselves manly airs at home with their younger brothers and sisters. Sometimes, when two or three boys were working together, they were too lively, and very little work was done. 'One boy's a boy; two boys be half a boy, and three boys be no boy at all', ran the old country saying. 'Little gallasses', the men called them when vexed; and, in more indulgent moods, 'young dogs'. 'Ain't he a regular young dog?' a fond parent would ask, when a boy, just starting work, would set his cap at an angle, cut himself an ash stick, and try to walk like a man.

They were lovable little fellows, in their stiff new corduroys and hobnailed boots, with their broad, childish faces, powdered with freckles and ready to break into dimples at a word. For a few years they were happy enough, for they loved their work and did not, as yet, feel the pinch of their poverty. The pity of it was that the calling they were entering should have been so unappreciated and underpaid. There was nothing the matter with the work, as work, the men agreed. It was a man's life, and they laughed scornfully at the occupations of some who looked down upon them; but the wages were ridiculously low and the farm labourer was so looked down upon and slighted that the day was soon to come when a country boy leaving school would look for any other way of earning a living than on the land.

At that time boys of a roving disposition who wanted to see a bit of the world before settling down went into the Army. Nearly every family in the hamlet had its soldier son or uncle or cousin, and it was a common sight to see a scarlet coat going round the Rise. After their Army service, most of the hamlet-bred young men returned and took up the old life on the land; but a few settled in other parts of the country. One was a policeman in Birmingham, another kept a public house, and a third was said to be a foreman in a brewery in Staffordshire. A few other boys left the hamlet to become farm servants in the North of England. To obtain such situations, they went to Banbury Fair and stood in the Market to be hired by an agent. They were engaged for a year and during that time were lodged and fed with the farmer's family, but received little or no money until the year was up, when they were paid in a lump sum. They were usually well treated, especially in the matter of food; but were glad to return at the end of the year from what was, to them, a foreign country where, at first, they could barely understand the speech.

At 'the hiring' the different grades of farm workers stood in groups, according to their occupations – the shepherds with their crooks, the carters with whips and tufts of horsehair in their hats, and the maid-servants relying upon their sex to distinguish them. The young boys, not as yet specialists, were easily picked out by their youth and their innocent, wondering faces. The maids who secured situations by hiring themselves out at the Fair were farm-house servants of the rougher kind. None of the hamlet girls attended the Fair for that purpose.

Squire at the Manor House, known as 'our Squire', not out of any particular affection or respect, but in contradistinction to the richer and more important squire in a neighbouring parish, was at that time unmarried, though verging on middle age, and his mother still reigned as Lady of the Manor. Two or three times a year she called at the school to examine the needlework, a tall, haughty, and still handsome old dame in a long, flowing, pale-grey silk dustcloak and small, close-fitting, black bonnet, with two tiny King Charles's spaniels on a leash.

It would be almost impossible for any one born in this century to imagine the pride and importance of such small country gentle-people in the 'eighties. As far as was known, the Bracewells were connected with no noble family; they had but little land, kept up but a small establishment, and were said in the village and hamlet to be 'poor as crows'. Yet, by virtue of having been born into a particular caste and of living in the 'big house' of the parish, they expected to reign over their poorer neighbours and to be treated by them with the deference due to royalty. Like royalty, too, they could be charming to those who pleased them. Those who did not had to beware.

A good many of the cottagers still played up to them, the women curtseying to the ground when their carriage passed and speaking in awed tones in their presence. Others, conscious of their own independence – for none of the hamlet people worked on their land or occupied their cottages – and having breathed the new free air of democracy, which was then beginning to percolate even into such remote places, were inclined to laugh at their pretensions. 'We don't want nothin' from they,' they would say, 'and us shouldn't get it if us did. Let the old gal stay at home and see that her own tea-caddy's kept locked up, not come nosing round here axin' how many spoonsful we puts in ours.'

Mrs Bracewell knew nothing of such speeches. If she had, she would probably have thought the world – her world – was coming to an end. Which it was. In her girlhood under the Regency, she had been taught her duty towards the cottagers, and that included reproving them for their wasteful habits. It also included certain charities. She was generous out of all proportion to her small means; keeping two aged women pensioners, doling out soup in the winter to those she called 'the deserving poor', and entertaining the school-children to a tea and a magic-lantern entertainment every Christmas.

Meanwhile, as the old servants in and about her house died or were pensioned off, they were not replaced. By the middle of the 'eighties only a cook and a house-parlourmaid sat down to meals in the vast servants' hall where a large staff had formerly feasted. Grass grew between the flagstones in the stable yard where generations of grooms and coachmen had hissed over the grooming of hunters and carriage horses, and the one old mare which drew her wagonette when she paid calls took a turn at drawing the lawn-mower, or even the plough, betweenwhiles.

As she got poorer, she got prouder, more overbearing in manner and more acid in tone, and the girls trembled when she came into school, especially Laura, who knew that her sewing would never pass that eagle eye without stern criticism. She would work slowly along the form, examining each garment, and exclaiming that the sewing was so badly done that she did not know what the world was coming to. Stitches were much too large; the wrong side of the work was not as well finished as the right side; buttonholes were bungled and tapes sewn on askew; and the feather-stitching looked as though a spider had crawled over the piece of work. But when she came to examine the work of one of the prize sewers her face would light up. 'Very neat! Exquisitely sewn!' she would say, and have the stitching passed round the class as an example.

The schoolmistress attended at her elbow, overawed, like the children, but trying to appear at her ease. Miss Holmes, in her day, had called Mrs Bracewell 'ma'am' and sketched a slight curtsey as she held open the door for her. The later mistresses called her 'Mrs Bracewell', but not very frequently or with conviction.

At that time the position of a village schoolmistress was a trying one socially. Perhaps it is still trying in some places, for it is not many years ago that the President of a Women's Institute wrote: 'We are very democratic here. Our Committee consists of three ladies, three women, and the village schoolmistress.' That mistress, though neither lady nor woman, was still placed. In the 'eighties the schoolmistress was so nearly a new institution that a vicar's wife, in a real dilemma said: 'I should like to ask Miss So-and-So to tea; but do I ask her to kitchen or dining-room tea?'

Miss Holmes had settled that question herself when she became engaged to the squire's gardener. Miss Shepherd was more ambitious socially. Indeed, democratic as she was in theory, the dear soul was in practice a little snobbish. She courted the notice of the betters, though, she was wont to declare, they were only betters when they were better men and women. An invitation to tea at the Rectory was, to her, something to be fished for before and talked about afterwards, and when the daughter of a poor, but aristocratic local family set up as a music teacher, Miss Shepherd at once decided to learn the violin.

Laura was once the delighted witness of a funny little display of this weakness. It was the day of the school treat at the Manor House, and the children had met at the school and were being marched, two and two, through garden and shrubbery paths to the back door. Other guests, such as the curate, the doctor's widow, and the daughters of the rich farmer, who were to have tea in the drawing-room while the children feasted in the servants' hall, were going to the front door.

Now, Miss Holmes had always marched right in with her pupils and sipped her own tea and nibbled her cake between attending to their wants; but Miss Shepherd was more ambitious. When the procession reached a point where the shrubbery path crossed the main drive which led to the front door, she paused and considered; then said, 'I think I will go to the front door, dears. I want to see how well you can behave without me,' and off she branched up the drive in her best brown frock, tight little velvet hip-length jacket, and long fur boa bound like a snake round her neck, followed by at least one pair of cynically smiling little eyes.

She had the satisfaction of ringing the front-door bell and drinking tea in the drawing-room; but it was a short-lived triumph. In a very few minutes she was out in the servants' hall, passing bread and butter to her charges and whispering to one of her monitors that 'Dear Mrs Bracewell gave me my tea first, because, as she said, she knew I was anxious to get back to my children.'

Squire himself called at the school once a year; but nobody felt nervous when his red, jovial face appeared in the doorway, and

smiles broke out all around when he told his errand. He was
arranging a concert, to take place in the schoolroom, and would like
some of the children to sing. He took his responsibilities less seriously
than his mother did hers; spending most of his days roaming the
fields and spinneys with a gun under his arm and a brace of spaniels
at his heels, leaving her to manage house and gardens and what was
left of the family estate, as well as to support the family dignity. His
one indoor accomplishment was playing the banjo and singing
Negro songs. He had trained a few of the village youths to support
him in his Negro Minstrel Troupe, which always formed the back-
bone of the annual concert programme. A few other items were
contributed by his and his mother's friends and the gaps were filled
up by the schoolchildren.

So, after his visit, the school became animated. What should be
sung and who should sing it were the questions of the moment.
Finally, it was arranged that everybody should sing something. Even
Laura, who had neither voice nor ear for music, was to join in the
communal songs.

They sang, very badly, mildly pretty spring and Nature songs
from the *School Song Book*, such as they had sung the year before
and the year before that, some of them actually the same songs.
One year Miss Shepherd thought it 'would be nice' to sing a Primrose
League song to 'please Squire'. One verse ran:

> O come, ye Tories, all unite
> To bear the Primrose badge with might,
> And work and hope and strive and fight
> And pray may God defend the right.

When Laura's father heard this, he wrote a stiffly polite little note
to the mistress, saying that, as a Liberal of pronounced views, he
could not allow a child of his to sing such a song. Laura did not tell
him she had already been asked to sing very softly, not to put the
other singers out of tune. 'Just move your lips, dear,' the mistress
had said. Laura, in fact, was to have gone on to help dress the stage,
where all the girls who were taking part in the programme sat in a

row throughout the performance, forming a background for the soloists. That year she had the pleasure of sitting among the audience and hearing the criticism, as well as seeing the stage and listening to the programme. A good three-pennyworth ('children, half-price').

When the great night came, the whole population of the neighbourhood assembled, for it was the only public entertainment of the year. Squire and his Negro Minstrel Troupe was the great attraction. They went on, dressed in red and blue, their hands and faces blackened with burnt cork, and rattled their bones and cracked their jokes and sang such songs as:

> A friend of Darwin's came to me,
> A million years ago said he
> You had a tail and no great toe.
> I answered him, 'That may be so,
> But I've one now, I'll let you know –
> G-r-r-r-r-r out!'

Very few in the audience had heard of Darwin or his theory; but they all knew what 'G-R-R-R-R-R out!' meant, especially when emphasized by a kick on Tom Binns's backside by Squire's boot. The schoolroom rocked. 'I pretty well busted me sides wi' laughin',' they said afterwards.

After the applause had died down, a little bell would ring and a robust curate from a neighbouring village would announce the next item. Most of these were piano pieces, played singly, or as duets, by young ladies in white evening frocks, cut in a modest V at the neck, and white kid gloves reaching to the elbow. As their contributions to the programme were announced, they would rise from the front seat in the audience; a gentleman – two gentlemen – would spring forward, and between them hand the fair performer up the three shallow steps which led to the platform and hand her over to yet another gentleman, who led her to the piano and held her gloves and fan and turned her music pages.

'Tinkle, tinkle, tinkle' went the piano, and 'Warble, warble, warble' went the voices, as the performers worked their conscientious way through the show piano pieces and popular drawing-room ballads of the moment. Each performer was greeted and dismissed with a round of applause, which served the double purpose of encouraging the singer and relieving the boredom of the audience. Youths and young men in the back seats would sometimes carry this too far, drowning the programme with their stamping and shouting until they had to be reprimanded, when they would subside sulkily, complaining, 'Us've paid our sixpences, ain't we?'

Once, when the athletic curate sang 'You should see Me dance the Polka' he accompanied the song with such violent action that he polked part of the platform down and left the double row of schoolgirls hanging in the air on the backmost planks while he finished his song on the floor:

> You should see me dance the polka,
>   You should see me cover the ground,
> You should see my coat tails flying
>   As I dance my way around.

Edmund and Laura had the words and actions by heart, if not the tune, and polked that night in their mother's bedroom until they woke up the baby and were slapped. A sad ending to an evening of pure bliss.

When the schoolchildren on the platform rose and came forward to sing they, also, were applauded; but their performance and those of the young ladies were but the lettuce in the salad; all the flavour was in the comic items.

Now, Miss Shepherd was a poet, and had several times turned out a neat verse to supplement those of a song she considered too short. One year she took the National Anthem in hand and added a verse. It ran:

> May every village school
> Uphold Victoria's rule,
> To Church and State be true,
> God save the Queen.

Which pleased Squire so much that he talked of sending it to the newspapers.

Going home with lanterns swinging down the long dark road, the groups would discuss the evening's entertainment. Squire's Minstrels and the curate's songs were always unreservedly praised and the young ladies' performances were tolerated, although, often, a man would complain, 'I don't know if I be goin' deaf, or what; but I couldn't hear a dommed word any of 'em said.' As to the school-children's efforts, criticism was applied more to how they looked than to their musical performance. Those who had scuffled or giggled, or even blushed, heard of it from their parents, while such remarks were frequent as: 'Got up to kill, that young Mary Ann Parish was!' or 'I declare I could see the hem o' young Rose Mitchell's breeches showin',' or 'That Em Tuffrey made a poor show. Whatever wer' her mother a thinkin' on?' Taken all in all, they enjoyed the concert almost as much as their grandchildren enjoy the cinema.

XIII

May Day

After the excitement of the concert came the long winter months, when snowstorms left patches on the ploughed fields, like scrapings of sauce on left-over pieces of Christmas pudding, until the rains came and washed them away and the children, carrying old umbrellas to school, had them turned inside out by the wind, and cottage chimneys smoked and washing had to be dried indoors. But at last came spring and spring brought May Day, the greatest day in the year from the children's point of view.

The May garland was all that survived there of the old May Day festivities. The maypole and the May games and May dances in which whole parishes had joined had long been forgotten. Beyond giving flowers for the garland and pointing out how things should be done and telling how they had been done in their own young days, the older people took no part in the revels.

For the children as the day approached all hardships were forgotten and troubles melted away. The only thing that mattered was the weather. 'Will it be fine?' was the constant question, and many an aged eye was turned skyward in response to read the signs of wind and cloud. Fortunately, it was always reasonably fine. Showers there were, of course, at that season, but never a May Day of hopelessly drenching rain, and the May garland was carried in procession every year throughout the 'eighties.

The garland was made, or 'dressed', in the schoolroom. Formerly it had been dressed out of doors, or in one of the cottages, or in someone's barn; but dressed it had been and probably in much the same fashion for countless generations.

The foundation of the garland was a light wooden framework of uprights supporting graduated hoops, forming a bell-shaped structure about four feet high. This frame was covered with flowers, bunched and set closely, after the manner of wreath-making.

On the last morning of April the children would come to school with bunches, baskets, arms and pinafores full of flowers – every blossom they could find in the fields and hedges or beg from parents and neighbours. On the previous Sunday some of the bigger boys would have walked six or eight miles to a distant wood where primroses grew. These, with violets from the hedgerows, cowslips from the meadows, and wallflowers, oxlips, and sprays of pale red flowering currant from the cottage gardens formed the main supply. A sweetbriar hedge in the schoolmistress's garden furnished unlimited greenery.

Piled on desks, table, and floor, this supply appeared inexhaustible; but the garland was large, and as the work of dressing it proceeded, it soon became plain that the present stock wouldn't 'hardly go nowheres', as the children said. So foraging parties were sent out, one to the Rectory, another to Squire's, and others to outlying farm-houses and cottages. All returned loaded, for even the most miserly and garden-proud gave liberally to the garland. In time the wooden frame was covered, even if there had to be solid greenery to fill up at the back, out of sight. Then the "Top-knot', consisting of a bunch of crown imperial, yellow and brown, was added to crown the whole, and the fragrant, bowering structure was sprinkled with water and set aside for the night.

While the garland was being dressed, an older girl, perhaps the May Queen herself, would be busy in a corner making the crown. This always had to be a daisy crown; but, meadow daisies being considered too common, and also possessing insufficient staying power, garden daisies, white and red, were used, with a background of dark, glossy, evergreen leaves.

The May Queen had been chosen weeks beforehand. She was supposed to be either the prettiest or the most popular girl in the parish; but it was more often a case of self-election by the strongest willed or of taking turns: 'You choose me this year and I'll choose you next.' However elected, the queens had a strong resemblance to each other, being stout-limbed, rosy-cheeked maidens of ten or eleven, with great manes of dark hair frizzed out to support the crown becomingly.

The final touches were given the garland when the children assembled at six o'clock on May Day morning. Then a large china doll in a blue frock was brought forth from the depths of the school needlework chest and arranged in a sitting position on a little ledge in the centre front of the garland. This doll was known as 'the lady', and a doll of some kind was considered essential. Even in those parishes where the garland had degenerated into a shabby nosegay carried aloft at the top of a stick, some dollish image was mixed in with the flowers. The attitude of the children to the lady is interesting. It was understood that the garland was her garland, carried in her honour. The lady must never be roughly handled. If the garland turned turtle, as it was apt to do later in the day, when the road was rough and the bearers were growing weary, the first question was always, 'Is the lady all right?' (Is it possible that the lady was once 'Our Lady', she having in her turn, perhaps, replaced an earlier effigy of some pagan spirit of the newly decked earth?)

The lady comfortably settled in front of the garland, a large white muslin veil or skirt, obviously borrowed from a Victorian dressing-table, was draped over the whole to act as drop-scene and sunshade combined. Then a broomstick was inserted between the hoops for carrying purposes.

All the children in the parish between the ages of seven and eleven were by this time assembled, those girls who possessed them wearing white or light coloured frocks, irrespective of the temperature, and girls and boys alike decked out with bright ribbon knots and bows and sashes, those of the boys worn crosswise over one shoulder. The queen wore her daisy crown with a white veil thrown over it, and the other girls who could procure them also wore white veils. White gloves were traditional, but could seldom be obtained. A pair would sometimes be found for the queen, always many sizes too large; but the empty finger-ends came in handy to suck in a bashful mood when later on, the kissing began.

The procession then formed. It was as follows:

Boy with flag.   Girl with money box.
THE GARLAND with two bearers.
King and queen.
Two maids of honour.
Lord and Lady.
Two maids of honour.
Footman and footman's lady.
Rank and file, walking in twos.
Girl known as 'Mother'.   Boy called 'Ragman'.

The 'Mother' was one of the most dependable of the older girls, who was made responsible for the behaviour of the garlanders. She carried a large, old-fashioned, double-lidded marketing basket over her arm, containing the lunches of the principal actors. The boy called 'Ragman' carried the coats, brought in case of rain, but seldom worn, even during a shower, lest by their poverty and shabbiness they should disgrace the festive attire.

The procession stepped out briskly. Mothers waved and implored their offspring to behave well; some of the little ones left behind lifted up their voices and wept; old people came to cottage gates and said that, though well enough, this year's procession was poor compared to some they had seen. But the garlanders paid no heed; they had their feet on the road at last and vowed they would not turn back now, 'not if it rained cats and dogs'.

The first stop was at the Rectory, where the garland was planted before the front door and the shrill little voices struck up, shyly at first, but gathering confidence as they went on:

A bunch of may I have brought you
    And at your door it stands.
It is but a sprout, but it's well put about
    By the Lord Almighty's hands.

God bless the master of this house
    God bless the mistress too,
And all the little children
    That round the table go.

And now I've sung my short little song
   I must no longer stay.
God bless you all, both great and small,
   And send you a happy May Day.

During the singing of this the Rector's face, wearing its mildest expression, and bedaubed with shaving lather, for it was only as yet seven o'clock, would appear at an upper window and nod approval and admiration of the garland. His daughter would be down and at the door, and for her the veil was lifted and the glory of the garland revealed. She would look, touch and smell, then slip a silver coin into the money-box, and the procession would move on towards Squire's.

There, the lady of the house would bow haughty approval and if there were visiting grandchildren the lady would be detached from the garland and held up to their nursery window to be admired. Then Squire himself would appear in the stable doorway with a brace of sniffing, suspicious spaniels at his heels. 'How many are there of you?' he would call. 'Twenty-seven? Well, here's a five-bob bit for you. Don't quarrel over it. Now let's have a song.'

'Not "A Bunch of May",' the girl called Mother would whisper, impressed by the five-shilling piece; 'not that old-fashioned thing. Something newer,' and something newer, though still not very new, would be selected. Perhaps it would be:

All hail gentle spring
   With thy sunshine and showers,
And welcome the sweet buds
   That burst in the bowers;
Again we rejoice as thy light step and free
Bring leaves to the woodland and flowers to the bee,
Bounding, bounding, bounding, bounding,
   Joyful and gay,
Light and airy, like a fairy
   Come, come away.

Or it might be:

> Come see our new garland, so green and so gay;
> 'Tis the firstfruits of spring and the glory of May.
> Here are cowslips and daisies and hyacinths blue,
> Here are buttercups bright and anemones too.

During the singing of the latter song, as each flower was mentioned, a specimen bloom would be pointed to in the garland. It was always a point of honour to have at least one of each named in the several verses; though the hawthorn was always a difficulty, for in the south midlands May's own flower seldom opens before the middle of that month. However, there was always at least one knot of tight green flower buds.

After becoming duty had been paid to the Rectory and Big House, the farm-house and cottages were visited; then the little procession set out along narrow, winding country roads, with tall hedges of blackthorn and bursting leaf-buds on either side, to make its seven-mile circuit. In those days there were no motors to dodge and there was very little other traffic; just a farm cart here and there, or the baker's white-tilted van, or a governess car with nurses and children out for their airing. Sometimes the garlanders would forsake the road for stiles and footpaths across buttercup meadows, or go through parks and gardens to call at some big house or secluded farmstead.

In the ordinary course, country children of that day seldom went beyond their own parish bounds, and this long trek opened up new country to most of them. There was a delightful element of exploration about it. New short cuts would be tried, one year through a wood, another past the fishponds, or across such and such a paddock, where there might, or might not, be a bull. On one pond they passed sailed a solitary swan; on the terrace before one mansion peacocks spread their tails in the sun; the ram which pumped the water to one house mystified them with its subterranean thudding. There were often showers, and to Laura, looking back after fifty years, the whole scene would melt into a blur of wet greenery, with rainbows and cuckoo-calls and, overpowering all other impressions, the wet wallflower and primrose scent of the May garland.

Sometimes on the road a similar procession from another village came into view; but never one with so magnificent a garland. Some of them, indeed, had nothing worth calling a garland at all; only nosegays tied mopwise on sticks. No lord and lady, no king and queen; only a rabble begging with money-boxes. Were the Fordlow and Lark Rise folks sorry for them? No. They stuck out their tongues, and, forgetting their pretty May songs, yelled:

> Old Hardwick skags!
> Come to Fordlow to pick up rags
> To mend their mothers' pudding-bags,
> Yah! Yah!

and the rival troop retaliated in the same strain.

At the front-door calls, the queen and her retinue stood demurely behind the garland and helped with the singing, unless Her Majesty was called forward to have her crown inspected and admired. It was at the back doors of large houses that the fun began. In country houses at that date troops of servants were kept, and the May Day procession would find the courtyard crowded with house-maids and kitchen-maids, dairy-maids and laundry-maids, footmen, grooms, coachmen, and gardeners. The songs were sung, the garland was admired; then, to a chorus of laughter, teasing and urging, one Maid of Honour snatched the cap from the King's head, the other raised the Queen's veil, and a shy, sheepish boy pecked at his companion's rosy cheek, to the huge delight of the beholders.

'Again! Again!' a dozen voices would cry and the kissing was repeated until the royal couple turned sulky and refused to kiss any more, even when offered a penny a kiss. Then the lord saluted his lady and the footman the footman's lady (this couple had probably been introduced in compliment to such patrons), and the money-box was handed round and began to grow heavy with pence.

The menservants, with their respectable side-whiskers, the maids in their little flat caps like crocheted mats on their smoothly parted hair, and their long, billowing lilac or pink print gowns, and the children in their ribbon-decked poverty, alike belong to a bygone order of things. The boys pulled forelocks and the girls dropped curtseys to the upper servants, for they came next in importance to 'the gentry'. Some of them really belonged to a class which would not be found in service today; for at that time there was little hospital nursing, teaching, typing, or shop work to engage the daughters of small farmers, small shopkeepers, innkeepers and farm bailiffs. Most of them had either to go out to service or remain at home.

After the mansion, there were the steward's, the head gardener's and the stud-groom's houses to visit with the garland; then on through gardens and park and woods and fields to the next stopping-place. Things did not always go smoothly. Feet got tired, especially when boots did not fit properly or were worn thin. Squabbles broke out among the boys and sometimes had to be settled by a fight. Often a heavy shower would send the whole party packing under trees for shelter, with the unveiled garland freshening outside in the rain; or some irate gamekeeper would turn the procession back from a short cut, adding miles to the way. But these were slight drawbacks to happiness on a day as near to perfection as anything can be in human life.

There came a point in the circuit when faces were turned towards home, instead of away from it; and at last, at long last, the lights in the Lark Rise windows shone clear through the spring twilight. The great day was over, for ever, as it seemed, for at ten years old a year seems as long as a century. Still, there was the May money to be shared out in school the next morning, and the lady to be stroked before being put back in her box, and the flowers which had survived to be put in water: even tomorrow would not be quite a common day. So the last waking thoughts blended with dreams of swans and peacocks and footmen and sore feet and fat cooks with pink faces wearing daisy crowns which turned into pure gold, then melted away.

XIV

To Church on Sunday

If the Lark Rise people had been asked their religion, the answer of nine out of ten would have been 'Church of England', for practically all of them were christened, married, and buried as such, although, in adult life, few went to church between the baptisms of their offspring. The children were shepherded there after Sunday school and about a dozen of their elders attended regularly; the rest stayed at home, the women cooking and nursing, and the men, after an elaborate Sunday toilet, which included shaving and cutting each other's hair and much puffing and splashing with buckets of water, but stopped short before lacing up boots or putting on a collar and tie, spent the rest of the day eating, sleeping, reading the newspaper, and strolling round to see how their neighbours' pigs and gardens were looking.

There were a few keener spirits. The family at the inn was Catholic and was up and off to early Mass in the next village before others had turned over in bed for an extra Sunday morning snooze. There were also three Methodist families which met in one of their cottages on Sunday evenings for prayer and praise; but most of these attended church as well, thus earning for themselves the name of 'Devil dodgers'.

Every Sunday, morning and afternoon, the two cracked, flat-toned bells at the church in the mother village called the faithful to worship. *Ding-dong, Ding-dong, Ding-dong*, they went, and, when they heard them, the hamlet churchgoers hurried across fields and over stiles, for the Parish Clerk was always threatening to lock the church door when the bells stopped and those outside might stop outside for all he cared.

With the Fordlow cottagers, the Squire's and farmer's families and maids, the Rectory people and the hamlet contingent, the congregation averaged about thirty. Even with this small number, the church was fairly well filled, for it was a tiny place, about the size of a barn, with nave and chancel only, no side aisles. The interior was almost as bare as a barn, with its grey, roughcast walls, plain-glass windows, and flagstone floor. The cold, damp, earthy odour common to old and unheated churches pervaded the atmosphere, with occasional whiffs of a more unpleasant nature said to proceed from the stacks of mouldering bones in the vault beneath. Who had been buried there, or when, was unknown, for, excepting one ancient and mutilated brass in the wall by the font, there were but two memorial tablets, both of comparatively recent date. The church, like the village, was old and forgotten, and those buried in the vault, who must have once been people of importance, had not left even a name. Only the stained-glass window over the altar, glowing jewel-like amidst the cold greyness, the broken piscina within the altar rails, and a tall broken shaft of what had been a cross in the churchyard, remained to witness mutely to what once had been.

The Squire's and clergyman's families had pews in the chancel, with backs to the wall on either side, and between them stood two long benches for the schoolchildren, well under the eyes of authority. Below the steps down into the nave stood the harmonium, played by the clergyman's daughter, and round it was ranged the choir of small schoolgirls. Then came the rank and file of the congregation, nicely graded, with the farmer's family in the front row, then the Squire's gardener and coachman, the schoolmistress, the maid-servants, and the cottagers, with the Parish Clerk at the back to keep order.

'Clerk Tom', as he was called, was an important man in the parish. Not only did he dig the graves, record the banns of marriage, take the chill off the water for winter baptisms, and stoke the coke stove which stood in the nave at the end of his seat; but he also took an active and official part in the services. It was his duty to lead the congregation in the responses and to intone the 'Amens'. The psalms were not sung or chanted, but read, verse and verse about, by the Rector and people, and in these especially Tom's voice so drowned the subdued murmur of his fellow worshippers that it sounded like a duet between him and the clergyman – a duet in which Tom won easily, for his much louder voice would often trip up the Rector before he had quite finished his portion, while he prolonged his own final syllables at will.

The afternoon service, with not a prayer left out or a creed spared, seemed to the children everlasting. The schoolchildren, under the stern eye of the Manor House, dared not so much as wriggle; they sat in their stiff, stuffy, best clothes, their stomachs lined with heavy Sunday dinner, in a kind of waking doze, through which Tom's 'Amens' rang like a bell and the Rector's voice buzzed beelike. Only on the rare occasions when a bat fluttered down from the roof, or a butterfly drifted in at a window, or the Rector's little fox terrier looked in at the door and sidled up the nave, was the tedium lightened.

Edmund and Laura, alone in their grandfather's seat, modestly situated exactly half-way down the nave, were more fortunate, for they sat opposite the church door and, in summer, when it was left open, they could at least watch the birds and the bees and the butterflies crossing the opening and the breezes shaking the boughs of the trees and ruffling the long grass on the graves. It was interesting, too, to observe some woman in the congregation fussing with her back hair, or a man easing his tight collar, or old Dave Pridham, who had a bad bunion, shuffling off a shoe before the sermon began, with one eye all the time upon the clergyman; or to note how closely together some newly married couple were sitting, or to see Clerk Tom's young wife suckling her baby. She wore a fur tippet in winter and her breast hung like a white heather bell between the soft blackness until it was covered up with a white handkerchief, 'for modesty'.

Mr Ellison in the pulpit was the Mr Ellison of the Scripture lessons, plus a white surplice. To him, his congregation were but children of a larger growth, and he preached as he taught. A favourite theme was the duty of regular churchgoing. He would hammer away at that for forty-five minutes, never seeming to realize that he was preaching to the absent, that all those present were regular attendants, and that the stray sheep of his flock were snoring upon their beds a mile and a half away.

Another favourite subject was the supreme rightness of the social order as it then existed. God, in His infinite wisdom, had appointed a place for every man, woman, and child on this earth and it was their bounden duty to remain contentedly in their niches. A gentleman might seem to some of his listeners to have a pleasant, easy life, compared to theirs at field labour; but he had his duties and responsibilities, which would be far beyond their capabilities. He had to pay taxes, sit on the Bench of Magistrates, oversee his estate, and keep up his position by entertaining. Could they do these things? No. Of course they could not; and he did not suppose that a gentleman could cut as straight a furrow or mow or thatch a rick as expertly as they could. So let them be thankful and rejoice in their physical strength and the bounty of the farmer, who found them work on his land and paid them wages with his money.

Less frequently, he would preach eternal punishment for sin, and touch, more lightly, upon the bliss reserved for those who worked hard, were contented with their lot and showed proper respect to their superiors. The Holy Name was seldom mentioned, nor were human griefs or joys, or the kindly human feelings which bind a man to man. It was not religion he preached, but a narrow code of ethics, imposed from above upon the lower orders, which, even in those days, was out of date.

Once and once only did inspiration move him. It was the Sunday after the polling for the General Election of 1886, and he had begun preaching one of his usual sermons on the duty to social superiors, when, suddenly something, perhaps the memory of the events of the past week, seemed to boil up within him. Flushed with anger – 'righteous anger', he would have called it – and his frosty blue eyes flashing like swords, he cast himself forward across the ledge of his pulpit and roared: 'There are some among you who have lately forgotten that duty, and we know the cause, the *bloody* cause!'

Laura shivered. Bad language in church! and from the Rector!

But, later in life, she liked to think that she had lived early enough to have heard a mild and orthodox Liberalism denounced from the pulpit as 'a bloody cause'. It lent her the dignity of an historical survival.

The sermon over, the people sprang to their feet like Jacks-in-a-box. With what gusto they sang the evening hymn, and how their lungs expanded and their tongues wagged as they poured out of the churchyard! Not that they resented anything that was said in the Rector's sermons. They did not listen to them. After the Bloody Cause sermon Laura tried to find out how her elders had reacted to it; but all she could learn was: 'I seems to have lost the thread just then,' or, more frankly, 'I must've been nodding'; the most she could get was one woman's, 'My! didn't th' old parson get worked up today!'

Some of them went to church to show off their best clothes and to see and criticize those of their neighbours; some because they loved to hear their own voices raised in the hymns, or because churchgoing qualified them for the Christmas blankets and coals; and a few to worship. There was at least one saint and mystic in that parish and there were several good Christian men and women, but the majority regarded religion as something proper to extreme old age, for which they themselves had as yet no use.

'About time he wer' thinkin' about his latter end,' they would say of one who showed levity when his head and beard were white, or of anybody who was ill or afflicted. Once a hunchback from another village came to a pig feast and distinguished himself by getting drunk and using bad language; and, because he was a cripple, his conduct was looked upon with horror. Laura's mother was distressed when she heard about it. 'To think of a poor afflicted creature like that cursing and swearing,' she sighed. 'Terrible! Terrible!' and when Edmund, then about ten, looked up from his book and said calmly, 'I should think if anybody's got a right to swear it's a man with a back like that,' she told him he was nearly as bad to say such a thing.

The Catholic minority at the inn was treated with respect, for a landlord could do no wrong, especially the landlord of a free house where such excellent beer was on tap. On Catholicism at large, the Lark Rise people looked with contemptuous intolerance, for they regarded it as a kind of heathenism, and what excuse could there be for that in a Christian country? When, early in life, the end house children asked what Roman Catholics were, they were told they were 'folks as prays to images', and further inquiries elicited the information that they also worshipped the Pope, a bad old man, some said in league with the Devil. Their genuflexions in church and their 'playin' wi' beads' were described as 'monkey tricks'. People who openly said they had no use for religion themselves became quite heated when the Catholics were mentioned. Yet the children's grandfather, when the sound of the Angelus bell was borne on the wind from the chapel in the next village, would take off his hat and, after a moment's silence, murmur, 'In my Father's house are many mansions.' It was all very puzzling.

Later on, when they came to associate more with the other children, on the way to Sunday school they would see horses and traps loaded with families from many miles around on their way to the Catholic church in the next village. 'There go the old Catholics!' the children would cry, and run after the vehicles shouting: 'Old Catholics! Old lick the cats!' until they had to fall behind for want of breath. Sometimes a lady in one of the high dogcarts would smile at them forbearingly, otherwise no notice was taken.

The horses and traps were followed at a distance by the young men and big boys of the families on foot. Always late in starting, yet always in time for the service, how they legged it! The children took good care not to call out after them, for they knew, whatever their haste, the boy Catholics would have time to turn back and cuff them. It had happened before. So they let them get on for quite a distance before they started to mock their gait and recite in a snuffling sing-song:

> 'O dear Father, I've come to confess.'
> 'Well, my child, and what have you done?'
> 'O dear Father, I've killed the cat.'
> 'Well, my child, and what about that?'
> 'O dear Father, what shall I do?'
> 'You kiss me and I'll kiss you.'

a gem which had probably a political origin, for the seeds of their ignorant bigotry must have been sown at some time. Yet, strange to say, some of those very children still said by way of a prayer when they went to bed:

> Matthew, Mark, Luke and John,
> Bless the bed where I lie on.
> Four corners have I to my bed;
> At them four angels nightly spread.
> One to watch and one to pray
> And one to take my soul away.

At that time many words, phrases, and shreds of customs persisted which faded out before the end of the century. When Laura was a child, some of the older mothers and the grandmothers still threatened naughty children with the name of Cromwell. 'If you ain't a good gal, old Oliver Crummell'll have 'ee!' they would say, or 'Here comes old Crummell!' just as the mothers of southern England threatened their children with Napoleon. Napoleon was forgotten there; being far from the sea-coast, such places had never known the fear of invasion. But the armies of the Civil War had fought ten miles to the eastward, and the name still lingered.

The Methodists were a class apart. Provided they did not attempt to convert others, religion in them was tolerated. Every Sunday evening they held a service in one of their cottages, and, whenever she could obtain permission at home, it was Laura's delight to attend. This was not because the service appealed to her; she really preferred the church service; but because Sunday evening at home was a trying time, with the whole family huddled round the fire and Father reading and no one allowed to speak and barely to move.

Permission was hard to get, for her father did not approve of 'the ranters'; nor did he like Laura to be out after dark. But one time out of four or five when she asked, he would grunt and nod, and she would dash off before her mother could raise any objection. Sometimes Edmund would follow her, and they would seat themselves on one of the hard, white-scrubbed benches in the meeting

house, prepared to hear all that was to be heard and see all that was
to be seen.

The first thing that would have struck any one less accustomed
to the place was its marvellous cleanliness. The cottage walls were
whitewashed and always fresh and clean. The everyday furniture
had been carried out to the barn to make way for the long white
wooden benches, and before the window with its drawn white blind
stood a table covered with a linen cloth, on which were the lamp, a
large Bible, and a glass of water for the visiting preacher, whose seat
was behind it. Only the clock and a pair of red china dogs on the
mantelpiece remained to show that on other days people lived and
cooked and ate in the room. A bright fire always glowed in the grate
and there was a smell compounded of lavender, lamp-oil, and packed
humanity.

The man of the house stood in the doorway to welcome each
arrival with a handshake and a whispered 'God bless you!' His wife,
a small woman with a slight spinal curvature which thrust her head
forward and gave her a resemblance to an amiable-looking frog,
smiled her welcome from her seat near the fireplace. In twos and
threes, the brethren filed in and took their accustomed places on
the hard, backless benches. With them came a few neighbours, not
of their community, but glad to have somewhere to go, especially
on wet or cold Sundays.

In the dim lamplight dark Sunday suits and sad-coloured Sunday
gowns massed together in a dark huddle against the speckless
background, and out of it here and there eyes and cheeks caught
the light as the brethren smiled their greetings to each other.

If the visiting preacher happened to be late, which he often was
with a long distance to cover on foot, the host would give out a
hymn from Sankey and Moody's Hymn-Book, which would be sung
without musical accompaniment to one of the droning, long-drawn-
out tunes peculiar to the community. At other times one of the
brethren would break into extempore prayer, in the course of which
he would retail the week's news so far as it affected the gathering,
prefacing each statement with 'Thou knowest', or 'As thou knowest,
Lord'. It amused Laura and Edmund to hear old Mr Barker telling

God that it had not rained for a fortnight and that his carrot bed was getting 'mortal dry'; or that swine fever had broken out at a farm four miles away and that his own pig didn't seem 'no great shakes'; or that somebody had mangled his wrist in a turnip cutter and had come out of hospital, but found it still stiff; for, as they said to each other afterwards, God must know already, as He knew everything. But these one-sided conversations with the Deity were conducted in a spirit of simple faith. 'Cast your care upon Him' was a text they loved and took literally. To them God was a loving Father who loved to listen to His children's confidences. No trouble was too small to bring to 'the Mercy Seat'.

Sometimes a brother or a sister would stand up to 'testify', and then the children opened their eyes and ears, for a misspent youth was the conventional prelude to conversion and who knew what exciting transgressions might not be revealed. Most of them did not amount to much. One would say that before he 'found the Lord' he had been 'a regular beastly drunkard'; but it turned out that he had only taken a pint too much once or twice at a village feast; another claimed to have been a desperate poacher, 'a wild, lawless sort o' chap'; he had snared an occasional rabbit. A sister confessed that in her youth she had not only taken a delight in decking out her vile body, forgetting that it was only the worm that perishes; but, worse still, she had imperilled her immortal soul by dancing on the green at feasts and club outings, keeping it up on one occasion until midnight.

Such mild sins were not in themselves exciting, for plenty of people were still doing such things and they could be observed at first hand; but they were described with such a wealth of detail and with such self-condemnation that the listener was for the moment persuaded that he or she was gazing on the chief of sinners. One man, especially, claimed that pre-eminence. 'I wer' the chief of sinners,' he would cry; 'a real bad lot, a Devil's disciple. Cursing and swearing, drinking and drabbing there were nothing bad as I didn't do. Why, would you believe it, in my sinful pride, I sinned against the Holy Ghost. Aye, that I did,' and the awed silence would be broken by the groans and 'God have mercy's of his hearers while he looked round to observe the effect of his confession before relating how he 'came to the Lord'.

No doubt the second part of his discourse was more edifying than the first but the children never listened to it; they were too engrossed in speculations as to the exact nature of his sin against the Holy Ghost, and wondering if he were really as thoroughly saved as he thought himself; for, after all, was not that sin unpardonable? He might yet burn in hell. Terrible yet fascinating thought!

But the chief interest centred in the travelling preacher, especially if he were a stranger who had not been there before. Would he preach the Word, or would he be one of those who rambled on for an hour or more, yet said nothing? Most of these men, who gave up their Sunday rest and walked miles to preach at the village meeting houses, were farm labourers or small shopkeepers. With a very few exceptions they were poor, uneducated men. 'The blind leading the blind,' Laura's father said of them. They may have been unenlightened in some respects, but some of them had gifts no education could have given. There was something fine about their discourses, as they raised their voices in rustic eloquence and testified to the cleansing power of 'the Blood', forgetting themselves and their own imperfections of speech in their ardour.

Others were less sincere, and some merely self-seeking *poseurs* who took to preaching as the only means of getting a little limelight shed on their undistinguished lives. One such was a young shop assistant from the market town, who came, stylishly dressed, with a bunch of violets in his buttonhole, smoothing his well-oiled hair with his hand and shaking clouds of scent from his large white handkerchief. He emphatically did not preach the Word. His perfume and buttonhole and pseudo-cultured accent so worked upon the brethren that, after he had gone, they for once forgot their rule of no criticism and exclaimed: 'Did you ever see such a la-de-da in all your draggings-up?'

Then there was the elderly man who chose for his text: 'I will sweep them off the face of the earth with the besom of destruction', and proceeded to take each word of his text as a heading. '*I* will sweep them off the face of the earth. I *will* sweep them off the face of the earth. I will *sweep* them off the face of the earth', and so on. By the time he had finished he had expounded the nature of God and justified His ways to man to his own satisfaction; but he made such a sad mess of it that the children's ears burned with shame for him.

Some managed to be sincere Christians and yet quicker of wit and lighter of hand. The host keeping the door one night was greeted by the arriving minister with 'I would rather be a doorkeeper in the house of my God,' and capped it with 'than dwell in the tents of the ungodly.'

Methodism, as known and practised there, was a poor people's religion, simple and crude; but its adherents brought to it more fervour than was shown by the church congregation, and appeared to obtain more comfort and support from it than the church could give. Their lives were exemplary.

Many in the hamlet who attended neither church nor chapel and said they had no use for religion, guided their lives by the light of a few homely precepts, such as 'Pay your way and fear nobody'; 'Right's right and wrong's no man's right'; 'Tell the truth and shame the devil', and 'Honesty is the best policy'.

Strict honesty was the policy of most of them; although there were a few who were said to 'find anything before 'tis lost' and to whom findings were keepings. Children were taught to 'Know it's a sin to steal a pin', and when they brought home some doubtful finding, saying they did not think it belonged to anybody, their mothers would say severely, 'You knowed it didn't belong to you, and what don't belong to you belongs to somebody else. So go and put it back where you found it, before I gets the stick to you.'

Liars were more detested than thieves. 'A liar did ought to have a good memory,' they would say, or, more witheringly, 'You can lock up from a thief, but you can't from a liar.' Any statement which departed in the least degree from plain fact was a lie; any one who ate a plum from an overhanging bough belonging to a neighbour's tree was a thief. It was a stark code in which black was black and white was white; there were no intermediate shades.

For the afflicted or bereaved there was ready sympathy. Had the custom of sending wreaths to funerals been general then, as it is today, they would certainly have subscribed their last half-penny for the purpose. But, at that time, the coffins of the country poor went flowerless to the grave, and all they could do to mark their respect was to gather outside the house of mourning and watch the clean scrubbed farm wagon which served as a hearse set out on its slow journey up the long, straight road, with the mourners following on foot behind. At such times the tears of the women spectators flowed freely; little children howled aloud in sympathy, and any man who happened to be near broke into extravagant praise of the departed. 'Never speak ill of the dead' was one of their maxims and they carried it to excess.

In illness or trouble they were ready to help and to give, to the small extent possible. Men who had been working all day would give up their night's rest to sit up with the ill or dying, and women would carry big bundles of bed-linen home to wash with their own.

They carried out St Paul's injunction to weep with those who weep; but when it came to rejoicing with those who rejoiced they were less ready. There was nothing they disliked more than seeing one of their number doing better or having more of anything than themselves. A mother whose child was awarded a prize at school, or whose daughter was doing better than ordinary in service, had to bear many pin-pricks of sarcasm, and if a specially devoted young married couple was mentioned, someone was bound to quote, 'My dear today'll be my devil tomorrow.' They were, in fact, poor fallible human beings.

The Rector visited each cottage in turn, working his way conscientiously round the hamlet from door to door, so that by the end of the year he had called upon everybody. When he tapped with his gold-headed cane at a cottage door there would come a sound of scuffling within, as unseemly objects were hustled out of sight, for the whisper would have gone round that he had been seen getting over the stile and his knock would have been recognized.

The women received him with respectful tolerance. A chair was dusted with an apron and the doing of housework or cooking was suspended while his hostess, seated uncomfortably on the edge of one of her own chairs, waited for him to open the conversation. When the weather had been discussed, the health of the inmates and absent children inquired about, and the progress of the pig and the prospect of the allotment crops, there came an awkward pause, during which both racked their brains to find something to talk about. There was nothing. The Rector never mentioned religion. That was looked upon in the parish as one of his chief virtues, but it limited the possible topics of conversation. Apart from his autocratic ideas, he was a kindly man, and he had come to pay a friendly call, hoping, no doubt, to get to know and to understand his parishioners better. But the gulf between them was too wide; neither he nor his hostess could bridge it. The kindly inquiries made and answered, they had nothing more to say to each other, and, after much 'ah-ing' and 'er-ing', he would rise from his seat, and be shown out with alacrity.

His daughter visited the hamlet more frequently. Any fine afternoon she might have been seen, gathering up her long, full skirts to mount the stile and tripping daintily between the allotment plots. As a widowed clergyman's only daughter, parochial visiting was, to her, a sacred duty; but she did not come in any district-visiting spirit, to criticize household management, or give unasked advice on the bringing up of children; hers, like her father's, were intended to be friendly calls. Considering her many kindnesses to the women, she might have been expected to be more popular than she was. None of them welcomed her visits. Some would lock their doors and pretend to be out; others would rattle their teacups when they saw her coming, hoping she would say, as she sometimes did, 'I hear you are at tea, so I won't come in.'

The only spoken complaint about her was that she talked too much. 'That Miss Ellison; she'd fair talk a donkey's hind leg off,' they would say; but that was a failing they tolerated in others, and one to which they were not averse in her, once she was installed in their best chair and some item of local gossip was being discussed.

Perhaps at the root of their unease in her presence was the subconscious feeling of contrast between her lot and theirs. Her neat little figure, well corseted in; her clear, high-pitched voice, good clothes, and faint scent of lily-of-the-valley perfume put them, in their workaday garb and all blowsed from their cooking or water-fetching, at a disadvantage.

She never suspected she was unwanted. On the contrary, she was most careful to visit each cottage in rotation, lest jealousy should arise. She would inquire about every member of the family in turn, listen to extracts from letters of daughters in service, sympathize with those who had tales of woe to tell, discuss everything that had happened since her last visit, and insist upon nursing the baby the while, and only smile good-naturedly when it wetted the front of her frock.

Her last visit of the day was always to the end house, where, over a cup of tea, she would become quite confidential. She and Laura's mother were 'Miss Margaret' and 'Emma' to each other, for they had known each other from birth, including the time when Emma was nurse to Miss Margaret's young friends at the neighbouring rectory.

Laura, supposed to be deep in her book, but really all ears, learnt that, surprisingly, Miss Ellison, the great Miss Ellison, had her troubles. She had a brother, reputed 'wild', in the parish, whom her father had forbidden the house, and much of their talk was about 'my brother Robert', or 'Master Bobbie', and the length of time since his last letter, and whether he had gone to Brazil, as he had said he should, or whether he was still in London. 'What I feel, Emma, is that he is such a boy, and you know what the world is – what perils –' Then Emma's cheerful rejoinder: 'Don't you worry yourself, Miss Margaret. He can look after himself all right, Master Bob can.'

Sometimes Emma would venture to admire something Miss Margaret was wearing. 'Excuse me, Miss Margaret, but that mauve muslin really does become you'; and Miss Ellison would look pleased. She had probably few compliments, for one of her type was not likely to be admired in those days of pink and white dollishness, although her clear, healthy pallor, with only the faintest flush of pink, her broad white brow, grey eyes, and dark hair waving back to the knot at her nape were at least distinguished looking. And she could not at that time have been more than thirty, although to Laura she seemed quite old, and the hamlet women called her an old maid.

Such a life as hers must have been is almost unimaginable now. Between playing the harmonium in church, teaching in Sunday school, ordering her father's meals and overseeing the maids, she must have spent hours doing needlework. Coarse, unattractive needlework, too, cross-over shawls and flannel petticoats for the old women, flannel shirts and long, thick knitted stockings for the old men, these, as well as the babies' print frocks, were all made by her own hands. Excepting a fortnight's visit a year to relatives, the only outing she was known to have was a weekly drive to the market town, shopping, in her father's high, yellow-wheeled dogcart, with the fat fox-terrier, Beppo, panting behind.

Half-way through the decade, the Rector began to feel the weight of his seventy odd years, and a succession of curates came to share his work and to provide new subjects of conversation for his parishioners. Several appeared and vanished without leaving any definite impression, beyond those of a new voice in church and an extraordinary bashfulness before the hamlet housewives; but two or three stayed longer and became, for a time, part of the life of the parish. There was Mr Dallas, who was said to be 'in a decline'. A pale, thin wraith of a man, who, in foggy weather wore a respirator, which looked like a heavy black moustache. Laura remembered him chiefly because when she was awarded the prize for Scripture he congratulated her – the first time she was ever congratulated upon anything in her life. On his next visit to her home he asked to see the prize prayer-book, and when she brought it, said: 'The binding is calf – my favourite binding – but it is very susceptible to damp. You must keep it in a room with a fire.' He was talking a language foreign to the children, who knew nothing of bindings or editions, a book to them being simply a book; but his expression and the gentle caressing way in which he turned the pages, told Laura that he, too, was a book-lover.

After he had left came Mr Alport; a big, fat-faced young man, who had been a medical student. He kept a small dispensary at his lodgings and it was his delight to doctor anyone who was ailing, both advice and medicine being gratis. As usual, supply created demand. Before he came, illness had been rare in the hamlet; now, suddenly, nearly everyone had something the matter with them. 'My pink pills', 'my little tablets', 'my mixture', and 'my lotion' became as common in conversation as potatoes or pig's food. People asked each other how their So-and-So was when they met, and, barely waiting for an answer, plunged into a description of their own symptoms.

Mr Alport complained to the children's father that the hamlet people were ignorant, and some of them certainly were, on the subjects in which he was enlightened. One woman particularly. On a visit to her house he noticed that one of her children, a tall, thin girl of eleven or twelve was looking rather pale. 'She is growing too fast, I expect,' he remarked. 'I must give her a tonic'; which he did. But she was not allowed to take it. 'No, she ain't a goin' to take that stuff,' her mother told the neighbours. 'He said she was growin' too tall, an' it's summat to stunt her. I shan't let a child o' mine be stunted. Oh, no!'

When he left the place and the supply of physic failed, all the invalids forgot their ailments. But he left one lasting memorial. Before his coming, the road round the Rise in winter had been a quagmire. 'Mud up to the hocks, and splashes up to the neck,' as they said. Mr Alport, after a few weeks' experience of mud-caked boots and mud-stained trouser-ends, decided to do something. So, perhaps in imitation of Ruskin's road-making at Oxford, he begged cartloads of stones from the farmer and, assisted by the hamlet youths and boys, began, on light evenings, to work with his own hands building a raised foot-path. Laura always remembered him best breaking stones and shovelling mud in his beautifully white shirt-sleeves and red braces, his clerical coat and collar hung on a bush, his big, smooth face damp with perspiration and his spectacles gleaming, as he urged on his fellow workers.

Neither of the curates mentioned ever spoke of religion out of church. Mr Dallas was far too shy, and Mr Alport was too busy ministering to peoples' bodies to have time to spare for their souls. Mr Marley, who came next, considered their souls his special care.

He was surely as strange a curate as ever came to a remote agricultural parish. An old man with a long, grey beard which he buttoned inside his long, close-fitting, black overcoat. Fervour and many fast days had worn away his flesh, and he had hollow cheeks and deep-set, dark eyes which glowed with the flame of fanaticism. He was a fanatic where his Church and his creed were concerned; otherwise he was the kindest and most gentle of men. Too good for this world, some of the women said when they came to know him.

He was what is now known as an Anglo-Catholic. Sunday after Sunday he preached 'One Catholic Apostolic Church' and 'our Holy Religion' to his congregation of rustics. But he did not stop at that: he dealt often with the underlying truths of religion, preaching the gospel of love and forgiveness of sins and the brotherhood of man. He was a wonderful preacher. No listener nodded or 'lost the thread' when he was in the pulpit, and though most of his congregation might not be able to grasp or agree with his doctrine, all responded to the love, sympathy, and sincerity of the preacher and every eye was upon him from his first word to his last. How such a preacher came to be in old age but a curate in a remote country parish is a mystery. His eloquence and fervour would have filled a city church.

The Rector by that time was bedridden, and a scholarly, easy-going, middle-aged son was deputizing for him; otherwise Mr Marley would have had less freedom in the church and parish. When officiating, he openly genuflected to the altar, made the sign of the cross before and after his own silent devotions, made known his willingness to hear confessions, and instituted daily services and weekly instead of monthly Communion.

This in many parishes would have caused scandal; but the Fordlow people rather enjoyed the change, excepting the Methodists, who, quite rightly according to their tenets, left off going to church, and a few other extremists who said he was 'a Pope's man'. He even made a few converts. Miss Ellison was one, and two others, oddly enough, were a navvy and his wife who had recently settled near the hamlet. The latter had formerly been a rowdy couple and it was strange to see them, all cleaned up and dressed in their best on a week-day evening, quietly crossing the allotments on their way to confession.

Of course, Laura's father said they were 'after what they could get out of the poor old fool'. That couple almost certainly were not; but others may have been, for he was a most generous man, who gave with both hands, '*and* running over', as the hamlet people said. Not only to the sick and needy, although those were his first care, but to anybody he thought wanted or wished for a thing or who would be pleased with it. He gave the schoolboys two handsome footballs and the girls a skipping-rope each – fine affairs with painted handles and little bells, such as they had never seen in their lives before. When winter came he bought three of the poorest girls warm, grey ulsters, such as were then fashionable, to go to church in. When he found Edmund loved Scott's poems, but only knew extracts from them, he bought him the *Complete Poetical Works*, and, that Laura might not feel neglected, presented her at the same time with *The Imitation of Christ*, daintily bound in blue and silver. These were only a few of his known kindnesses; there were signs and rumours of dozens of others, and no doubt many more were quite unknown except to himself and the recipient.

He once gave the very shoes off his feet to a woman who had pleaded that she could not go to church for want of a pair, and had added, meaningly, that she took a large size and that a man's pair of light shoes would do very well. He gave her the better of the two pairs he possessed, which he happened to be wearing, stipulating that he should be allowed to walk home in them. The wearing of them home was a concession to convention, for he would have enjoyed walking barefoot over the flints as a follower of his beloved St Francis of Assisi, towards whom he had a special devotion twenty years before the cult of the Little Poor Man became popular. He gave away so much that he could only have kept just enough to keep himself in bare necessaries. His black overcoat, which he wore in all weathers, was threadbare, and the old cassock he wore indoors was green and falling to pieces.

Laura's mother, whose religion was as plain and wholesome as the food she cooked, had little sympathy with his 'bowings and crossings'; but she was genuinely fond of the old man and persuaded him to look in for a cup of tea whenever he visited the hamlet. Over this simple meal he would tell the children about his own childhood. He had been the bad boy of the nursery, he said, selfish and self-willed and given to fits of passionate anger. Once he had hurled a plate at his sister (here the children's mother frowned and shook her head at him and that story trailed off lamely); but on another day he told them of his famous ride, which ever after ranked with them beside Dick Turpin's.

The children of his family had a pony which they were supposed to ride in turn; but, in time, he so monopolized it that it was known as his Moppet, and once, when his elders had insisted that another brother should ride that day, he had waited until the party had gone, then taken his mother's riding horse out of the stable, mounted it with the help of a stable boy who had believed him when he said he had permission to do so, and gone careering across country, giving the horse its head, for he had no control over it. They went like the wind, over rough grass and under trees, where any low-hanging bough might have killed him, and, at that point in the story, the teller leaned forward with such a flush on his cheek and such a light in his eye that, for one moment, Laura could almost see in the ageing man the boy he had once been. The ride ended in broken knees for the horse and a broken crown for the rider. 'And a mercy 'twas nothing worse,' the children's mother commented.

The moral of this story was the danger of selfish recklessness: but he told it with such relish and so much fascinating detail that had the end house children had access to anybody's stable they would have tried to imitate him. Edmund suggested they should try to mount Polly, the innkeeper's old pony, and they even went to the place where she was pegged out to reconnoitre; but Polly had only to rattle her tethering chain to convince them they were not cut out for Dick Turpins.

All was going well and Mr Marley was talking of teaching Edmund Latin, when, in an unfortunate moment, finding the children's father at home, he taxed him with neglect of his religious duties. The father, who never went to church at all and spoke of himself as an agnostic, resented this and a quarrel arose, which ended in Mr Marley being told never to darken that door again. So there were no more of those pleasant teas and talks, although he still remained a kind friend and would sometimes come to the cottage door to speak to the mother, scrupulously remaining outside on the doorstep. Then, in a few months, the Rector died, there were changes, and Mr Marley left the parish.

Five or six years afterwards, when Edmund and Laura were both out in the world, their mother, sitting by her fire one gloomy winter afternoon, head a knock at her door and opened it to find Mr Marley on her doorstep. Ignoring the old quarrel, she brought him in and insisted upon making tea for him. He was by that time very old and she thought he looked very frail; but in spite of that he had walked many miles across country from the parish where he was doing temporary duty. He sat by the fire while she made toast and they talked of the absent two and of her other children and of neighbours and friends. He stayed a long time, partly because they had so much to say to each other and partly because he was very tired and, as she thought, ill.

Presently the children's father came in from his work and there was a strained moment which ended, to her great relief, in a polite handclasp. The old feud was either forgotten or repented of.

The father could see at once that the old man was not in a fit state to walk seven or eight miles at night in that weather and begged him not to think of doing so. But what was to be done? They were far from a railway station, even had there been a convenient train, and there was no vehicle for hire within three miles. Then some one suggested that Master Ashley's donkey-cart would be better than nothing, and the father departed to borrow it. He brought it to the garden gate, for he had to drive it himself, and this, surprisingly, he was ready to do although he had just come in tired and damp from his work and had had no proper meal.

With his knees wrapped round in an old fur coat that had once belonged to the children's grandmother and a hot brick at his feet, the visitor was about to say 'Farewell', when the mother, Martha like, exclaimed: 'I'm sorry it's such a poor turn-out for a gentleman like you to ride in.'

'Poor!' he exclaimed. 'I'm proud of it and shall always remember this day. My Master rode through Jerusalem on one of these dear patient beasts, you know!'

A fortnight afterwards she read in the local paper that the Rev Alfred Augustus Peregrine Marley, who was relieving the Vicar of Such-and-such a parish, had collapsed and died at the altar while administering Holy Communion.

XV

Harvest Home

If one of the women was accused of hoarding her best clothes instead of wearing them, she would laugh and say: 'Ah! I be savin' they for high days an' holidays an' bonfire nights.' If she had, they would have lasted a long time, for there were very few holidays and scarcely any which called for a special toilet.

Christmas Day passed very quietly. The men had a holiday from work and the children from school and the churchgoers attended special Christmas services. Mothers who had young children would buy them an orange each and a handful of nuts; but, except at the end house and the inn, there was no hanging up of stockings, and those who had no kind elder sister or aunt in service to send them parcels got no Christmas presents.

Still, they did manage to make a little festival of it. Every year the farmer killed an ox for the purpose and gave each of his men a joint of beef, which duly appeared on the Christmas dinner-table together with plum pudding – not Christmas pudding, but suet duff with a good sprinkling of raisins. Ivy and other evergreens (it was not a holly country) were hung from the ceiling and over the pictures; a bottle of home-made wine was uncorked, a good fire was made up, and, with doors and windows closed against the keen, wintry weather, they all settled down by their own firesides for a kind of super-Sunday. There was little visiting of neighbours and there were no family reunions, for the girls in service could not be spared at that season, and the few boys who had gone out in the world were mostly serving abroad in the Army.

There were still bands of mummers in some of the larger villages, and village choirs went carol-singing about the countryside; but none of these came to the hamlet, for they knew the collection to be expected there would not make it worth their while. A few families, sitting by their own firesides, would sing carols and songs; that, and more and better food and a better fire than usual, made up their Christmas cheer.

The Sunday of the Feast was more exciting. Then strangers, as well as friends, came from far and near to throng the houses and inn and to promenade on the stretch of road which ran through the hamlet. On that day the big ovens were heated and nearly every family managed to have a joint of beef and a Yorkshire pudding for dinner. The men wore their best suits, complete with collar and tie, and the women brought out their treasured finery and wore it, for, even if no relatives from a distance were expected, some one might be 'popping in', if not to dinner, to tea or supper. Half a crown, at least, had been saved from the harvest money for spending at the inn, and the jugs and beer-cans went merrily round the Rise. 'Arter all, 'tis the Feast,' they said; 'an't only comes once a year,' and they enjoyed the extra food and drink and the excitement of seeing so many people about, never dreaming that they were celebrating the dedication five hundred years before of the little old church in the mother village which so few of them attended.

Those of the Fordlow people who liked to see life had on that day to go to Lark Rise, for, beyond the extra food, there was no celebration in the mother village. Some time early in that century the scene of the Feast had shifted from the site of the church to that of the only inn in the parish.

At least a hundred people, friends and strangers, came from the market town and surrounding villages; not that there was anything to do at Lark Rise, or much to see; but because it was Fordlow Feast and a pleasant walk with a drink at the end was a good way of spending a fine September Sunday evening.

The Monday of the Feast – for it lasted two days – was kept by women and children only, the men being at work. It was a great day for tea parties; mothers and sisters and aunts and cousins coming in droves from about the neighbourhood. The chief delicacy at these teas was 'baker's cake', a rich, fruity, spicy dough cake, obtained in the following manner. The housewife provided all the ingredients excepting the dough, putting raisins and currants, lard, sugar, and spice in a basin which she gave to the baker, who added the dough, made and baked the cake, and returned it, beautifully browned in his big oven. The charge was the same as that for a loaf of bread the same size, and the result was delicious. 'There's only one fault wi' these 'ere baker's cakes,' the women used to say; 'they won't keep!' And they would not; they were too good and there were too many children about.

The women made their houses very clean and neat for Feast Monday, and, with hollyhocks nodding in at the open windows and a sight of the clean, yellow stubble of the cleared fields beyond, and the hum of friendly talk and laughter within, the tea parties were very pleasant.

At the beginning of the 'eighties the outside world remembered Fordlow Feast to the extent of sending one old woman with a gingerbread stall. On it were gingerbread babies with currants for eyes, brown-and-white striped peppermint humbugs, sticks of pink-and-white rock, and a few boxes and bottles of other sweets. Even there, on that little old stall with its canvas awning, the first sign of changing taste might have been seen, for, one year, side by side with the gingerbread babies, stood a box filled with thin, dark brown slabs packed in pink paper. 'What is that brown sweet?' asked Laura, spelling out the word 'Chocolate'. A visiting cousin, being fairly well educated and a great reader, already knew it by name. 'Oh, that's chocolate,' he said off-handedly. 'But don't buy any; it's for drinking. They have it for breakfast in France.' A year or two later, chocolate was a favourite sweet even in a place as remote as the hamlet; but it could no longer be bought from the gingerbread stall, for the old woman no longer brought it to the Feast. Perhaps she had died. Except for the tea-drinkings, Feast Monday had died, too, as a holiday.

The younger hamlet people still went occasionally to feasts and club walkings in other villages. In larger places these were like small fairs, with roundabouts, swings, and coconut shies. At the club walkings there were brass bands and processions of the club members, all wearing their club colours in the shape of rosettes and wide sashes worn across the breast. There was dancing on the green to the strains of the band, and country people came from miles around to the village where the feast or club walking was being held.

Palm Sunday, known locally as Fig Sunday, was a minor hamlet festival. Sprays of soft gold and silver willow catkins, called 'palm' in that part of the country, were brought indoors to decorate the houses and be worn as buttonholes for churchgoing. The children at the end house loved fetching in the palm and putting it in pots and vases and hanging it over the picture frames. Better still, they loved the old custom of eating figs on Palm Sunday. The week before, the innkeeper's wife would get in a stock to be sold in pennyworths in her small grocery store. Some of the more expert cooks among the women would use these to make fig puddings for dinner and the children bought pennyworths and ate them out of screws of blue sugar paper on their way to Sunday school.

The gathering of the palm branches must have been a survival from old Catholic days, when, in many English churches, the willow served for palm to be blessed on Palm Sunday. The original significance of eating figs on that day had long been forgotten; but it was regarded as an important duty, and children ordinarily selfish would give one of their figs, or at least a bite out of one, to the few unfortunates who had been given no penny.

No such mystery surrounded the making of a bonfire on 5 November. Parents would tell inquiring children all about the Gunpowder Plot and 'that unked ole Guy Fawkes in his black mask', as though it had all happened recently; and, the night before, the boys and youths of the hamlet would go round knocking at all but the poorest doors and chanting:

> Remember, remember, the fifth of November,
>   The gunpowder treason and plot.
> A stick or a stake, for King James's sake
>   Will you please to give us a faggot?
> If you won't give us one, we'll take two!
> The better for us and the worse for you.

The few housewives who possessed faggot stacks (cut from the undergrowth of woods in the autumn and sold at one and sixpence a score) would give them a bundle or two; others would give them hedge-trimmings, or a piece of old line-post, or anything else that was handy, and, altogether, they managed to collect enough wood to make a modest bonfire which they lit on one of the open spaces and capered and shouted around and roasted potatoes and chestnuts in the ashes, after the manner of boys everywhere.

Harvest time was a natural holiday. 'A hemmed hard-worked 'un,' the men would have said; but they all enjoyed the stir and excitement of getting in the crops and their own importance as skilled and trusted workers, with extra beer at the farmer's expense and extra harvest money to follow.

The 'eighties brought a succession of hot summers and, day after day, as harvest time approached, the children at the end house would wake to the dewy, pearly pink of a fine summer dawn and the *swizzh, swizzh* of the early morning breeze rustling through the ripe corn beyond their doorstep.

Then, very early one morning, the men would come out of their houses, pulling on coats and lighting pipes as they hurried and calling to each other with skyward glances: 'Think weather's a-gooin' to hold?' For three weeks or more during harvest the hamlet was astir before dawn and the homely odours of bacon frying, wood fires and tobacco smoke overpowered the pure, damp, earthy scent of the fields. It would be school holidays then and the children at the end house always wanted to get up hours before their time. There were mushrooms in the meadows around Fordlow and they were sometimes allowed to go picking them to fry for their breakfast. More often they were not; for the dew-soaked grass was bad for their boots. 'Six shillingsworth of good shoe-leather gone for six-pen'orth of mushrooms!' their mother would cry despairingly. But some years old boots had been kept for the purpose and they would dress and creep silently downstairs not to disturb the younger children, and with hunks of bread and butter in their hands steal out into the dewy, morning world.

Against the billowing gold of the fields the hedges stood dark, solid and dew-sleeked; dewdrops beaded the gossamer webs, and the children's feet left long, dark trails on the dewy turf. There were night scents of wheat-straw and flowers and moist earth on the air and the sky was fleeced with pink clouds.

For a few days or a week or a fortnight, the fields stood 'ripe unto harvest'. It was the one perfect period in the hamlet year. The human eye loves to rest upon wide expanses of pure colour: the moors in the purple heyday of the heather, miles of green downland, and the sea when it lies calm and blue and boundless, all delight it; but to some none of these, lovely though they all are, can give the same satisfaction of spirit as acres upon acres of golden corn. *There* is both beauty and bread and the seeds of bread for future generations.

Awed, yet uplifted by the silence and clean-washed loveliness of the dawn, the children would pass along the narrow field paths with rustling wheat on each side. Or Laura would make little dashes into the corn for poppies, or pull trails of the lesser bindweed with its pink-striped trumpets, like clean cotton frocks, to trim her hat and girdle her waist, while Edmund would stump on, red-faced with indignation at her carelessness in making trails in the standing corn.

In the fields where the harvest had begun all was bustle and activity. At that time the mechanical reaper with long, red, revolving arms like windmill sails had already appeared in the locality; but it was looked upon by the men as an auxiliary, a farmers' toy; the scythe still did most of the work and they did not dream it would ever be superseded. So while the red sails revolved in one field and the youth on the driver's seat of the machine called cheerily to his horses and women followed behind to bind the corn into sheaves, in the next field a band of men would be whetting their scythes and mowing by hand as their fathers had done before them.

With no idea that they were at the end of a long tradition, they still kept up the old country custom of choosing as their leader the tallest and most highly skilled man amongst them, who was then called 'King of the Mowers'. For several harvests in the 'eighties they were led by the man known as Boamer. He had served in the Army and was still a fine, well-set-up young fellow with flashing white teeth and a skin darkened by fiercer than English suns.

With a wreath of poppies and green bindweed trails around his wide, rush-plaited hat, he led the band down the swathes as they mowed and decreed when and for how long they should halt for 'a breather' and what drinks should be had from the yellow stone jar they kept under the hedge in a shady corner of the field. They did not rest often or long; for every morning they set themselves to accomplish an amount of work in the day that they knew would tax all their powers till long after sunset. 'Set yourself more than you can do and you'll do it' was one of their maxims, and some of their feats in the harvest field astonished themselves as well as the onlooker.

Old Monday, the bailiff, went riding from field to field on his long-tailed, grey pony. Not at that season to criticize, but rather to encourage, and to carry strung to his saddle the hooped and handled miniature barrel of beer provided by the farmer.

One of the smaller fields was always reserved for any of the women who cared to go reaping. Formerly all the able-bodied women not otherwise occupied had gone as a matter of course; but, by the 'eighties, there were only three or four, beside the regular field women, who could hand the sickle. Often the Irish harvesters had to be called in to finish the field.

Patrick, Dominick, James (never called Jim), Big Mike and Little Mike, and Mr O'Hara seemed to the children as much a part of the harvest scene as the corn itself. They came over from Ireland every year to help with the harvest and slept in the farmer's barn, doing their own cooking and washing at a little fire in the open. They were a wild-looking lot, dressed in odd clothes and speaking a brogue so thick that the natives could only catch a word here and there. When not at work, they went about in a band, talking loudly and usually all together, with the purchases they had made at the inn bundled in blue-and-white check handkerchiefs which they carried over their shoulders at the end of a stick. 'Here comes they jabberin' old Irish,' the country people would say, and some of the women pretended to be afraid of them. They could not have been serious, for the Irishmen showed no disposition to harm any one. All they desired was to earn as much money as possible to send home to their wives, to have enough left for themselves to get drunk on a Saturday night, and to be in time for Mass on a Sunday morning. All these aims were fulfilled; for, as the other men confessed, they were 'gluttons for work' and more work meant more money at that season; there was an excellent inn handy, and a Catholic church within three miles.

After the mowing and reaping and binding came the carrying, the busiest time of all. Every man and boy put his best foot forward then, for, when the corn was cut and dried it was imperative to get it stacked and thatched before the weather broke. All day and far into the twilight the yellow-and-blue painted farm wagons passed and repassed along the roads between the field and the stack-yard. Big cart-horses returning with an empty wagon were made to gallop like two-year-olds. Straws hung on the roadside hedges and many a gate-post was knocked down through hasty driving. In the fields men pitchforked the sheaves to the one who was building the load on the wagon, and the air resounded with *Hold tights* and *Wert ups* and *Who-o-oas*. The *Hold tight!* was no empty cry; sometimes, in the past, the man on top of the load had not held tight or not tight enough. There were tales of fathers and grandfathers whose necks or backs had been broken by a fall from a load, and of other fatal accidents afield, bad cuts from scythes, pitchforks passing through feet, to be followed by lockjaw, and of sunstroke; but, happily, nothing of this kind happened on that particular farm in the 'eighties.

At last, in the cool dusk of an August evening, the last load was brought in, with a nest of merry boys' faces among the sheaves on the top, and the men walking alongside with pitchforks on shoulders. As they passed along the roads they shouted:

> Harvest home! Harvest home!
> Merry, merry, merry harvest home!

and women came to their cottage gates and waved, and the few passers-by looked up and smiled their congratulations. The joy and pleasure of the labourers in their task well done was pathetic, considering their very small share in the gain. But it was genuine enough; for they still loved the soil and rejoiced in their own work and skill in bringing forth the fruits of the soil, and harvest home put the crown on their year's work.

As they approached the farmhouse their song changed to:

> Harvest home! Harvest home!
> Merry, merry, merry harvest home!
> Our bottles are empty, our barrels won't run,
> And we think it's a very dry harvest home.

and the farmer came out, followed by his daughters and maids with jugs and bottles and mugs, and drinks were handed round amidst general congratulations. Then the farmer invited the men to his harvest home dinner, to be held in a few days' time, and the adult workers dispersed to add up their harvest money and to rest their weary bones. The boys and youths, who could never have too much of a good thing, spent the rest of the evening circling the hamlet and shouting 'Merry, merry, merry harvest home!' until the stars came out and at last silence fell upon the fat rickyard and the stripped fields.

On the morning of the harvest home dinner everybody prepared themselves for a tremendous feast, some to the extent of going without breakfast, that the appetite might not be impaired. And what a feast it was! Such a bustling in the farmhouse kitchen for days beforehand; such boiling of hams and roasting of sirloins; such a stacking of plum puddings, made by the Christmas recipe; such a tapping of eighteen-gallon casks and baking of plum loaves would astonish those accustomed to the appetites of today. By noon the whole parish had assembled, the workers and their wives and children to feast and the sprinkling of the better-to-do to help with the serving. The only ones absent were the aged bedridden and their attendants, and to them, the next day, portions, carefully graded in daintiness according to their social standing, were carried by the children from the remnants of the feast. A plum pudding was considered a delicate compliment to an equal of the farmer; slices of beef or ham went to the 'bettermost poor'; and a ham-bone with plenty of meat left upon it or part of a pudding or a can of soup to the commonalty.

Long tables were laid out of doors in the shade of a barn, and soon after twelve o'clock the cottagers sat down to the good cheer, with the farmer carving at the principal table, his wife with her tea urn at another, the daughters of the house and their friends circling the tables with vegetable dishes and beer jugs, and the grandchildren, in their stiff, white, embroidered frocks, dashing hither and thither to see that everybody had what they required. As a background there was the rickyard with its new yellow stacks and, over all, the mellow sunshine of late summer.

Passers-by on the road stopped their gigs and high dog-carts to wave greetings and shout congratulations on the weather. If a tramp looked wistfully in, he was beckoned to a seat on the straw beneath a rick and a full plate was placed on his knees. It was a picture of plenty and goodwill.

It did not do to look beneath the surface. Laura's father, who did not come into the picture, being a 'tradesman' and so not invited, used to say that the farmer paid his men starvation wages all the year and thought he made it up to them by giving that one good meal. The farmer did not think so, because he did not think at all, and the men did not think either on that day; they were too busy enjoying the food and the fun.

After the dinner there were sports and games, then dancing in the home paddock until twilight, and when, at the end of the day, the farmer, carving indoors for the family supper, paused with knife poised to listen to the last distant 'Hooray!' and exclaimed, 'A lot of good chaps! A lot of good chaps, God bless 'em!' both he and the cheering men were sincere, however mistaken.

But these modest festivals which had figured every year in everybody's life for generations were eclipsed in 1887 by Queen Victoria's Golden Jubilee.

Up to the middle of the 'eighties the hamlet had taken little interest in the Royal House. The Queen and the Prince and Princess of Wales were sometimes mentioned, but with little respect and no affection. 'The old Queen', as she was called, was supposed to have shut herself up in Balmoral Castle with a favourite servant named John Brown and to have refused to open Parliament when Mr Gladstone begged her to. The Prince was said to be leading a gay life, and the dear, beautiful Princess, afterwards Queen Alexandra, was celebrated only for her supposed make-up.

By the middle of the decade a new spirit was abroad and had percolated to the hamlet. The Queen, it appeared, had reigned fifty years. She had been a good queen, a wonderful queen, she was soon to celebrate her Jubilee, and, still more exciting, they were going to celebrate it, too, for there was going to be a big 'do' in which three villages would join for tea and sports and dancing and fireworks in the park of a local magnate. Nothing like it had ever been known before.

As the time drew nearer, the Queen and her Jubilee became the chief topic of conversation. The tradesmen gave lovely coloured portraits of her in her crown and garter ribbon on their almanacks, most of which were framed at home and hung up in the cottages. Jam could be bought in glass jugs adorned with her profile in hobnails and inscribed '1837 to 1887. Victoria the Good', and, underneath, the national catchword of the moment: 'Peace and Plenty'. The newspapers were full of the great achievements of her reign: railway travel, the telegraph, Free Trade, exports, progress, prosperity, Peace: all these blessings, it appeared, were due to her inspiration.

Of most of these advantages the hamlet enjoyed but Esau's share; but, as no one reflected upon this, it did not damp the general enthusiasm. 'Fancy her reigning fifty years, the old dear, her!' they said, and bought paper banners inscribed 'Fifty Years, Mother, Wife, and Queen' to put inside their window panes. 'God Bless Her. Victoria the Good. The Mother of Her People.'

Laura was lucky enough to be given a bound volume of *Good Words* – or was it *Home Words*? – in which the Queen's own journal, *Leaves From Her Majesty's Life in the Highlands*, ran as a serial. She galloped through all the instalments immediately to pick out the places mentioned by her dear Sir Walter Scott. Afterwards the journal was re-read many times, as everything was re-read in that home of few books. Laura liked the journal, for although the Queen kept to the level of meals and drives and seasickness and the 'civility' of her hosts and hostesses, and only mentioned the scenery (Scott's scenery!) to repeat what 'Albert said' about it – and he always compared it to some foreign scene – there was a forthright sincerity about the writing which revealed a human being behind all the glitter and fuss.

By the end of May everybody was talking about the weather. Would it be fine for the great drive through London; and, still more important, would it be fine for the doings in Skeldon Park? Of course it would be fine, said the more optimistic. Providence knew what He was about. It was going to be a glorious June. Queen's weather, they called it. Hadn't the listener heard that the sun always shone when the Queen drove out?

Then there were rumours of a subscription fund. The women of England were going to give the Queen a Jubilee present, and, wonder of wonders, the amount given was not to exceed one penny. 'Of course we shall give,' they said proudly. 'It'll be our duty an' our pleasure.' And when the time came for the collection to be made they had all of them their pennies ready. Bright new ones in most cases, for, although they knew the coins were to be converted into a piece of plate before reaching Her Majesty, they felt that only new money was worthy of the occasion.

The ever-faithful, ever-useful clergyman's daughter collected the pence. Thinking, perhaps, that the day after pay-day would be most convenient, she visited Lark Rise on a Saturday, and Laura, at home from school, was clipping the garden hedge when she heard one neighbour say to another: 'I want a bucket of water, but I can't run round to the well till Miss Ellison's been for the penny.'

'Lordy, dear!' ejaculated the other. 'Why, she's been an' gone this quarter of an hour. She's a-been to my place. Didn't she come to yourn?'

The first speaker flushed to the roots of her hair. She was a woman whose husband had recently had an accident afield and was still in hospital. There were no Insurance benefits then, and it was known she was having a hard struggle to keep her home going; but she had her penny ready and was hurt, terribly hurt, by the suspicion that she had been purposely passed over.

'I s'pose, because I be down on me luck, she thinks I ain't worth a penny,' she cried, and went in and banged the door.

'There's temper for you!' the other woman exclaimed to the world at large and went about her own business. But Laura was distressed. She had seen Mrs Parker's expression and could imagine how her pride was hurt. She, herself, hated to be pitied. But what could she do about it?

She went to the gate. Miss Ellison had finished collecting and was crossing the allotments on her way home. Laura would just have time to run the other way round and meet her at the stile. After a struggle with her own inward shrinking which lasted about two minutes, but was ridiculously intense, she ran off on her long, thin legs, and popped up, like a little jack-in-the-box, on the other side of the stile which the lady was gathering up her long frilly skirts to mount.

'Oh, please, Miss Ellison, you haven't been to Mrs Parker's, and she's got her penny all ready and she wants the Queen to have it so much.'

'But, Laura,' said the lady loftily, surprised at such interference, 'I did not intend to call upon Mrs Parker today. With her husband in hospital, I know she has no penny to spare, poor soul.'

But, although somewhat quelled, Laura persisted: 'But she's got it all polished up and wrapped in tissue paper, Miss Ellison, and 'twill hurt her feelings most awful if you don't go for it, Miss Ellison.'

At that, Miss Ellison grasped the situation and retraced her steps, keeping Laura by her side and talking to her as to another grown-up person.

'Our dear Queen,' she was saying as they passed Twister's turnip patch, 'our dear, good Queen, Laura, is noted for her perfect tact. Once, and I have this on good authority, some church workers were invited to visit her at Osborne. Tea was served in a magnificent drawing-room, the Queen actually partaking of a cup with them, and this, I am told, is very unusual – a great honour, in fact; but no doubt she did it to put them at their ease. But in her confusion, one poor lady, unaccustomed to taking tea with royalty, had the misfortune to drop her slice of cake on the floor. Imagine that,

Laura, a slice of cake on the Queen's beautiful carpet; you can understand how the poor lady must have felt, can't you dear? One of the ladies-in-waiting smiled at her discomfiture, which made her still more nervous and trembling; but our dear Queen – she has sharp eyes, God bless her! – saw at once how matters stood. She asked for a slice of cake, then purposely dropped it, and commanded the lady who had smiled to pick up both pieces at once. Which she did quickly, you may be sure, Laura, and there were no more smiles. What a lesson! What a lesson, Laura!'

Cynical little Laura wondered for whom the lesson was intended; but she only said meekly: 'Yes, indeed, Miss Ellison,' and this brought them to Mrs Parker's door, where she had the satisfaction of hearing Miss Ellison say: 'Oh, dear, Mrs Parker, I nearly overlooked your house. I have come for your contribution to the Queen's Jubilee present.'

The great day dawned at last and most of the hamlet people were up in time to see the sun burst in dazzling splendour from the pearly pink east and mount into a sky unflecked by the smallest cloud. Queen's weather indeed! And as the day began it continued. It was very hot; but nobody minded that, for the best hats could be worn without fear of showers, and those who had sunshades put by for just such an occasion could bring them forth in all their glory of deep lace or long, knotted, silk fringe.

By noon all the hamlet children had been scrubbed with soap and water and arrayed in their best clothes. 'Every bit clean, right through to the skin,' as their mothers proudly declared. Then, after a snack, calculated to sustain the family during the walk to the park, but not to spoil the appetite for tea, the mothers went upstairs to take out their own curl papers and don their best clothes. A strong scent of camphor and lavender and closely shut boxes pervaded the atmosphere around them for the rest of the day. The colours and styles did not harmonize too well with the midsummer country scene, and many might have preferred to see them in print frocks and sunbonnets; but they dressed to please themselves, not to please the artistic taste of others, and they were all the happier for it.

Before they started there was much running from house to house and asking: 'Now, *should* you put on another bow just here!' or 'Do you think that ostrich tip our young Em sent me'd improve my hat, or do you think the red roses and black lace is enough?' or 'Now, tell me true, do you like my hair done this way?'

The men and boys with shining faces and in Sunday suits had gone on before to have dinner at the farm before meeting their families at the cross-roads. They would be having cuts off great sirloins and Christmas pudding washed down with beer, just as they did at the harvest home dinner.

The little party from the end house walked alone in the straggling procession; the mother, still rather pale from her recent confinement, pushing the baby carriage with little May and baby Elizabeth; Laura and Edmund, on tiptoe with excitement, helping to shove the carriage over the rough turf of the park. Their father had not come. He did not care for 'do's', and had gone to work at his bench at the shop alone while his workmates held high holiday. There were as yet no trade union laws to forbid such singularity.

There were more people in the park than the children had ever seen together, and the roundabouts, swings, and coconut shies were doing a roaring trade. Tea was partaken of in a huge marquee in relays, one parish at a time, and the sound of the brass band, roundabout hurdy-gurdy, coconut thwacks, and showmen's shouting surged round the frail, canvas walls like a roaring sea.

Within, the mingled scents of hot tea, dough cake, tobacco smoke, and trampled grass lent a holiday savour to a simple menu. But if the provisions were simple in quality, the quantity was prodigious. Clothes baskets of bread and butter and jam cut in thick slices and watering cans of tea, already milked and sugared, were handed round and disappeared in a twinkling. 'God bless my soul,' one old clergyman exclaimed. 'Where on earth do they put it all!' They put three-fourths of it in the same handy receptacle he himself used for his four-course dinners; but the fourth part went into their pockets. That was their little weakness – not to be satisfied with a bellyful, but to manage somehow to secure a portion to take home for next day.

After tea there were sports, with races, high jumps, dipping heads into tubs of water to retrieve sixpences with the teeth, grinning through horse-collars, the prize going to the one making the most grotesque face, and, to crown all, climbing the greased pole for the prize leg of mutton. This was a tough job, as the pole was as tall and slender as a telephone post and extremely slippery. Prudent wives would not allow their husbands to attempt it on account of spoiling their clothes, so the competition was left to the raga-muffins and a few experts who had had the foresight to bring with them a pair of old trousers. This competition must have run concurrently with the other events, for all the afternoon there was a crowd around it, and first one, then another, would 'have a go'. It was painful to watch the climbers, shinning up a few inches, then slipping back again, and, as one retired, another taking his place, until, late in the afternoon, the champion arrived, climbed slowly but steadily to the top and threw down the joint, which, by the way, must have been already roasted after four or five hours in the burning sun. It was whispered around that he had carried a bag of ashes and sprinkled them on the greasy surface as he ascended.

The local gentlepeople promenaded the ground in parties: stout, red-faced squires, raising their straw hats to mop their foreheads; hunting ladies, incongruously garbed in silks and ostrich-feather boas; young girls in embroidered white muslin and boys in Eton suits. They had kind words for everybody, especially for the poor and lonely, and, from time to time, they would pause before some sight and try to enter into the spirit of the other beholders; but everywhere their arrival hushed the mirth, and there was a sigh of relief when they moved on. After dancing the first dance they disappeared, and 'now we can have some fun', the people said.

All this time Edmund and Laura, with about two hundred other children, had been let loose in the crowd to spend their pennies and watch the fun. They rode on the wooden horses, swung in the swing-boats, pried around coconut shies and shooting booths munching coconut or rock or long strips of black liquorice, until their hands were sticky and their faces grimed.

Laura, who hated crowds and noise, was soon tired of it and looked longingly at the shady trees and woods and spinneys around the big open space where the fair was held. But before she escaped a new and wonderful experience awaited her. Before one of the booths a man was beating a drum and before him two girls were posturing and pirouetting. 'Walk up! Walk up!' he was shouting. 'Walk up and see the tightrope dancing! Only one penny admission. Walk up! Walk up!' Laura paid her penny and walked up, as did about a dozen others, the man and girls came inside, the flap of the tent was drawn, and the show began.

Laura had never heard of tightrope dancing before and she was not sure she was not dreaming it then. The outer tumult beat against the frail walls of the tent, but within was a magic circle of quiet. As she crossed to take her place with the other spectators, her feet sank deep into sawdust; and, in the subdued light which filtered through the canvas, the broad, white, pockmarked face of the man in his faded red satin and the tinsel crowns and tights of the girls seemed as unreal as a dream.

The girl who did the tightrope dancing was a fair, delicate-looking child with grey eyes and fat, pale-brown ringlets, a great contrast to her dark, bouncing gipsy-looking sister, and when she mounted to the rope stretched between two poles and did a few dance steps as she swayed gracefully along it, Laura gazed and gazed, speechless with admiration. To the simple country-bred child the performance was marvellous. It came to an end all too soon for her; for not much could be done to entertain a house which only brought a shilling or so to the box office; but the impression remained with her as a glimpse into a new and fascinating world. There were few five-barred gates in the vicinity of Laura's home on which she did not attempt a little pirouetting along the top bar during the next year or two.

The tightrope dancing was her outstanding memory of the great Queen's Jubilee; but the merrymaking went on for hours after that. All the way home in the twilight, the end house party could hear the popping of fireworks behind them and, turning, see rockets and showers of golden rain above the dark tree-tops. At last, standing at their own garden gate, they heard the roaring of cheers from hundreds of throats and the band playing 'God save the Queen'.

They were first home and the hamlet was in darkness, but the twilight was luminous over the fields and the sky right round to the north was still faintly pink. A cat rubbed itself against their legs and mewed; the pig in the sty woke and grunted a protest against the long day's neglect. A light breeze rustled through the green corn and shivered the garden bushes, releasing the scent of stocks and roses and sunbaked grass and the grosser smells of cabbage beds and pigsties. It had been a great day – the greatest day they were ever likely to see, however long they lived, they were told; but it was over and they were home and home was best.

After the Jubilee nothing ever seemed quite the same. The old Rector died and the farmer, who had seemed immovable excepting by death, had to retire to make way for the heir of the landowning nobleman who intended to farm the family estates himself. He brought with him the new self-binding reaping machine and women were no longer required in the harvest field. At the hamlet several new brides took possession of houses previously occupied by elderly people and brought new ideas into the place. The last of the bustles disappeared and leg-o'-mutton sleeves were 'all the go'. The new Rector's wife took her Mothers' Meeting women for a trip to London. Babies were christened new names; Wanda was one, Gwendolin another. The innkeeper's wife got in cases of tinned salmon and Australian rabbit. The Sanitary Inspector appeared for the first time at the hamlet and shook his head over the pigsties and privies. Wages rose, prices soared, and new needs multiplied. People began to speak of 'before the Jubilee' much as we in the nineteen-twenties spoke of 'before the war', either as a golden time or as one of exploded ideas, according to the age of the speaker.

And all the time boys were being born or growing up in the parish, expecting to follow the plough all their lives, or, at most, to do a little mild soldiering or go to work in a town. Gallipoli? Kut? Vimy Ridge? Ypres? What did they know of such places? But they were to know them, and when the time came they did not flinch.

Eleven out of that tiny community never came back again. A brass plate on the wall of the church immediately over the old end house seat is engraved with their names. A double column, five names long, then, last and alone, the name of Edmund.

Penguin Modern Classics

OVER TO CANDLEFORD
FLORA THOMPSON

In the little hamlet of Lark Rise times are changing and Laura is growing up. Although she must attend the nearby village school, she would far rather read and make up stories in her head. Real-life excitement comes, however, when she and her beloved younger brother Edmund are allowed to walk on their own to the grand market town of Candleford to stay with their relatives one summer. There, Laura discovers the joys of the shops, the ways of boy-talk with her cousins and the secret world of 'Bookworms Ltd' with her Uncle Tom, before an offer arrives that will determine her future.

A story of friendships, rivalries and a young girl finding her place in the world, this is the second part of Flora Thompson's endearing *Lark Rise to Candleford* trilogy on country life, which evokes the passage from childhood to adolescence and a society on the cusp of transformation.

PENGUIN MODERN CLASSICS

CANDLEFORD GREEN
FLORA THOMPSON

Laura is now fourteen-and-a-half and setting off for a new life in the sleepy village of Candleford Green, as assistant to the clever, dapper Miss Dorcas Lane, who runs the Post Office.

In Candleford Green new ideas and new ways are coming in from the outside world, from Dorcas's famous telegraph machine to the scandalous sight of ladies riding bicycles. There are also new people entering Laura's life: the curmudgeonly old servant Zillah, the grand Sir Thomas, the Irish harvesters and the ardent young gamekeeper Philip White. As Laura adjusts to this world, the traditions and ways of her country childhood seem further and further away – and a different future beckons.

In this final part of Flora Thompson's charming and evocative *Lark Rise to Candleford* trilogy, the old finally gives way to the new.

PENGUIN MODERN CLASSICS

MAPP AND LUCIA
E. F. BENSON

'Enchanting ... even at their worst-behaved, his characters never stop being lovable' Philip Hensher

When the recently widowed Mrs Emmeline Lucas (Lucia to her friends) desires a change of scene, she determines on the picturesque seaside town of Tilling for an extended break. There, with her ever-faithful friend and accomplice Georgie Pillson in tow, she sets forth to wrest the reins of Tilling society from Miss Elizabeth Mapp. But the Machiavellian Lucia has not reckoned on the indomitable Mapp, who has no intention of giving up her supremacy. Has Lucia at last met her match?

Battle-lines are swiftly drawn as the ladies strive to outdo each other, using invitations to delightful garden parties and, above all, the recipe for 'Lobster *à la Riseholme*' as their deadly weapons (to the fascinated horror of their friends), for the position of doyenne of Tilling.

'We will pay anything for Lucia books' Noël Coward, Gertrude Lawrence, Nancy Mitford, W. H. Auden

With an Introduction by Philip Hensher

PENGUIN MODERN CLASSICS

THE GO-BETWEEN
L. P. HARTLEY

'Magical and disturbing' *Independent*

When one long, hot summer, young Leo is staying with a school-friend at Brandham Hall, he begins to act as a messenger between Ted, the farmer, and Marian, the beautiful young woman up at the hall. He becomes drawn deeper and deeper into their dangerous game of deceit and desire, until his role brings him to a shocking and premature revelation. The haunting story of a young boy's awakening into the secrets of the adult world, *The Go-Between* is also an unforgettable evocation of the boundaries of Edwardian society.

'On a first reading, it is a beautifully wrought description of a small boy's loss of innocence long ago. But, visited a second time, the knowledge of approaching, unavoidable tragedy makes it far more poignant and painful' *Express*

Edited with an Introduction and Notes by Douglas Brooks-Davies

PENGUIN MODERN CLASSICS

UNDER MILK WOOD
DYLAN THOMAS

'[Its] great strength is the Chaucerian life and liveliness of its sixty or more characters, enjoyed in all their spontaneous eccentricity' Walford Davies

As the inhabitants of Llareggub lie sleeping, their dreams and fantasies deliciously unfold. There is Captain Cat surrounded by fish that 'nibble him down to his wishbone', Mog Edwards, 'a draper mad with love' for shy dressmaker Miss Price, Organ Morgan, listening to the music in Coronation Street with 'spouses … honking like geese and the babies singing opera', while at the sea-end of town, Mr and Mrs Floyd lie in their bed 'side by side … like two old kippers in a box'. Waking up, their dreams turn to bustling activity as a new day begins.

In this classic modern pastoral, the 'dismays and rainbows' of the imagined seaside town become, within the cycle of one day, 'a greenleaved sermon on the innocence of men'.

Edited with an Introduction and Notes by Walford Davies

PENGUIN MODERN CLASSICS

BRIDESHEAD REVISITED
EVELYN WAUGH

'Lush and evocative ... the one Waugh which best expresses at once the profundity of change and the indomitable endurance of the human spirit'
The Times

The most nostalgic and reflective of Evelyn Waugh's novels, *Brideshead Revisited* looks back to the golden age before the Second World War. It tells the story of Charles Ryder's infatuation with the Marchmains and the rapidly disappearing world of privilege they inhabit. Enchanted first by Sebastian at Oxford, then by his doomed Catholic family, in particular his remote sister, Julia, Charles comes finally to recognize his spiritual and social distance from them.

Penguin Modern Classics

OFFICERS AND GENTLEMEN
EVELYN WAUGH

'A literary innovator, inventor of modern black comedy in the novel'
Malcolm Bradbury, *Mail on Sunday*

Guy Crouchback is now attached to a Commando unit undergoing training on the Hebridean Isle of Mugg, where the whisky flows freely and HM forces have to show proper respect for the omnipotent Laird. But the high comedy of Mugg is followed by the bitterness of Crete – and the chaos and indignity of total withdrawal or surrender.

Officers and Gentlemen is the second volume of Waugh's trilogy, *Sword of Honour*, which chronicles the fortunes of Guy Crouchback. The first and third volumes, *Men at Arms* and *Unconditional Surrender*, are also published in Penguin.

PENGUIN MODERN CLASSICS

THE POORHOUSE FAIR
JOHN UPDIKE

'A work of art' *The New York Times*

Published just four years after John Updike graduated from Harvard, *The Poorhouse Fair* is a brilliant allegory about charity. The setting is a poorhouse – repository of the old, the infirm, and the impoverished – on the day of the annual summer fair. The people are the vividly realized, unforgettable characters that only Updike can create. Short and succinct, *The Poorhouse Fair* speaks to those fears all of us have of growing not old, but dependent.

'A first novel of rare precision and real merit ... A rich poorhouse indeed'
Newsweek

With a new afterword by John Updike

Contemporary ... Provocative ... Outrageous ...
Prophetic ... Groundbreaking ... Funny ... Disturbing ...
Different ... Moving ... Revolutionary ... Inspiring ...
Subversive ... Life-changing ...

What makes a modern classic?

At Penguin Classics our mission has always been to make the best
books ever written available to everyone. And that also means
constantly redefining and refreshing exactly what makes a 'classic'.
That's where Modern Classics come in. Since 1961 they have been an
organic, ever-growing and ever-evolving list of books from the last
hundred (or so) years that we believe will continue to be read over and
over again.

They could be books that have inspired political dissent, such as
Animal Farm. Some, like *Lolita* or *A Clockwork Orange*, may have
caused shock and outrage. Many have led to great films, from *In Cold
Blood* to *One Flew Over the Cuckoo's Nest*. They have broken down
barriers – whether social, sexual, or, in the case of *Ulysses*, the
boundaries of language itself. And they might – like *Goldfinger* or
Scoop – just be pure classic escapism. Whatever the reason, Penguin
Modern Classics continue to inspire, entertain and enlighten millions
of readers everywhere.

'No publisher has had more influence on reading habits than Penguin'
Independent

'Penguins provided a crash course in world literature'
Guardian

The best books ever written

PENGUIN (🐧) CLASSICS

SINCE 1946

Find out more at www.penguinclassics.com